THE
BACHELORETTE
PARTY

THE
BACHELORETTE
PARTY

A NOVEL

CAMILLA STEN

MINOTAUR
BOOKS
NEW YORK

First published in the United States by Minotaur Books, an imprint of St. Martin's Publishing Group

THE BACHELORETTE PARTY. Copyright © 2025 by Camilla Sten. All rights reserved. Printed in the United States of America. For information, address St. Martin's Publishing Group, 120 Broadway, New York, NY 10271.

www.minotaurbooks.com

Designed by Steven Seighman

The Library of Congress Cataloging-in-Publication Data is available upon request.

ISBN 978-1-250-86850-3 (hardcover)
ISBN 978-1-250-86851-0 (ebook)

Our books may be purchased in bulk for promotional, educational, or business use. Please contact your local bookseller or the Macmillan Corporate and Premium Sales Department at 1-800-221-7945, extension 5442, or by email at MacmillanSpecialMarkets@macmillan.com.

First Edition: 2025

10 9 8 7 6 5 4 3 2 1

To Mark,
For teaching me to dream bigger. Every day.
This book would not exist if not for you.

THE
BACHELORETTE
PARTY

PROLOGUE

May 12, 2012

The bonfire was starting to die out. It had been a pitiful attempt at a fire to begin with, fueled by optimism and vodka. The few skinny, damp branches they'd managed to find on the island had barely agreed to catch flame after half an hour of gentle coercion at the beginning of the night.

Not that they had needed a bonfire, anyway. Summer was almost upon them. The sky was still high and blue, the sun hanging low over the horizon, stubbornly refusing to set. The few trees that had managed to defy the odds and maintain their grip on the stony surface of the small island seemed to glow in the soft summer light.

If only the temperature had been as obliging. This early in the season the ground still held on to the cold, and even though Matilda was sitting on a half-rotten log they'd dragged over to the cliffside, she could still feel the chill emanating from below.

The fire was tradition, though. No matter how small or pathetic. Everything about the party was tradition.

Matilda took another sip of her beer. It had gone warm and flat in her hand, the glass clammy against her palm. She was tired enough to feel cold, but too antsy and self-conscious to do anything about it. Wondering if this had been a mistake.

She could have been at home with Carl. They'd have gone to bed by now. Carl wasn't much for late evenings. He was one of those early risers, the kind of person who liked to get a run in before breakfast and didn't sleep in even on the weekends. Neat hair, smallish hands, perpetually fresh and organized. So very different from her. He was all logic and rationality, carefully made plans followed to the letter, with contingencies upon contingencies to ensure nothing would go wrong.

It would have been enough to drive her mad if she hadn't somehow managed to fall in love with him. One surprisingly successful hungover date, scheduled last minute over Match.com, and two years later they were looking at wedding venues.

God, if her teenage self could see her now.

Matilda smiled, small and tight-lipped.

Something about the trip always made her nostalgic.

Maybe that was why they kept doing them. Despite everything.

Over by the dying fire Linnea and Evelina were dancing, hair flying, plastic wineglasses in hand. The small, rounded speaker Linnea had brought for the evening was fighting the good fight, attempting to transcend its physical limitations and fill the night with '90s nostalgia.

They had been coming here every May for eleven years now. It sounded to Matilda like an impossibly long time. In her memory, the trips tended to bleed into one another. They had aged, their hairstyles had changed, they'd gone to university and found jobs and rectified youthful mistakes like piercings and boyfriends in bands, but out here on Isle Blind, time seemed to stand still.

Someone always cried. Someone always threw up. Someone always had a life-changing realization.

It was here that Anna had come out to them. It was here that Linnea had told them about her dad's cancer. It was to Isle Blind they'd come when Evelina landed the job in Paris, for one last big hurrah before she left, and it was on Isle Blind they'd seen her again for the first time after she came back home.

When it started, they had all been teenagers throbbing with angst and sexual frustration. Desperate to feel like their real lives were about to begin. Wanting more than anything a space to call their own, if only for a night.

Isle Blind had been Anna's idea. The naked, barren little sliver of land in the Baltic Sea belonged to her parents, as part of the fishing waters her dad had inherited along with the big summerhouse on Harö. According to Anna, her father had looked into building a house on the island but failed to get a permit, and so it wasn't worth anything to anyone. It wasn't beautiful enough to be a destination, and the rocky beaches weren't appealing enough to draw any sailors. Isle Blind had been sitting there, the wilting wallflower of the Baltic, since it rose from the sea a couple of hundred years previously.

It was theirs for the taking.

Matilda noticed without much surprise that her beer bottle was empty. She couldn't remember drinking the last of it. She didn't particularly want another one but knew that the others would protest if she didn't have a drink in her hand. She was already far behind Evelina, and Linnea looked to be catching up rather than slowing down.

The log she was sitting on thumped as Anna sat down next to her, and Matilda started.

"Where have you been?" Matilda asked.

Anna handed her another beer, already open. Matilda pretended to take a sip, felt the burn of the bubbles on her lips.

"Had to take a piss," Anna said.

The cold humidity of the archipelago made Anna's long blond hair hang heavy against her shoulders. Her mascara had smudged a bit, echoing the kohl-heavy look she'd preferred as a teenager, back when Anna had attempted to tattoo "Baby Goth" on the inside of her wrist with a needle and a ballpoint pen, and when Matilda's preferred choice of jewelry had been safety pins.

"How are you holding up?" Anna asked her.

Matilda smiled.

"Tired," she said. "I don't have the stamina I used to."

"That's not what Carl's made it sound like," Anna said and pumped her eyebrows at Matilda with a dirty chuckle.

Matilda rolled her eyes.

"Please," she said. "Don't start. We're old and stale by now. Eleven minutes of missionary twice a week if I'm lucky."

It was an old refrain, worn and comfortable. Whichever one of them was in a relationship had to make it out like it was dying on the vine, floundering under the weight of monogamy and routine, so as not to make the other one feel left out.

Maybe that's what had made her hang on to Anna, Matilda thought, why she'd put in the effort with her in a way she hadn't with the other two. Anna was the linchpin that kept them coming back, both to one another and to Isle Blind, even though they'd grown apart over the years. When you were a teenager, all you needed to have in common was time and circumstance. Who could have guessed when they were all running wild and ragged that Linnea would end up gleaming and polished, that Evelina would shoot up and turn out cold and statuesque? Who could have foreseen that Matilda herself would go from an angry little hissing ball of eyeliner and studded jackets to a junior executive with an apartment in central Stockholm where the countertops gleamed and the kitchen chairs cost more than some of her old classmates made in a month?

Sometimes she wondered what she'd lost, leaving that girl behind. It hadn't been dramatic. It had been incremental, piece by piece, a haircut here and a blazer there.

She liked who she was now. She liked her life. Sometimes she even loved it.

But that untamed quality, that feral lust for something else, something different—that she could miss.

Sometimes when she couldn't sleep, she could feel that girl whispering in her ear. Breath hot and ragged.

You could just leave. Run far, far away and start over. Let it all go.

And that was the answer, wasn't it? That was why she kept responding in the affirmative every year when the group chat came back to life in early spring, even as she groaned inwardly at the thought of the long trip out to the cold island.

The trip was the last thing connecting her to that girl. The girl she'd been.

"How are you feeling?" she asked Anna, suspecting she'd duck and deflect.

Anna had her gaze fastened on the other two, who were still dancing, albeit slower.

Evelina wasn't looking too steady. She must have been drinking more than usual; she had seemed a bit stressed and standoffish all night, but with her job, that was probably to be expected. She'd almost flaked out of the trip this year, citing work, and Matilda was happy she'd managed to convince her otherwise.

Might be time to pour some chips down her throat to soak up the alcohol. With her running and swimming and biking Evelina didn't have enough body fat to sustain even mild drunkenness for long.

"Eh," Anna said. "Not great." She shrugged.

"Thinking about the ex?" Matilda asked.

Anna shook her head, then sighed.

"I don't know," she said. "Not really. Sigrid was great." She paused.

"*Is* great. She'll make someone really happy, I'm sure." There was a bitter twist to her mouth that contradicted her breezy tone.

"But?" Matilda coaxed.

She knew you had to be careful with Anna. Her happy-go-lucky, mildly vulgar front was a defense that could easily turn into an offense if she sensed you were trying to pry.

But on Isle Blind, it was okay to ask.

It was where they'd come to escape the adults, and the boys, and the girls who didn't understand. The place where they had been able to drop all pretenses for a while. Where they had been able to stop trying so hard and just exist.

"It wasn't Sigrid," Anna said. "It was the whole thing. You know, my mom thinks I have attachment issues. She offered to pay for a therapist if I want to, and I quote, work out my 'kinks.'" Anna mimicked her mom's dry upper-class tone, made air quotes with one hand and put her middle finger up on the other one.

"I don't think there's a therapist on earth who can handle your kinks," Matilda said, and Anna hooted with laughter.

"Would you mind repeating that to my mother?"

"I don't have a death wish," Matilda replied, and they grew silent.

"I don't think I have attachment issues," Anna eventually said. "I've managed to stay attached to you guys, right?"

Matilda weighed her words carefully.

"Yeah," she settled on. "You have. You've kept us together."

"But?" Anna said.

Frightfully perceptive, even after having a few. As she always had been.

"Well, I guess it depends on what you want," Matilda said. "Friendships and relationships are different, right? I mean, I think I'm pretty good at relationships, but I'm kind of shit at friendships. I do well with acquaintances and work friends. But aside from you guys I'm not sure I have a lot of close friends." She paused.

"Maybe I need therapy for bad friend-attachment," Matilda added.

"So you're saying I have crap attachment when it comes to girl-friends?" Anna said, and Matilda groaned.

"Jesus, Anna, not everything is about you," she said.

Anna shot Matilda a shrewd look. Matilda wasn't quite sure how to interpret it.

"So," Anna said, setting her gaze on the dying fire. "When are you going to tell them?"

Matilda stilled. She suddenly felt acutely aware of the fact that she needed to pee. Or throw up. Possibly both.

Her mouth felt very dry. Sort of fuzzy, as though she'd been chewing on a ball of cotton.

"Carl told you?" she asked Anna, who shook her head.

"Come on, Mattie," she said, the old nickname fitting snugly in Matilda's ear. "I knew. You've gone all weird and quiet on me lately."

Anna still wasn't looking at her. Matilda could see the fire reflected in her eyes, a mild glow that for a moment seemed to grant her an otherworldly quality.

"Also," she added, suddenly snapping out of it and smirking, "I know what alcohol-free beer looks like."

She clinked her own bottle against Matilda's.

"That was just my final test. You thought I wouldn't see you fake-sipping?" She laughed, snorting a bit, and the knot in Matilda's chest loosened.

"Fuck you," she said easily, laughing as she rested her head against Anna's shoulder for a second.

"How far along are you?" Anna asked her.

"Nine weeks," Matilda replied. It felt weird talking about it, oddly forbidden, like she was telling a secret she'd sworn to keep. So far it hadn't quite felt real. It felt more like a game she was playing with Carl, making lists of names and looking at bigger places, discussing pros and cons of getting married before or after the baby came.

The baby. What a strange thought. What an odd, foreign thing to imagine.

"Ah," Anna said. "So we're not telling them yet, then?"

Matilda rolled her eyes.

"It's 'we' now, is it?"

"Of course," Anna said easily. "As resident auntie I naturally get a say in anything to do with my future niece or nephew."

"God, you're impossible," Matilda said, wanting to say more but falling silent.

The breeze had picked up in the last few minutes. The sky had gone a couple of shades darker, a mild indigo patterned by the few stars brave enough to pierce through the northern summer sky. When she concentrated, Matilda could hear the soft lapping of the waves against the rocky shore a couple of hundred yards away.

She wanted to say it. She *needed* to say it, or she was sure she was going to break; in the last few weeks she had felt the words bubbling under her skin, clawing their way up her throat, had sometimes had to clap her hand over her mouth to prevent them from escaping.

"I'm not sure about it," Matilda said, so quietly it was barely louder than the whisper from the waves.

She fastened her eyes on the fire. It was almost fully out now. Nothing but dying embers under skinny, twisted branches of wet and blackened wood. The mark it left on the cliff would get washed away by the rain within a couple of weeks.

"Okay," Anna said, slowly.

Matilda waited for her to continue before she realized that Anna wasn't going to say anything at all. She was listening.

"I think I want it," Matilda said. "It's the right time." She paused.

"Carl *really* wants it."

She almost took a sip from the beer Anna had given her before she remembered and stopped herself. The nonalcoholic ones she'd brought for herself were just a few yards away, but she felt that if she stood up now, broke the spell, she wouldn't have the guts to try again. She'd just swallow it all down again, keep trying to make it not true, plaster a joyous smile over the cracks.

"Is it because you're scared?" Anna asked. "Or because it doesn't feel right?"

Matilda shook her head.

"I don't know," she whispered. "I have no idea. I just . . . I thought I'd have more time. It wasn't like we were trying or anything. I mean, it took my parents two years to get pregnant with my sister! And then four more to have me, even though they started trying again almost immediately. I always assumed I'd be the same. I thought I'd have some time to make up my mind, or get used to the idea, or . . . something."

Anna nodded.

"Of course, Carl would have type A, overachieving super-sperm," she said.

Matilda stared at her. Then she burst out laughing, louder than she'd expected, surprising both herself and Anna, who raised her eyebrows before smiling.

Out of the corner of her eye Matilda saw Evelina look over at them, and she smiled at her, trying to look normal, and drunk, and like they weren't talking about anything important. Evelina didn't smile back. She'd never liked being left out of the joke.

"Are you guys ready to go skinny-dipping yet?" Evelina yelled, louder than necessary. Her face was very red, and very shiny, courtesy of both the alcohol and the joint she'd shared with Anna and Linnea earlier. Her short, caramel-colored hair was hanging frizzy around her face, and she had spilled beer on her sweater. She would have been mortified if she'd known.

"Yeah, let's do it," Linnea said, pulling her thick, chestnut curls into a ponytail at the nape of her neck. Matilda had been surprised when she'd seen Linnea had dyed her hair, but it suited her.

Linnea was just one of those girls. Always had been. Once upon a time, it used to make Matilda feel self-conscious about her own appearance.

Oh, what the hell. It still made her feel self-conscious.

"Maybe wait to undress till we're down by the beach, Evie," Anna pointed out, and Evelina, who had been in the process of unzipping her hoodie, let go of the zipper.

"Good point," Evelina said. "But yeah, let's go! Before it gets too cold!"

It was always too cold this time of year. That was sort of the point. But Matilda couldn't help but smile at her, anyway, at the enthusiasm that was breaking through.

"You guys go ahead," she told Evelina and Linnea. "I'll be right behind you."

Evelina and Linnea took off toward the beach, weaving drunkenly over the cliffs between the sparse trees.

Anna leaned in a little closer to Matilda.

"Are you okay to go swimming?" she asked quietly. "Or is the embryo going to get freezer burn?"

Matilda snorted.

"Dear God, woman, what did they teach you in Sex Ed? No, it's fine." She paused. "Actually, I don't know if I'm allowed to go swimming in cold water or not," she said.

Anna smirked.

"Exactly," she said. "Anyway, it doesn't matter. You can stay on the shore. We'll just say you have a cold. I'll keep them distracted."

Matilda smiled. Lopsided and a little wobbly.

"Thank you," she said.

"We can talk about it more later," Anna said. "Linnea always passes out first, and Evelina won't last more than a couple more hours." She stood up from the log and stretched, her short form elongating against the blue of the sky.

They left their shoes by the fire, walked barefoot down the path that the other two had staked for them. The isle always felt larger at night, as though all the little shadowy crevices in the harsh terrain added some unknown dimension to the rocky surface. Matilda felt herself breathing deeper, smelling the sweet and the salt of the brackish water that surrounded them on all sides, the smoke in her own hair, the non-alcoholic beer on her breath.

Would they be back here again next year? Or would she be at home, sleep-deprived and hollow-eyed, trying to figure out how to keep a tiny, screaming bundle alive?

It was so hard to imagine.

Anna, and Linnea, and Evelina, and Isle Blind; those all felt real, more so, sometimes, than anything else in her life. There was a continuity here that everything else seemed to lack. Something binding her to the past, something she had always assumed would keep on stretching into her future, the thread running through her life.

Would she have to let go of this? For some new person she'd never met who had the audacity to grow inside her?

It seemed absurd.

The shore wasn't more than a stone's throw away now, the water glittering softly in the dark. They had anchored the jetty on the other side of the island, but this was the best place to swim, the cliffs sloping gently into the water.

"What is she doing?" Anna muttered, and Matilda tore herself away from the view of the deep black of the sea, saw Linnea lying on her back on the shore just a couple of feet from the waterline.

"You were right, she does always pass out first," Matilda said.

Anna shook her head.

"We'll pour some water on her face," she said, "that should wake her up enough to get her back to the tent. God, she's going to snore like a bear tonight. That should be fun."

Matilda crouched down by Linnea while Anna stayed a couple of steps behind, looking around.

"Where's Evelina? You don't think she went into the water on her own, do you? I know she's drunk, but she should know better."

Matilda was still laughing as she reached over to touch Linnea's cheek.

"Hey, Linnea," Matilda said. She patted her softly on the cheek. "Are you awake? You can't sleep here, you're going to get cold."

Linnea didn't respond.

Matilda's eyes were registering the details, even as she was rejecting them. The oddness of the way her head was resting against the stone. The very geometry of it was wrong.

Linnea's eyes were open, staring up into the sky. They were gleaming but devoid of luster, like shards of glass polished to dullness by the sand.

Oh, and the stillness of her. That terrible lack of movement.

Her body reacted before her mind had time to catch up. She felt herself withdrawing her hand, as though she'd been burned. She felt the blood, thick and sticky on her fingertips. She felt her breath catch, as though the air itself had gained mass, lodged itself in her throat.

Her thoughts grew smaller and seemed to shrink back, make themselves unreachable.

Linnea had been dancing, just a few minutes ago. She was such a bad dancer. It always made Matilda smile.

She wanted to say Linnea's name, but it would not let itself be spoken. The silence was the only thing protecting her against the truth.

The scream started building in her throat but was cut short by a sudden, horrible gurgling. Matilda grabbed Linnea's shoulders, leaned down over her, only half aware of the tears streaming soundlessly down her cheeks.

"Linnea? It's going to be okay, sweetie, okay, we're going to call for an ambulance, or an—an ambulance boat, we'll get you to a hospital, I promise. What happened, did you fall? Did Evelina run to get help?"

Linnea's head lolled. Her eyes half closed, only the whites showing. Her lips weren't moving.

"Linnea?"

Still that awful, wet sound.

But it wasn't coming from Linnea.

Matilda raised her eyes to Anna, wanting her to make sense of it, wanting her to take charge, like she always did. Wanting her to already be on her phone, calling for a boat or a helicopter, wanting her to know what to do. To tell Matilda what to do.

But Anna wasn't on her phone. Anna wasn't speaking at all.

The blade protruding from her throat just under her jaw was thick and flat, almost as wide as her slim, pale neck. The blood was steadily drenching the front of her white T-shirt. The rivulets at the corners of her mouth had already reached her strong, beautiful jawline, dripping down onto those tresses of blond hair.

How Matilda had coveted that hair when they had been teenagers.

Matilda knew she had to do something. She should scream, or run. But she just sat there as the black-clad figure behind Anna pulled the knife back, sending her best friend crumpling to the ground.

Things like this didn't happen. Not in real life.

When the figure in black approached, the knife firmly clasped in gloved hand, Matilda sat next to Linnea and looked out at the water.

She should run. She should scream for her life. She should beg, say she was pregnant, promise not to tell. Do anything and everything to get away.

Maybe the girl she had once been would have had the strength to do that.

Instead, she looked out over the water. Feeling her breath coming in small, shallow gulps, the tears drying on her cheeks, her muscles locked in rigid shock, until she felt the metal against her neck.

It wasn't cold like she would have expected. It was warm and wet.

She looked out over the waves and felt with absolute certainty that this wasn't real. She was about to wake up at any moment.

When she turned her head, she started, and for a moment, everything seemed so very clear.

But the insight had come too late.

There was no time to fight, or to plead.

When the blade slid through her skin, the pain of realization was almost greater than the pain of the cut.

Almost.

Subject: IT'S FINALLY TIME!

Hey ladies!

Can you believe it's almost time? After all of the prep and planning it's finally happening! I am SO excited to see you all and celebrate the end to Anneliese's single life!

I assume you've all checked out the gorgeous hotel that's booked for just us the whole weekend. Baltic Vinyasa is an ultraluxe new yoga resort, with in-house vegan catering, and we will be the first guests to EVER get to experience it!

Extra thanks to Lena for finding this fantastic deal! We all owe you one, girl!

Since it has yet to open to the public, there will be minimal staff (so don't do anything crazy in your rooms, as there will be no house-keeping . . . well, don't do anything crazy without inviting the Maid of Honor!!)

As I mentioned in the previous two emails, the Baltic Vinyasa philos-ophy is all about living in the moment and making memories. As such, there is no Wi-Fi on the island, and our phones will be collected on arrival. The owner has requested that we all follow the policy for the sake of our collective experience, so please, no fussing when it's time! Work can wait until our gorgeous once-in-a-lifetime weekend is over. And if you're worried about pictures, don't fret, because our lovely Natalie has donated her services as a photographer!

Attached is a suggested packing list, your schedule for the week-end, as well as different ways of getting to Stavsnäs Harbor, where a private ferry will be picking us up at 10:00 Thursday morning to bring us out to Isle Blind. I hate to be a nag, but please make sure to be there at 09:30, as the schedule depends on the boat actually departing on time.

I hope you are all ready for a weekend of yoga, bonding, beauty and cava! Can't wait!!!

Xoxo,

Mikaela (Maid of Honor)

SUGGESTED PACKING

TO BRING:
Four sets of athletic clothing
Three party dresses (can't phone it in just because it's on an island in
    the middle of the archipelago, girls! I want to see GLAMOUR!)
Comfortable shoes for meditative walks
Two sweaters (it gets cold out there!)
Moisturizer (the air in the archipelago is very dry, and we don't want
    flaking faces in the pictures!)
Sunscreen
Bridal gift(s)
Any funny stories or anecdotes you might have about the bride

LEAVE AT HOME:
Yoga mat (this will be provided)
Any "party favors" (Anneliese has requested the only drug at the party
    be joy)
Laptops
Tablets
Negative thoughts
Bad vibes

CHAPTER 1

April 14, 2022

If I kill myself, I don't have to go.

The rays of the early-morning sun are filtering in through the cheap, gauzy curtains that are one of the few things remaining in the bedroom, and the hangover is threatening to push its way up my throat. Whisky is never kind to the system, and cheap whisky even less so. But it helps me sleep, these days.

I don't think I'm an alcoholic. Not yet, at least. But with some more practice, who knows?

As I sit up in my bed, I catch sight of my suitcase on the floor, still gaping suspiciously empty. I've got less than forty minutes before it's time to go. I had intended to pack last night, but wallowing held more appeal, and so far all I've managed to fit into it is an old, worn pair of jeans and a few pairs of underwear.

Don't go, then. It'll be horrible. Humiliating.

Just make up an excuse and stay here.

Anneliese probably doesn't even want you to come.

Oh, but the appeal of my worst self is tempting.

A four-day yoga-themed bachelorette party on a tiny island in the middle of the archipelago would not have been high on my list of wants even at the best of times. And the last few months have been very far from the best of times.

When Anneliese first invited me to be part of her bridal party, I'd felt all the emotions I was supposed to feel. Pride, and joy, and nostalgia. All that stuff.

But, sure. There was a pinprick of something else.

I have known these women half a lifetime, and for most of those years, I had been the fuckup. The one who was never going to amount to anything. The one who dropped out of college, the one who couldn't hold down a partner, the one who skipped from job to job while endlessly having to move back home over and over again due to lack of funds.

And then it finally happened for me. I made something of myself. I created something people liked, and it started growing, and I found myself someone who was, if not admired, then at least respected.

When Anneliese told me she wanted me to be a bridesmaid, it seemed like an excellent opportunity to show everyone what kind of person I had become.

The memory has a bitter taste to it now.

The plan had been to drop out of the wedding. Drop off the face of the Earth, actually. Anneliese called me and begged me to participate, and even the voice of my oldest, if not closest, friend would not have been enough to convince me.

Until she told me where the bachelorette party was going to be.

I've been trying to get access to Isle Blind for years now. But it's privately owned, and the owners always refused to answer my emails.

This could be my chance. My one, final chance to take back what was lost, to re-create what I'd ruined.

So I'm going, no matter how little I want to.

My phone beeps, and I pick it up.

Lena
I'll be at yours in 30. Ready to go?

I stare at the message for a couple of seconds before I send her a quick thumbs-up back. Then I start picking stuff off the floor and throwing it in the suitcase. Hopefully my truly god-awful yoga skills will distract from my threadbare exercise wear.

I've got less than two hundred kronor in my bank account. I've missed my last two mortgage payments. I've had to sell most of my furniture just to be able to buy food and cheap booze.

And I'm about to go on a luxury yoga weekend at a private hotel in the archipelago.

As I pack, I can hear my own podcasting voice in my head—slightly deeper than my speaking voice, to add some much-needed richness.

"They thought they were going to spend the weekend celebrating their friend's upcoming wedding. They had it all planned out; ninety-six hours of yoga, cava, and female bonding. What could possibly go wrong?

"Welcome to The Witching Hour. *This is Tessa Nilsson, and today we bring you the story . . . of the Bachelorette Party."*

CHAPTER 2

April 14, 2022

The sun is bright in that very specific way that only seems to happen in Stockholm in April, a light so strong it almost seems to have its own smell. The sky is high and painfully blue, the sidewalk full of new moms strolling with their beautiful babies, shiny ponytails bouncing and takeaway coffee cups held high.

I wish I hadn't had that last drink last night.

I wish I had a drink right now.

Hangovers always make me feel at odds with the world. I've never felt quite at home in Stockholm, even though I grew up here. It always felt like a club that was slightly too cool to let me join, satisfied to have me hanging around the edges but not quite generous enough to let me in.

Minna always used to say that nothing marked me more as a child of Stockholm than the fact that I didn't feel like I belonged. Her theory was that people like her, who'd moved to the city as adults, took to it immediately, while people like me who were born and raised here never managed to figure it out.

I remember telling her that didn't make any sense. She laughed at me, her teeth glinting in the dim light.

I can't remember which bar we were at. I just remember that we were happy. Celebrating something or other.

There was so much to celebrate, back then.

I was drunk on success, drunk on her, drunk on the champagne that always seemed to be flowing like water. There was always somewhere to be. Someone to be.

God, but the memory hurts. I pull back from it, force myself to focus on the headache that's building behind my left eyebrow.

Where is Lena?

She's usually so punctual. She's always been the well-organized sister, the high achiever. Usually she's the one scolding me for being two minutes late. I wish I could look forward to making fun of her for not being exactly on time, but if Lena is late, then she's got a very good, very important reason to be late, and I will end up looking like an idiot for ever having questioned her.

And then I see her.

Her little, black, electric BMW takes the corner and pulls up neatly to the sidewalk. Even the car is so perfectly Lena.

I drag my sad little wheelie bag to the trunk, check the license plate to make doubly sure that I'm not stuffing my luggage in some stranger's car, and pop it open.

"Hey," I call out while I put my bag next to Lena's Louis Vuitton–emblazoned carryall.

"Hey, yourself," she calls back, and immediately follows it up with, "Come on, hurry up, we don't want to miss the boat."

Lena is sitting in the driver's seat. Her hair is hanging in thick, glossy hazel-brown ropes down her back, and a pair of gigantic sunglasses are sitting daintily on the bridge of her nose. She's perfectly decked out in loose-fitting clothes that would look sloppy on anyone who'd dare to wear them with an ounce less confidence.

I wish I could resent her for it, but even in my state of general self-loathing, the sight of my sister brightens my mood. I smile, despite myself, as I climb into the passenger seat.

Lena does not smile. She looks at me and raises her eyebrows.

"Is that what you're wearing?" she asks.

"Wow, your impression of Mom is really coming along," I respond.

Lena sighs.

"I could have lent you something, you know," she says, her chiding me stinging all the more because of her gentle tone.

Lena has always been the one relationship I don't have to overthink—she is just my big sister, the dynamic set in stone since the moment of my conception—but I haven't seen much of her in the last few months. Been too busy hating myself and hiding from the world, which is not really an excuse.

"I didn't want to put you out," I say.

Lena presses her lips together, hard enough to create lines radiating from the corners of her mouth, and I feel a small pang of tenderness at the sight of them, a feeling I can't quite explain even to myself.

"Are you sure you're up for this?" she asks me.

She's always been able to read me a little too well.

"Of course I am," I respond, my attempt at a casual, upbeat tone convincing no one.

"I know it's been . . . hard," Lena says, ever the diplomat. "Everyone would understand if you didn't want to come."

"What could be better than a weekend surrounded by old friends?" I'd like to say my smile looks natural and convincing; I can tell from her expression that it is not.

"I just think it might be a bit much for you, right now," Lena presses on. "You haven't been answering your phone. You haven't been answering my texts. Even Franz is worried about you."

"Oh, even Franz, you say?"

Her husband has never been my biggest fan. The feeling is mutual. It's not so much that I dislike Franz, and I don't think he has anything against me either, not really. We are just such fundamentally different people that there is no overlap whatsoever in our personalities. Whenever I try to make conversation with Franz, it's like I'm speaking Human and he is speaking Corporate.

Or maybe I'm just a bit of a bitch.

"Tessa, please," Lena says. "Look, I don't want to fight. If you want to go, we can go. I just want to say that, as someone who cares about you, you don't seem well. I mean, look at you."

I look away, not wanting her to see the tears welling up.

It's not that I'm upset at her comment; it's nothing more and nothing less than an accurate observation.

But there's a reason I haven't seen Lena for a while. At the first sight of care or kindness, I can feel my fragile façade start to crack. It's easier, and more comfortable, to stick with solitude and self-loathing, to keep trying to build an exoskeleton of feigned indifference.

After a couple of seconds I can feel Lena's well-groomed hand softly squeezing mine.

I say nothing. I squeeze back.

She releases me, and I hear her start the car.

"All right," she says, performing joie de vivre much more successfully than I did. "Let's go."

Eager to avoid conversation, I dive into my phone. My fingers move without my consent, bringing me to the social media app I should have deleted weeks ago, and find Minna's account.

She's posted two new stories since I last checked right before falling asleep. I manage to not click them, but it takes near-superhuman strength of will, and I don't have enough effort left in me to stop myself from scrolling through her feed.

Here, a selfie with a new short, pastel-pink haircut, one I've never seen in person; there, a picture of her and a former colleague of mine raising their glasses to celebrate another milestone reached.

She's changed her bio. It used to read "Minna Jacobssen. Soon-to-be legend. Producer for @thewitchinghourwithtessanilsson, @whatsupwiththat, and @linnhellströminterviews."

Now it says, "Minna J. Woman, Warrior, Legend. Producer for @whatsupwiththat and @linnhellströminterviews. Email: mjacobssen@newgenerationproductions.com."

Even the email address is new.

I wonder how much of the hate that came my way reached her.

There's a reason I've shut down all my old accounts. The one I'm on now is a burner account. An anonymous profile without anything identifiable.

It's possible it's more like a creeper account, but I prefer not to think about it that way.

"Stop cyber-stalking your ex," Lena says.

"Keep your eyes on the road," I respond. "And she's not my ex."

"Ex-producer, then," Lena says. "Trust me. Doesn't matter what kind of ex it is. It's not going to make you feel better."

I don't want to argue with Lena, especially not when I know I won't be able to win, so I exit the app and put my phone away.

Minna isn't my ex. Not really. In order to be my ex, we would have had to formally be together, and we never were. Not in any official capacity.

We were never even exclusive. Two years of spending long mornings in bed and long nights at different industry events, and I don't even have a name for what we were.

I loved her.

I think.

In retrospect, it's hard to say what I felt. I don't know whether I grieve losing her as a partner or as a producer, or if those feelings are too tied to the whole train wreck to ever get to exist independently. Maybe she just represents something I am never going to get back.

As the cityscape around us gives way first to brick houses and then to dreamy, rolling fields showing the first colorful bursts of spring, I decide to turn to the only thing capable of making me feel something other than dread.

I've been preparing for the past few weeks. Scouring articles, digging into my old notes.

If I can pull this off—if I can find something on Isle Blind this weekend—it might just turn out to be my salvation.

NACKA-VÄRMDÖ COURIER
June 4, 2012

BOAT FOUND DRIFTING IDENTIFIED
AS BELONGING TO MISSING WOMEN

The search for the four women reported missing on the morning of May 17th has taken a new turn after a small dinghy was found drifting outside of Harö early this morning.

According to a statement from the Nacka Police, Arvid Wittenberg, father of Anna Wittenberg, has identified the dinghy as belonging to him. While police have confirmed that they are still searching for the four women, an inside source has stated that investigators are now focusing on attempted recovery.

"No one is expecting to find them alive," says the local resident who found the boat and who has requested to remain anonymous.

"Considering the state of the boat and the weather the night after they were reported missing, it seems most likely that the girls decided to take the boat out while drunk, had an accident, and went down. It's sad, but it happens. It really just shows the importance of not going out on the sea while intoxicated. These tourists think a boat is like a bicycle, but it's just not safe. This was a wholly preventable accident. I just hope they find the bodies so their families can get some peace of mind."

CHAPTER 3

April 14, 2022

L ena parks the car, and I look up.

In front of the car is the Baltic Sea. Small, fierce waves of blue and iron, a small red cottage housing a bakery seemingly not yet open for the season. There's a boat anchored in the harbor; too big to be a private ship, too small to be a ferry.

In front of it, I see two tall women with handbags slung over their shoulders and expensive, slouchy jeans talking animatedly.

"Are we already here?" I ask Lena, my voice squeaky.

"Yup," she says. "Right on time."

If she's taken notice of my high pitch, she's not letting on. I don't know whether or not to be grateful for that.

Jesus. I got lost in my notes. Over an hour went by without me noticing.

Research always was my biggest weakness; back when I used to run every aspect of the show myself, I'd lose hours and hours to it, poring over obscure webpages from 2003 and old articles I'd dug up from the Wayback Machine archive.

My stomach drops. I'm not sure I'm ready for this.

For the last few weeks, I've been focusing on the task at hand. On the prospect of figuring out what happened to the Nacka Four that evening ten years ago.

I've been keeping my mind off the actual bachelorette party.

Suddenly, the prospect of having to spend the weekend pretending to be having a delightful time with a group of women I haven't seen since most of us were still stuffing our bras is very real. And it dawns on me that I'm scared.

Terrified, in fact.

I swallow, tasting bile in the back of my throat.

Lena clicks away on her phone with furious efficiency, and with a little swoosh sound she puts it away in her purse.

"Okay," she says. "Parking's taken care of for the weekend. Let's go."

I waver.

This is the last moment we've got before we're swallowed up by a whirlwind of pink confetti, sparkling wine, and vegan brunch food. Before ninety-six full hours of having to perform normalcy, of having to pretend like I have my shit even remotely together among women who actually do.

This is my last opportunity to back out.

I square my shoulders, open the door, and step out.

CHAPTER 4

April 14, 2022

My wheelie bag isn't taking to the gravel very well as I walk toward the marina from the parking lot, and my scuffed, heeled, impractical boots are slowing me down. Lena is a couple of steps behind me.

"Oh my God, Theresa!" Mikaela exclaims. "I feel like I haven't seen you in ages!"

She throws her arms around me, and I breathe in a heavy gust of vanilla bean perfume.

"Hi," I manage to squeak out. "Yeah, it's been far too long!"

Nine years, give or take.

Mikaela pulls back, her hands still firm on my shoulders, and she smiles at me through pink-framed Celine sunglasses. Her lacquered beauty still has the power to shock me. When we were teenagers, she wore jeans so low the laws of physics should have stopped them from buttoning, but I never remember her showing as much as half an inch of butt crack.

The flat-ironed hair has been replaced by beachy, highlighted waves, the low-riders by wide-legged Levi's, but she still looks the very image of the girl I used to have an intense, hate-filled crush on.

Of course she's the maid of honor. I couldn't imagine anyone better suited to the role. She'll run the weekend with an iron fist, and we'll all thank her for it, in the end.

"God, you look so different," Mikaela says. "Still the same old Theresa, though, I assume?" Her teeth are very, very straight. It's hypnotizing.

"I go by Tessa now," I say, and try to soften the sentiment with a smile. "But, yeah. Other than that."

"God," Mikaela says, looking me over.

I can't help but wonder what she's seeing. If I am what she expected.

"Hey, Theresa." The other woman waves at me, smiles a bit, and it takes me a moment to recognize her as Natalie. The new girl.

She's the only one I've never met before; the only one of us who didn't grow up in the same circles, in the moneyed Stockholm suburb infamous for the fact that half the population could trace bona fide aristocratic lineage and the other half had made enough money to fit right in.

"It's nice to meet you," she says, and thrusts her hand out to shake mine.

She's got a couple of inches on me, even with my stupid, impractical boots, and she looks almost offensively healthy, as though she lives off rainbows and kale. Her hair is long and corn-silk blond, and when she smiles, her teeth look very white against the golden tan she's somehow managed to attain in Sweden in April.

"Nice to meet you too," I say, and when I shake her hand, I'm surprised by her strong grip.

Natalie looks at me, expectantly, and I realize I'm supposed to say something.

Just make a comment, Tessa. Or ask a question.

Be charming. Be normal.

Yet I find myself frozen in place. It's like I've never met a new person before. I can't remember how social interactions are supposed to work.

Mikaela comes to my rescue. She fastens her gaze on a point right above my shoulder and straightens up.

I imagine Lena has done the same, behind me. Two alpha females recognizing each other.

"You must be Lena, Theresa's sister!" Mikaela says, and steps around me, her arms already wide.

"Yes! Hello!" I hear Lena say, and when I turn, I see they are hugging.

"I've heard so much about you! I'm so excited you could make it. I know Anneliese was worried, what with your job. I mean, I could barely find the time, not with two little ones at home, but I managed to wrangle my husband into taking them!"

Lena just smiles at this.

They separate, and Mikaela turns back to me, saving me from the ongoing awkwardness with Natalie and immediately plunging me into something worse.

"Oh my God, Theresa," she says and grabs me again by the shoulders. She sighs and squeezes my upper arms.

"How are you holding up?"

If I had held on to any hope that the rest of the group would have somehow managed to miss what had happened, that they hadn't read the papers or watched the news, that is now gone.

I desperately want to respond with something snarky, lash out and protect myself, but I try to remind myself that even if I was okay with being a bitch to someone who has, so far, done nothing but ask a fairly obvious question, I really don't want to be the person to fuck up this weekend for Anneliese by making everyone uncomfortable.

I might have ulterior motives for coming, but Anneliese has never been anything but a good friend to me. No matter my own moral shortcomings, I want to try to repay that.

"I'm okay," I say. "It's rough, you know. But I don't want to focus on all that. It's Anneliese's weekend, after all."

Mikaela doesn't let go. She's taken her sunglasses off, and she's fixated those big, blue eyes on me, sadness and understanding almost managing to camouflage the hint of greedy curiosity hiding underneath.

Before she has time to start probing, I turn and make a show of looking around, breaking out of her grip in a way that hopefully looks accidental.

"Where is Anneliese, by the way? I'm so excited to see her!"

"She should be here soon," Natalie says. "She just wrote in the group chat, she's only ten minutes out."

"The group chat?" The question is reflexive, and I realize the answer as I'm asking it.

I look to Lena, but I can't see her eyes behind those damn sunglasses.

Goddamn it. We're two minutes in, and I can already feel my stomach sinking, an echo of my thirteen-year-old self curling in and willing herself not to take it personally.

"Oh my God!" Mikaela says. "Did I forget to add you to the group chat? I'm such an idiot! You know, we almost haven't used it at all yet, it's more for wedding-day stuff anyway. I'll add you right now!"

"Oh, that's okay," I say and smile, refusing to let myself be upset. "It's not like we're going to have our phones out there anyway, right? If I remember correctly, it'll be all about 'living in the moment.'"

"Right," Mikaela says, and she shoots me a smile that almost looks grateful. "But I'll add you anyway. I feel really, really bad, and I don't want to forget again!"

She seems so sincere that I decide to believe her. Maybe she really did just forget.

"Oh, I think that's Caroline!" Natalie says, and I turn around.

A small, impossibly cool red car has turned into the parking lot. I don't know enough about cars to be able to tell what kind it is; all I know is that it looks vintage, with clean, organic lines and a sloping silhouette.

"Wow," Lena says next to me, and I see her pushing her sunglasses down to get a better look.

"God, I would love to have a cute little number like that." Mikaela sighs. "It's just so hard with kids, you know. You tell yourself you're never going to be one of those moms who keep talking about how practical it is with an SUV and then, poof! One day you're standing there and you hear yourself sounding like a sponsored ad for Volvo."

On the plus side, Caroline hasn't chosen to wear what appears to be the uniform of the weekend—straight-legged jeans, flat shoes, light knitwear—but is instead in spiky boots the exact same red as the car and black slacks that seem painted on her slim legs.

Anneliese mentioned that she's a family therapist now. She doesn't look like any therapist I've ever met.

"Caro!" Natalie is waving at her, and Caroline raises a hesitant hand, smiling a small, secret smile. Her lips are bare, and I immediately want to wipe off the smear of lipstick I painted on a couple of hours ago thinking it would give some color to my worn face.

"Hey," she says, stopping just a little further away from the rest of us. It makes her seem apart from the group.

"God, look at you!" Mikaela exclaims. "You look like a completely different person!"

"Well," Caroline says. She doesn't say anything more than that.

It seems I'm not the only person who's lost touch with the group. It should make me feel better, but instead it makes me feel some combination of lovesick and crushed.

Back in the day, Caroline was quiet and studious, another one of Anneliese's projects. I remember her as having been funny, in a dark, understated way, which, if I had been less focused on my own adolescent angst, would have signaled to me that she had yet to hit her stride; that she'd find herself in the years to come. After we'd all shed our braces and switched Clearasil for retinol.

With her black, cat eye glasses and short, choppy, expertly highlighted haircut, she looks cool, and slightly mysterious. Exactly the kind of woman I'd let ruin my life.

My admiration is interrupted by Lena exclaiming:

"There she is!"

We all turn toward the road.

Anneliese.

The bride.

I can't help but laugh, despite myself.

The limo is utterly out of place, both in the beautiful, rural environment and in the year of our Lord 2022. It's way too long to turn gracefully on the narrow road, and so it's driving slowly enough that I can imagine the chauffeur sweating.

Anneliese is sticking out of the roof, an unopened bottle of champagne in one hand and a bouquet of flowers in the other, with a tiara perched on top of her caramel curls and a huge, beaming smile on her lips. I can't stop myself from laughing, and it's only when I feel it that I realize the rest of them are laughing with me.

"Hey, ladies!" I hear Anneliese's voice coming faintly from the road. "Who's ready to party?"

CHAPTER 5

April 14, 2022

I hang back a bit as the others descend on Anneliese, watch her interact with them through hugs and squeals. Even Lena gives her a big hug, and I feel my stomach twist, just a little bit. There is a small, angry child inside of me, whining that Lena is supposed to be *my* sister, Anneliese *my* friend.

Odd as it may seem, I've always sorted them into different categories, even knowing that they have a friendship of their own. I've never actually spent time with the two of them together; I don't know anything about their dynamic.

Honestly, when Lena told me Anneliese had asked her to be a bridesmaid, I was surprised. I'd never understood them to be quite that close. Certainly, Lena never talked much about Anneliese to me.

But maybe I was never as subtle about feeling territorial as I thought I was.

That doesn't make me feel any better.

Watching Anneliese, I'm reminded of something I'd managed to forget, that special brand of magic she's always possessed. After all these years, some part of me is still surprised we're friends.

It would have been so easy to hate her, after all. Not just for her tall, slim figure or that halo of springy, golden curls, not just for her wealthy origins or her seemingly effortless professional success, but for that easy laugh, the way everything always seems to go her way.

The secret to it all, as I discovered some fifteen years ago, is that Anneliese is genuinely nice. Ever since I met her, she's always delighted in the people around her. I'm not her only weird friend; her social network stretches far and wide, and she never forgets a name.

For the first time since I got that final email, I feel bad about how I'm planning on spending the weekend.

I shouldn't be here to investigate a ten-year-old cold case, hoping to resurrect my dead career. I should be here to celebrate my friend.

"Tessa!" Anneliese exclaims, as if on cue, and she throws her arms around me.

Natalie has already picked up her bags; yet another Anneliese trademark. People always seem to just do things for her, without her ever having to ask.

"Hey," I laugh, and hug her back, feeling the surprising strength in her long, skinny arms.

She whispers in my ear, so close I can feel her hair tickling my cheek.

"I'm so glad you came. I wasn't sure you would."

I swallow, hard.

"Of course," I manage to croak out. "I wouldn't miss it."

Anneliese pulls back, a crooked little smile on her perfectly glossed lips.

"Liar," she says, but there's no rancor in her voice.

"Annie?" I hear Mikaela say. "Honey, I think we should all start to board. We don't want to get off schedule."

Anneliese releases me and salutes.

"You all heard the maid of honor! To sea!"

The boat in question looks like it might have been confiscated from a Russian oligarch, all dark, gleaming wood and swooping lines. I'm last to get on, and when I step onto the gleaming wooden deck a man hands me a glass full of pale sparkling wine. He looks like an AI-generated image of a handsome man: tall, broad-shouldered, clean jawline, and thick reddish-brown hair sparkling in the sun.

Not my usual type, but I still find myself hoping he'll join us at the hotel. I could do with some half-drunken sloppy sex with someone I'll never see again; even if he's terrible in bed, which seems like a near certainty given his looks, it would still make me feel better.

"Thank you," I say, hold his gaze a second too long, and then smile. Can't hurt to start laying the groundwork if I want something to happen tomorrow night.

"Of course," he says, smiling with perfect teeth. "Welcome aboard the *Gull*."

"Delighted to be here," I say, surprised to find that I kind of mean it.

I drop my luggage next to the neat pile of suitcases and ascend the narrow staircase to the upper deck. The sun is near blinding up here, reflecting off the small, cheery waves below. Aside from a mild breeze smelling like a promise of summer, there's no wind; until we get going, nobody's hair is getting messed up.

I take a sip of my sparkling wine, the smooth, cold flavor momentarily fighting my nausea and winning, and then I walk up to Lena, who's standing by the railing talking to Natalie.

". . . sounds really exciting," I hear Lena finish her sentence. Her posture is ramrod-straight, and she's taken off her sunglasses so as to be able to fully look Natalie in the eyes. Lena in full social mode has always been a sight to behold, but she seems slightly more manic than usual.

It suddenly dawns on me that she's nervous. I've been so focused on my own shit I've completely failed to notice.

But maybe I can help.

"I see you guys have gotten to talking!" I say, clinking my glass against Natalie's with a bit more force than I intended.

Natalie's eyes narrow, making her tiny nose crease. She resembles nothing so much as a small cartoon mouse. Something by Disney or Pixar, a cutesy creature to be mass-produced for the adoration of one million toddlers.

"Natalie was just telling me about her photography business," Lena says. "You guys should talk, actually! Natalie had to start over from scratch. It's honestly really inspiring."

Natalie smiles, close-lipped, her line of sight skidding off to the side.

I look around, searching for some kind of escape, some other conversation to join, and come up empty. Anneliese and Mikaela are locked in a tight huddle, whispering and giggling, shutting the whole world out, and Caroline is nowhere to be seen.

"Not that inspiring," Natalie says. "You do what you have to."

"So what happened?" I ask. "Did you get laid off from work and decide to pursue your dreams?"

Lena's smile grows slightly stiffer, and Natalie attempts a small laugh.

"Oh, you know," she says. "I got divorced, and fell out with my business partner, so now I'm trying to make it work on my own."

"I'm sorry," I say, and swallow.

Shit. I've managed to make it awkward.

"No, God, don't worry," she says. "Worse things have happened to better people. It's going well. I've got a new apartment, and it's pretty nice. People get divorced every day. I still have my career, and my reputation, and . . ."

Her voice dies out.

She flushes.

"I'm so sorry," Natalie says, her voice only slightly squeaky. "I didn't mean . . ."

"It's okay," I say, waving her off, not meaning it but trying to sound like I do. "It's not like it's a secret or anything."

Of course she knows. Everyone knows.

Natalie takes a swig from her glass and, with a bold glint in her eyes, asks me:

"How are you—I mean, how is everything? Are you doing okay?"

For a split second I imagine being honest. It might be freeing, telling the truth to a virtual stranger.

Well, the bank is about to seize my apartment, I've lost my job, I have no formal skills or, for that matter, a degree to fall back on. None of the people I thought of as friends will take my calls, my producer and not-girlfriend has blocked me, and I'm completely out of money. I'm fairly certain I couldn't get hired at a McDonald's at the moment.

"You know, I'm getting by," I say.

"Is it true that they are . . . I mean . . ." Natalie has apparently run out of audacity. I imagine she'll regain it after a little bit more champagne.

"The lawsuit?" I rip off the figurative Band-Aid. "Nothing has been filed yet, as far as I know. We'll see."

I smile. Natalie smiles back. I have successfully turned the worst thing that has ever happened to me into cocktail party conversation.

How's that for progress?

The boat starts to hum under my feet.

"Oh, we're going!" Lena lights up, clearly relieved to have something else to talk about.

The wind picks up a bit now that we're pushing away from the harbor. The movement is slight, the boat steady on the water, but it's still making me wish I had skipped that wine.

Lena takes a quick look at her phone, and Natalie laughs.

"Are you feeling the pre-withdrawals yet?" she says to Lena.

"God, yes," Lena responds. "I wish I wasn't so addicted to my devices. But I think this will be good for me. I've never made it more than four hours into a digital detox on my own."

"We'll have to start passing notes again," Natalie says. "Like in high school."

"Oh, I like that!" Lena says and lights up. "Or, well, I wasn't in high school with the rest of them. Though neither were you, so I guess that's okay. But the passing of the notes is great. I'm sure Irene will have papers or Post-it notes or something."

Natalie fishes her own phone out of her pocket and looks at it.

"What's the island called again?" Natalie asks, thumbing at her phone. "My brother said something about having sailed by there."

"Isle Blind," I say.

It feels strange, saying it out loud, having read it so many times over the past ten years. Almost as though I'm breaking a promise. Revealing a secret.

"That's a strange name for an island," Lena says.

"It's an old sailor's term," I respond. "A 'blind isle' is an underwater rock or cliff right under the surface of the water. Back in the day, it was considered one of the most dangerous parts of navigating the coast-line, since it was so easy to run aground on one of them or scrape a hole in the hull. Especially at night. If you didn't know it was there, you'd never see it in time. Ergo, blind isle. Isle Blind."

Natalie shudders.

"God, that's creepy," she says.

I'm finding it difficult to stop, now that I've started talking about it.

"There's an old poem about it," I say. "Well, not about Isle Blind, in particular, but about blind isles." I draw a deep breath.

"*A crack, a crash, a swallowed shout; the sudden swell of silence; of yellowed teeth, a naked smile; resting beneath the blind isle—*"

"Gosh, Tessa, you don't have to prove how much more cultural you are than the rest of us," Lena interrupts me with a brittle laugh.

She turns to Natalie.

"It's supposed to be gorgeous," she says. "All this raw natural beauty, paired with pure luxury. I know the owner, and she's really transformed the place."

When Natalie laughs, it's tinged with relief.

"I hope so," she says. "I could really use some pampering."

I bite my tongue, feeling the burn of blushing on my cheeks. Lena has taken over the conversation, chatting on about how she met the owner of the hotel, what a lovely woman she is, and I take another sip of champagne. It tastes mostly of metal, at this point.

I could have kept talking. I could have kept telling them about Isle Blind.

About how it rose from the depths of the sea over the course of millennia, just one of many small islands making up an archipelago. How it never held any value to anyone before this, sold and traded as part of the fishing waters that surrounded it. Too small to support a community, to barren to bear any crops.

No point of interest to anyone.

Not even the police, ten years ago, when four women went missing around those parts. The Nacka Four, as they were called.

Everyone assumed they had gotten drunk, taken the boat out, and drowned.

The boat was found drifting. The bodies were never recovered.

It was never thought to be anything more than a tragic accident.

The police never looked into any other possibilities.

They never even took a look at Isle Blind, owned, at the time, by the father of one of the women. Despite reports from the year before by the volunteer coastal rescue service of loud music coming from the island, late at night. Despite the friends and families of the presumed deceased confirming that the four women had gone on a trip out to the archipelago that very weekend, every year, to an unknown location. Despite two of the women having grown up around the sea and one of them having worked as a boating instructor, making it unlikely that they'd be so stupid as to take a boat out while drunk and not wearing life jackets.

If I am right—if the Nacka Four, named for the last place they were seen alive, did, in fact, spend that fateful night on Isle Blind, and if something much more sinister than an accidental drowning happened to them—Isle Blind is not just the site of a gorgeous new boutique hotel.

It's the site of a massacre.

Which would be bad news for the owner. But very, very good news for me.

May 8, 2012

"**H**oney? You okay?"

Carl's voice floated through the thin, wooden door, worried and slightly nasal. He always got congested, this time of year.

Matilda spat one final time, then reached up to flush the toilet without looking at the disgusting mess within.

Just the smell was enough to set her off again, but there was nothing left in her stomach.

"Tilly, are you okay?" he asked again, and Matilda felt a surge of irritation, sudden and choking, something white hot building in her throat.

She swallowed it down.

"I'm fine," she forced herself to say. "Guess the oatmeal didn't agree with me."

The nausea hadn't been too bad, so far. Certainly not as bad as the internet had suggested it would be.

"Sweetie, can you open the door?"

Matilda felt a tear making its way down her cheek, and she closed her eyes hard, so hard it made her face hurt.

She didn't want to open the door. She didn't want Carl to see her like this.

She didn't want anyone to see her like this.

She didn't want to feel like this.

"Tilly?" he asked again, and his voice was oh-so-soft, and the rage threatened to push its way up from her innards again, burst out through her mouth and take her whole relationship down with it.

"I brought you some ginger. I think you're supposed to chew on it. I peeled it and cut it up and sprinkled it with sugar. I googled it, and it's supposed to help with the nausea."

The rage receded.

"Okay," she whispered, grabbed ahold of the sink to hoist herself up, and opened the bathroom door.

Carl was standing just outside, holding a small bowl full of neatly cut up ginger, with that worried little wrinkle between his eyebrows she knew so well. Matilda felt herself well up again.

"Oh, honey," Carl said, and opened his arms.

She didn't want a hug. Not really. She was sweaty, and her mouth tasted like puke, and she was so tired.

She wanted her mom. She wanted to be five years old again, and to be in bed, sick, and to have her mom bring her minestrone with the beans picked out. She didn't want to be an adult, didn't want to have to go to work with her stomach still roiling and the world assaulting her with smells, didn't want to have to smile bravely and pretend it was all okay since it was all for a small lump of cells that would, at some point, turn into a baby.

But she couldn't resist him worrying about her. She'd always been powerless in the face of that sad little frown.

So she let him hug her.

"It's going to be okay," Carl said. "I can call the office for you. Tell them you have food poisoning. I'll say you have it coming out both ends. They won't ask any questions about that."

Matilda laughed, despite herself, and sniffled.

"I wish I could do this for you," Carl muttered. "I wish I was the one feeling shitty and run-down. It doesn't seem fair, that you're the one who has to do all the work."

Matilda wiped her face with the back of her hand and took a step back. She exhaled hard.

"No, I can do it," she said, trying to sound brave. "I can't miss the end-of-quarter meeting today. Hand me that bowl of raw ginger."

Carl smiled softly as she put a cube in her mouth and bit down, grimacing from the flavor.

"That's my girl," he said.

Matilda chewed, breathing through her nose, and tried to smile.

Maybe he was right.

Maybe it would all be okay.

If she just kept on pretending.

CHAPTER 6

April 14, 2022

Back when I first started recording *The Witching Hour with Tessa Nilsson,* I called the podcast *Sweden After Dark.* Minna made me switch it when we signed the distribution deal, since she said "Sweden After Dark" sounded like a '70s VHS porno.

I never did feel quite comfortable with the new title. I guess it was at that point that I lost control over the whole thing. Easy to spot with hindsight, but at the time, I was blind to it.

I got hooked on true crime as a teenager. The Nacka Four case was the inciting incident to a lifelong love affair. I was a teenager when it happened, and it rocked the small community I grew up in. Things like that simply weren't supposed to happen to people like them.

Or, people like us, as my parents would have put it.

At the time, I couldn't explain what it was that captivated me so about the case. I had always been interested in the macabre, had always been drawn to movies I was not allowed to watch and books that made the school librarian purse her lips; but those had all been fiction. Death appeared to me, at the time, as something that happened far away from me, something so strange and dramatic that it could never touch a life as miserably mundane as mine.

In the end, I guess I wanted to be interesting. And when the Nacka Four disappeared after departing from Nacka Beach, never to be seen again, it seemed to grant them a kind of mystery I could never hope to attain.

I scoured the details of their lives, hoping to find a clue, any clue, as to what might have happened to them. They were older than me and my sister, sure, but they were made from the same mold. At least the same mold as Lena. Beautiful, and talented, and destined for an easy, beautiful life.

Until something happened.

I got to know them through bits and pieces of articles and interviews, held on feverishly to every detail. Linnea, and Evelina, and Matilda, and Anna—they felt like my friends. More real to me than the people around me. I felt close to them, in some strange way. I felt like I had a responsibility. As if I, nineteen-year-old Tessa Nilsson, was going to be the one to figure it out. To find them. To save them.

When my mother mentioned that one of them, Matilda, had babysat me and Lena when we were kids, it only inflamed my interest. Lena remembered her as "Tilly," and I hounded Lena for details for days, until Lena finally, unusually, lost her patience and snapped at me. She told me to stop; told me that I was being creepy, and morbid.

But I couldn't. It horrified me. And fascinated me.

The idea that someone I'd met, someone who'd grown up close to our house, someone who'd had everything going for them, could meet with a sudden, mysterious end filled me with a longing to understand. To research. To learn, in order to make sure it would never, ever happen to me.

I spent my days kind-of-sort-of hanging out with Anneliese and her friends and my nights searching out old user-created Tumblr pages detailing gruesome murders and horrifying unsolved cases. My babysitter caught me a couple of times and ratted me out to my parents, who tried to deal with it by denying me computer privileges for two weeks. Those two weeks seemed like an eternity. Staring at the compact screen of our sturdy family computer without being able to access that beautiful, magical, horrifying online world felt like an itch under my skin.

There was something about horror and true crime that made me feel better about myself, as though I was in control. All that anxiety I was struggling with would finally come in handy if I was in that situation, I'd think, because I would be prepared. I would know what to do and what not to do. I would never run up the stairs if the murderer came in through the front door—I would throw something in his path and run to the kitchen door, or lock myself in the bathroom and crawl out the window.

I never thought I would end up turning it into a career. That was never the goal. The podcast was more something I stumbled into than anything else. It started with me getting annoyed at never finding any good sources on Swedish cold cases. I'd find a detail here, a witness statement there, but there was no one compiling them into something readable.

Sure, there were blogs chronicling horrible cases from the U.S., Britain, and Australia—the English-speaking internet was drowning in lurid accounts of violent crime—but they didn't quite do it for me. They were too far removed from my reality, from being a young millennial living in Stockholm. I couldn't imagine being an Arizona millionaire assaulted in his home, nor an eccentric sheep farmer living two hundred miles outside of Melbourne wondering who'd been cutting up his livestock.

So I started doing write-ups on my own. It wasn't meant for anyone but me, at the beginning. I toyed with the idea of starting a blog, but this was when blogs were already past their prime, and some part of my brain didn't like the idea of attaching my name to what I was doing. I knew enough to know I was supposed to be ashamed of this part of my life, this digging into the traumas of others, of losing hours engrossed in the details of the worst day of someone else's life. I knew it was weird and undesirable.

So I kept it to myself. For a while.

I called my podcast *Sweden After Dark* and kept it anonymous. I didn't promote it much, just posted links in a couple of the small Swedish true-crime forums I'd been hanging out in for the previous few years.

I didn't expect much to come of it. I wasn't even sure I'd keep doing it for very long. But it was the only thing that gave me any joy. I hated my job, temping at various offices, my schedule at the mercy of the agency manager. I hated never having enough money, having had to once again move back in with my parents. I hated not really having any real friends, hated the mechanical sex I'd indulge in bimonthly with near strangers I'd find on Tinder or in cheap bars with sticky floors.

I felt stuck in a way everyone in my life seemed to look down on with either pity or vague distaste.

So, I kept doing the podcast. The view count stayed steadily under the one-hundred mark for each episode. It wasn't much, but it was something.

And then, one day, one of my episodes got over a thousand listens.

When I first saw it, I thought I'd misread the number. The rush of realizing I hadn't was better than any orgasm I'd had up to that point. It would turn out to be a lucky combination of two factors: there had been an unexpected development in the old case I had been talking about, and a C-list influencer had somehow stumbled over my little podcast in a quest for content to recommend to her followers.

Two things I never could have predicted or controlled. But it was enough. It started the podcast growing. I started putting in more work, used my temp-job money to buy better recording equipment to get a cleaner sound.

And then, one day, her email popped up in my inbox. From mjacobssen@allinmedia.com. The subject line read "Do you want to make some money?"

I'd tease her about that, later. Ask her what kind of a corny fucking thing that was to ask someone you wanted to sign as a creator. When I asked her that, Minna just raised her eyebrows at me, cigarette smoke curling up past her inky-dark eyebrows in the blue light of the Stockholm sunset.

It worked, didn't it?

It did. I never could argue with that.

CHAPTER 7

April 14, 2022

"**W**elcome to Baltic Vinyasa!" The woman standing on the small, sturdy wooden pier is wearing slim, black jeans and a white linen shirt. She's waving enthusiastically at us, and her voice is strong enough to carry over the sound of the others scrambling to help the handsome captain hang boat bumpers off the side of the ship.

Over the last hour, as the levels in the bottles of sparkling wine had gotten lower, the mood had shot right past happy and turned much too quickly into outright rowdiness. The captain seemed to handle it in stride, though his smile grew significantly more rigid over the course of the ride.

Anneliese, who's hanging half off the boat, the pink tulle of her dress fluttering in the wind, catches sight of the woman on the pier and straightens up.

"Irene! Hi!" she yells, waving back with the enthusiasm of the very happy or the very intoxicated.

The captain manages to get the attention of the group and informs us, voice only slightly strained, that we will disembark through the same lower-deck spot that we boarded through. The fact that the whole group tries to rush down the stairs at the same time creates a momentary human pileup, and I bump into Anneliese, who turns to me with shining eyes and a wide smile.

"Can you believe it, Tessa?" she asks me, grabbing my hand and squeezing it. Her fingers are cold and a tiny bit sticky.

"We're finally here!"

Her joy is impossible to resist. I feel a smile pulling on my lips.

"Are you excited?" I ask her, and she squeals. If anyone else had attempted to squeal as an adult, professionally well-established woman, it would have come off as silly, but Anneliese somehow just manages to sound happy.

"I've just been looking forward to this for such a long time," she says. "I can't believe Lena found this place for us. It's perfect. It's everything I wanted. Just the six of us, spending four whole days together." She sighs and looks out at the island.

"It's just . . . it's so hard, sometimes. You know? I feel like I never get to see anyone as much as I want. There's never enough time. I always feel like I'm letting someone down. This is such a gift, getting to go on this trip with my best friends. Because I'm guessing I won't exactly have more free time after me and Samuel are married."

She turns back to me.

"I want to talk to you this weekend," she adds. "Like, really talk. About what happened. I hope you know you can talk to me about hard stuff, too."

"Of course I do," I lie, feeling every ounce of the weight in my stomach.

"But first," Anneliese says, the first step of the stairs freeing up as Mikaela manages to make her way down, "we're going to have *so much fun!*"

She lets go of my hand and runs down the stairs.

I'm the last to make it onto the pier, and I see the woman, who I recognize from countless pictures, chatting with Mikaela and Anneliese. There is a small dinghy tied to the pier on the other side, bobbing serenely on the small waves, completing the picture of Baltic perfection.

I haul the shoulder strap of my bag higher up and make my way up to the group, and the woman turns to me and smiles.

"And this must be the last one! Theresa, is that right?" she asks, smiling a charming, close-lipped smile.

"I go by Tessa," I say.

And she nods and repeats:

"Tessa. That's lovely."

I have no idea how to respond to that, so I choke out an awkward "Thanks."

"I'm Irene," she says to me, and then looks around the group, clasping her hands in front of her.

"Well, since we're all finally here, it's my pleasure to welcome you to Isle Blind!"

As if on cue, we all look beyond her, to the island and the hotel.

It's stunning in a stark, startling way, a different kind of beauty than the pictures told me to expect. The island is small, hardly more than a mile across, and the vegetation is sparse. Small, crooked pine trees cover the middle of the island, shooting defiantly from the thin layer of soil at odd angles. The sky seems higher and bluer out here than it did at the harbor, the clouds appearing to hang lower, nuances of white and lilac depicted in shockingly sharp contours.

The hotel looks unnatural where it sits to the left of the pier, a modern building of stone and glass shooting from the unprocessed natural beauty of the island. But it's undeniably impressive. A large veranda faces the ocean, and there's music coming from the open doors on the bottom floor.

"Wow," Lena says, and turns to Irene. "Jesus, Irene, it's just . . ."

Irene's lips split into a huge smile.

"I know, right?" she says, her voice full of glee. "I can hardly believe it myself."

Lena has pulled her sunglasses off to get a proper look.

Mikaela looks at Irene.

"How long did it take you to build this?" she asks. "I mean, a project of this size—me and my husband just redid our mountain chalet, and it took almost a year. And that was just a remodel!"

Irene laughs.

"Well, in a way it's easier to build from scratch," she says. "It's all about trusting the architects, really. But it took almost eighteen months, from start to finish."

"And it's all ready now?" Mikaela inquires.

"Almost," Irene says. "Still got a few details to sort out. But not to worry, that won't impact your experience here."

"Please!" Anneliese interjects. "I mean, with the deal you gave us . . ."

"Anything for friends of Lena's," Irene says, with a little smile that turns into a smirk. "And I can't deny that the marketing boost I'm hoping to get from you posting about us is going to more than make up for it!"

Mikaela laughs, the same deep, surprisingly throaty sound that used to give me heart palpitations in high school.

"Oh, trust me," she says. "I will post the shit out of this. There won't be a single one of my six hundred thousand followers who won't be clamoring for a room here once I'm done."

Irene smiles at her.

"I hope you're right," she says. "It was an expensive project. But all worth it. I'm so excited for you guys to see it."

She looks around the group.

"Does anyone need help with their luggage?" she asks. "I thought we'd get you guys set up in your rooms and then go straight into lunch. Adam should have it all ready for us in about fifteen minutes, he's been hard at work for a couple of hours now."

"Adam?" I ask, and Irene responds:

"The chef. We're not fully staffed yet, so I will be taking care of you guys, but I made sure to have him start early. Trust me, I wouldn't want to ruin the bachelorette weekend by forcing you lovely ladies to eat my cooking."

This gets a laugh from the group, and we start making our way up to the hotel.

I hang back a little, watching Irene from a distance. I can't see any likeness, but sisters don't always look alike. Lena and I are a fine example of that.

Irene looks like what she is, a yoga instructor in her early forties.

She's prettier than her pictures and, at least at first glance, not nearly as breathy and spiritual as I would have thought.

I don't know if that bodes well or not. I'm going to have to spend some more time with her and see whether or not she'd be amenable to talking to me.

Irene was the tipping point, after all. The final reason I decided to go on the trip.

When I googled the hotel and realized it was on Isle Blind, I got excited. But when I saw the name of the owner, I knew I had to come.

If I could find some kind of proof that the Nacka Four spent their final hours on this island, it would be huge.

But if I could get Matilda Sperling's older sister, Irene, to help me with the investigation?

It could be much bigger than that.

CHAPTER 8

April 14, 2022

I sit down gingerly on the bed and look out the window.

The room is large and white and full of light. There is really no color here to compete with the stark iron blue of the Baltic Sea outside the high windows; the art on the walls is all black-and-white photographs of women contemplating something deep and profound, the floor is naked, pale wood lacquered to slick perfection, the bedspread woven white linen. Everything feels crisp and new to the touch.

I've already put my worn, slightly stained makeup case in the bathroom, taken the mandatory forty-five seconds to admire the claw-foot tub, the raised granite sink, and the small, identical bottles of organic oatmeal body wash, shampoo, conditioner, and body lotion, all informing me that the packaging is made from recycled sea glass. I rubbed some of the body lotion on the inside of my wrist, and now I raise it to my face to take a whiff.

According to the bottle, it was supposed to smell like hawthorn, sea salt, and cloudberries. I have no idea what that would smell like. But it's nice.

Credit where credit's due; Irene has done a fantastic job with the place. I know the others must be busy chatting and unpacking in their rooms, but sitting here with the door closed, I might as well be the only person in the hotel. The only person on the island.

For a moment, I feel a stab of panic, low in my belly. Looking out through the window, I see only water with no end. The wide, open space outside makes me feel like I'm shrinking, becoming smaller and weaker.

If I wanted to leave, if I walked down to the beach and started to swim, I could swim until my arms and legs grew numb from the cold, until the sun glinting off the waves was replaced by moonlight reflecting off the surface, until my muscles started to give out, without ever seeing land.

We're all alone, out here, on this small, barren rock that used to pull sailors to their graves. If something were to go wrong . . .

I shake my head, trying to cast the feeling out. I'm being ridiculous. This is a beautiful weekend in a luxury hotel I could never hope to afford on my own. There is no reason to be afraid of anything.

It's just the hangover, combined with the champagne during the boat ride. Nothing but chemicals swirling in my bloodstream. I have to focus on why I'm here; on the Nacka Four, and on Anneliese. On trying to find a balance between fact-finding and showing up for my oldest friend.

I catch a glimpse of myself in the big, round mirror on the wall opposite the bed, and I see my twin's mouth twisting. My hair is tangled and frizzy from the wind, my cheeks flushed in a way that seems to spell intoxication rather than excitement, and I've left enough lipstick on various cups and glasses to make it look like I've merely outlined my mouth in Ruby Woo.

Or, if I'm being honest with myself, a Ruby Woo knockoff.

I dearly wish I had my phone. The itch has already settled deep in my bones, despite no more than seven minutes having passed since Irene collected our cell phones and various electronic accoutrements in a woven basket by the door and solemnly promised us she'd take good care of them.

Irene assured us that we're not completely cut off from the world.

She mentioned that there is a landline in her office, and in case of a true emergency, the dinghy I saw tied to the pier apparently has enough gas in the engine to make it all the way back to the harbor where the ferry picked us up.

Still. There's no other word for it. I feel . . . cornered. Like a small animal lured into a trap, stepping in voluntarily, so entranced by the bait that I've failed to notice the door about to lock behind me.

"Tessa?" A knock on the door, and I stand up from the bed.

"Come in!"

Lena is standing in the doorway. Somehow, she's managed to fix herself back into perfection in the fifteen minutes or so that's passed since we were shown to our rooms. She's even added a touch of muted pink lipstick. It makes me want to rub the remaining cheap red off my lips immediately.

"Can you believe these rooms?" Lena asks.

"Yeah, they are just . . . ," I say, trying to find the appropriate adjective. "It's . . . gorgeous."

"Are you ready for lunch?" Lena asks. "Mikaela asked me to gather everybody up. Make sure no one had fallen asleep while unpacking."

"Sounds nice," I say. "I could use some food."

Lena looks me over.

"Do you want to borrow a comb?" she asks. "I've got one in my purse."

"I'm good," I say, resisting the urge to flatten down my hair with my hands. "We all just came off the boat, right?"

"Sure," Lena says, sounding anything but.

I pull the elastic out of my ragged ponytail and quickly gather it into something resembling a bun instead.

"You and Irene go way back, huh?" I ask her, doing my best to sound casual, as I study my efforts in the mirror.

"Not that long," Lena responds. "Are you good to go?"

"Almost," I say. "I'm just going to fix my lipstick."

"Just wipe it off," Lena says. "The food is going to mess it up, anyway."

I hesitate before grabbing one of the soft, perfumed paper napkins out of the box that's placed perfectly and intuitively just below the mirror, wipe my lips, and throw it in the wastebasket under the small, asymmetrical wooden table.

"Better," Lena says. "You looked like Grandma after a cigarette."

"Don't be a dick," I tell her, and she laughs.

Lena turns to leave, and I follow her out in the hallway. I can hear voices coming from downstairs; we must be the last two to arrive for lunch.

"You knew her sister too, right? Matilda?" I ask Lena as she starts down the reclaimed-wood staircase.

Lena stops and turns. She purses her lips and lowers her voice.

"Please, Tessa," she says, in what is hardly more than a whisper. "Don't be so . . ."

"What?" I ask.

"Don't start asking Irene about Tilly," Lena says. "It's a really painful and personal thing. This is a work event for her. And the rest of us just want to have fun."

"I know that," I say, stung by the truth of it.

"Just . . ." Lena sighs. ". . . try to dial down the Tessa of it all this weekend. Okay?"

My heart thumps painfully in my chest.

"Okay," I say, and Lena shakes her head before continuing downstairs.

I wait a couple of seconds, wait for my eyes to stop stinging, wait for the guilt to recede, before I follow her down.

CHAPTER 9

April 14, 2022

My mouth tastes like truffles and the crisp, slightly tart notes of white wine. My skin feels slightly clammy, wrapped a little too tightly around my body, the muggy warmth of a room full of bodies offset by the cool air from the open glass doors over by the patio.

Lunch took almost three hours, followed by a quick break and then a session of sunset yoga. Irene turned out to be an excellent teacher, at least in the sense that she managed to make all the positions look smooth and easy. I can't blame her teaching for me failing to do a proper downward dog; that comes down to my stiff tendons and terrible posture, something I've come by honestly through years of hunching over computers.

The table is covered in medium-size plates, now half empty and picked over. I see a couple of pencils forgotten on the table between the plates, after the exercise we started dinner off with, where we each had to write a letter to Anneliese full of advice and good fortunes for her to read on her first anniversary. Mikaela seemed to get really into it, writing furiously, and Natalie took so long with hers, her face closed and focused, that Anneliese threatened to read it immediately, which made Natalie go pink and Mikaela laugh.

I did the best I could. In the end, I'm not sure I managed to give Anneliese any good advice for marriage. I don't exactly have years of successful relationships to pull from. But I wrote about what a lovely person she is, and how lucky Samuel is to have found her, and I hope that she'll know that I mean it, even though my attempts at eloquence might have left something to be desired.

Where lunch was a light, lemony pasta and a crisp salad, the concept for dinner was, as Irene explained it, "France meets Scandinavia." Swedish mushrooms flambéed in cognac and covered in black truffle, silk tofu mini quiches with golden beets, dill, and seaweed pearls, Pommes Anna cooked with avocado oil and served in small cast-iron pots, and several loaves of crusty sourdough baguettes.

The dress I pulled on after a quick shower feels uncomfortably tight, and I'm more tired than I expected. For a few minutes, I've been able to relax into the weekend, forget about the outside world, about what I'm planning.

I'm seated in between Mikaela and Caroline at the table. The dining room is decorated in the same fresh, clean style as the bedrooms: white walls, natural wood, and monochrome art, though in here the photographs from the rooms have been replaced with large abstract oil paintings, the slashes of black over the white canvases so thick and glossy they look as though they're about to drip onto the floor.

"The whole point of yoga," Irene says, gesturing with her glass of wine. "It's not just about exercise, it's about feeling at home in your body. If you need a break from your thoughts, yoga can provide that. If you want to lose weight, yoga can help you."

"And if you want the ass of a twenty-one-year-old, yoga can do that!" Mikaela interrupts, and Irene throws her head back and laughs.

"Yeah, that, too," she says to Mikaela and winks at her.

Irene has joined us for dinner, and she is blending beautifully with the group. She's changed from the loose white pants and sports bra she wore for the class into a fitted white button-down and a short, red, wrap skirt, and her legs make a convincing argument for why miniskirts should not solely be the purview of the under-thirties.

"You must have done a lot of yoga, though," Irene says to Mikaela. "I mean, either that or you're a natural. I felt like you could have been leading the class instead of me!"

Mikaela laughs. Her hair is loose around her shoulders, sweat lightly dusting the skin over her collarbones. Looking at the pictures on her Instagram one might have thought that she'd be one of those women who are just very photogenic, who might look slightly generic in person, but Mikaela doesn't. There's something about the way her features fit together that makes her pleasant to look at, makes you want to rest your eyes on her face, study the details of it so as to make sense of the whole.

"I'm very into holistic fitness," Mikaela says. "I've got two kids under five, so I'm on my feet all day. I do yoga, I swim, I do Krav Maga, I go running . . . it just feels so important for them, you know? I want to be as healthy as I can for my little guys."

Her voice hitches at the last word.

"God, of course," Irene says. "Two kids, though! You look absolutely phenomenal."

"Do you have kids?" Mikaela asks her.

I don't think I'm imagining it; Irene's face seems to freeze, for just a second, before she shakes her head.

"No, it wasn't in the cards for me," she says. "I chose to focus on other things."

Mikaela doesn't appear to notice the sudden change in Irene's mood, because she says:

"That's so awesome for you! I love that. Women's choices are always valid."

I pull my gaze away from Irene, see Lena deep in conversation with Caroline to the left of me, Natalie taking pictures of Anneliese on the other side of the table as she pretends not to notice the camera. It's enough to make me smile.

I reach for the bottle of white wine and find that it's empty. A quick look around the table reveals that they all are.

Irene notices and starts getting up from her chair.

"I really should have gotten six bottles!" she says. "I knew four wouldn't be enough. I'll just pop downstairs and get a couple more. Unless someone wants something else?"

"God, no, this wine is gorgeous," Mikaela exclaims. "What is it, a young Riesling? I had something similar in Switzerland last year. Me and my husband went on a little babymoon to Zermatt."

Irene shakes her head.

"It's a white Grenache from Catalonia," she says. "It's one of my favorites. I can give you the name of the vineyard, it's well worth a visit if you're in the area."

I get up from my chair as well, and Irene raises her impeccable eyebrows.

"I can get them," I say. "You've been on your feet all night."

She laughs.

"I mean, I am the host," she says.

"Please," I say. "You're running the whole operation yourself. You deserve some time to sit down and enjoy the fruits of your labor."

Irene hesitates, but then smiles and sits down, to the sound of whooping from Mikaela and Anneliese.

"Thank you, Tessa," she says. "That is very kind. There's more in the kitchen. Just down the stairs, at the end of the hallway. And if you could tell Adam that we will be ready for dessert in about . . ." She takes stock of the table. ". . . fifteen minutes, that would be so lovely."

"Your wish is my command," I tell her, and she laughs again.

The sounds of their voices grow quieter as I make my way into the back of the building, teetering slightly on my too-high heels. The staircase down to the basement isn't as nice as the one from the first to the second floor, clearly meant for staff as opposed to guests, and I feel a small thrill at getting a glimpse behind the scenes.

I've always been that way. Whenever our parents took us on vacation to some lavish location they could neither fully afford nor enjoy, I'd wonder about the staff, trying to study them covertly as my parents checked their email from the pool loungers and Lena tanned and flirted. I wanted to know what was going on when the guests weren't around, what happened in the kitchen after dinner was over, if there was some secret I wasn't privy to as one of the ever-interchangeable guests.

The basement is a stark contrast to the serene beauty of the rest of the building. The glossy woods and rough linen fabrics are nowhere to be seen. Here, the walls are concrete, unpainted and unadorned, and it's markedly cooler down here than just one floor up. I can smell the lingering odor of food cooking down here, the memory of onions sweating in oil and the sweetness of sugar burning in the oven.

The only source of light is the naked fluorescent industrial tubes at the ceiling. Had they been flickering, you could have easily imagined it as a set for a B-horror movie from the early aughts. Images show up in my mind—bare feet, running, blood splatter drying on the wall. For a second, I can taste the imagined fear of it.

I do my best to shake it off. I've been in a strange mood ever since we got here. Maybe Lena was right about what she often said.

Typical Tessa. Having to conjure up ghouls and monsters just to feel something.

I'm not here to fantasize. I'm here to help.

After just a few steps, I come upon a closed door with a built-in window. I put my hands against it to push it open, and I'm either exerting more force than I thought, or the hinges are very well oiled indeed, because it swings open and hits the wall on the other side.

The man standing by the metal counter starts, lifting the small blowtorch he's holding, and my pulse ratchets up.

I put my hands up and half yell:

"Sorry! Sorry. I'm so sorry. I didn't mean to startle you."

The flame turns off, and he lowers the torch, allowing me to get a good look at his face.

He's of medium height, somewhere in between my age and Irene's, with short dark sweat-slicked hair and strong features. A Roman nose balances out his heavy brow, and even from a distance I can see that he's got long, dark lashes, the kind women pay for and men neglect.

"I'm sorry," I say again. "You must be Adam?"

"You're one of the guests?" he asks, in a tone of voice that one couldn't, even charitably, call friendly.

"I'm Tessa," I say. "I—Irene sent me down here to get a couple more bottles of wine."

Adam sighs and looks back to the small white bowls on the counter.

"Do you mind if I finish the crème brûlées first?" he says. "They need to cool down before I can transfer them onto the pineapple carpaccio."

I notice he's got the same vaguely posh north Stockholm accent as the rest of us; muted, sure, but it's there.

"No problem," I say. "You're the boss."

I'm hoping to get a smile. That hope is dashed as he turns back to the counter and turns the torch back on.

I take in the kitchen as he works. It's big, and very neat, with gleaming new appliances and an industrial dishwasher next to the gigantic sink. I recognize it from my own short, failed career in the service industry. I never managed to get the lingo down, and one missed shout of "Behind!" resulted in sixteen smashed crystal glasses, which led, with remarkable speed and efficiency, to my immediate firing.

"You keep it clean in here," I say, as Adam once again turns the torch off.

"Easy with only six guests," he responds. He then turns to the wine fridge and pulls out two bottles I recognize as the white we've been drinking with dinner, takes a few steps, and hands them to me.

"Thank you," I say. "By the way, Irene told me to tell you that she thought we'd be ready for dessert in about fifteen minutes."

This earns a smile. Not for me, though.

"I know," he says. "You can tell Irene we're right on schedule."

Something prevents me from leaving, even as I can tell he's in no way interested in talking to me.

"How did you come to work here?" I ask him.

I could chalk it up to that same nosiness, the urge to pry, peek behind the curtain. But it's not just that.

It's this place. Isle Blind. The whisper of the Nacka Four, deep in my mind, running under my skin like a live wire.

Adam folds his arms across his chest. He's got a tattoo just above his wrist. Something with wings.

"Irene was hiring," he says, clipped. "I needed a job."

"Well, you're doing great," I say, and then I feel myself blush at the condescending tone of it. "I mean, the food is great. Really excellent. I usually don't eat a lot of vegan food, but this was . . . great."

"Glad to have changed your mind," he says.

He turns around, marking a clear end to our short interaction, and I start to turn around, but the alcohol in my bloodstream propels me to ask him:

"Did you know about Irene's sister?"

This causes him to stop in his tracks.

He doesn't turn around. But I can still hear him, clear as day, when he says:

"Matilda?"

"Yes," I say, suddenly breathless.

"She was murdered," he says, and I suddenly wish I could see his face, because it sounds like a challenge. "Right?"

Despite the chill, my face suddenly feels hot, my skin clammy.

"I don't . . ." I stop, and then I say, "Yeah. I think so."

"Sad thing, that," Adam says. He's picked up the blowtorch again, and when he turns it on, I stare, entranced, at the small, focused flame. Unable not to imagine what it would feel like to have it turn on me. How the small, fine hairs would glow before evaporating. How the skin would blister, and bubble, and burn.

"I wouldn't bring that up with Irene, if I were you," he says, ever so casually. "I don't think she'd like to be reminded of it."

"Right," I say, and I swallow. "I'll keep that in mind."

I back out through the door, nearly stumbling as it swings shut again, the window showing a flickering series of pictures before it stills again.

The kitchen wall. The prep station.

And Adam's face, having turned to look at me as I left, his face set in a scowl.

She was murdered. Right?

I think she was. But no one else did. Not the police. Not the families. They all thought the four women had drowned in an accident.

He must have been misremembering. It's easy to mix up different tragedies, when you haven't been obsessing about this single one since you were a teenager.

That's what I tell myself, as I speed up my steps, wanting suddenly, desperately and with animal fervor, to be back upstairs, with my friends, in their warmth and company.

As opposed to down here, in the dark. With him.

CHAPTER 10

April 14, 2022

I'm met by applause when I return to the dinner table, and as I sit down, I hand one bottle to Irene and one to Caroline. Mikaela reaches to high-five me, and I laugh as our palms meet with a pathetic little *thwack,* some of the discomfort from downstairs evaporating in the face of the ebullient mood around the table.

"Do you want some more?"

Caroline's voice is sudden and startling in my ear, and I glance over at her. She's holding the now-open bottle of wine, leaning in over my shoulder, and there's a slight smile on her lips. For dinner she's added a bold streak of eyeliner, giving her a vaguely dangerous look, and the little pendant around her neck is dangling freely over her neckline.

Don't look, I chide myself, and I straighten up and nod.

The cold bottle is sweating in the warm air, and I see the condensation dripping down on the thick tablecloth as she pours.

For a moment, I wonder if I've had enough; when I turn my head, my vision seems to be lagging behind for half a second.

"Cheers," Caroline says.

"Cheers." We drink. There's a soft sweetness to the wine, a near-effervescence that lingers in the mouth.

I wait for her to talk. It seems safest, that way. We haven't spoken much during dinner. Caroline has, once again, not said much to any-one. I've been trying to remember whether she used to be this quiet back in school, but it's hard to marry this Caroline to the one I remember, the serious girl who never so much as untucked her shirt from her ironed slacks.

"I can't stand it when people start talking about their kids," Caroline mutters under her breath, low enough so only I can hear it, and I nearly choke on my mouthful of wine.

She smiles conspiratorially at me.

"What?" she asks. "Too much?"

"Aren't you a family psychologist?" I ask her. "Aren't you supposed to be super into kids?"

"Eh," Caroline says, shrugging as she deposits her wineglass back on the table. "I like puzzles. You know, when you're treating one patient, there's always factors you can't see, things you have to try to intuit or guess. When you see the whole family, you can start untangling the patterns. That's what I like about it."

"Interesting," I say. "What made you get into psychology? I thought you wanted to be a lawyer."

Caroline raises her eyebrows.

"Oh, you remember!" she says. I can't tell if she's teasing or not, but I feel my face heating up.

"I guess I do," I say, trying to play it off, hoping she can't see the flush on my cheeks. "If I recall, you were very set on it when we were kids."

"Things change," Caroline says, flashing a quick smile that reveals a crooked incisor. "They did for you, too, if I interpreted what Anneliese said correctly? You run a podcast, right?"

I can't tell what's on her face, if it's sincere interest or if she's baiting me.

"I . . . *had* a true-crime podcast," I say. "That's over now."

"Still," Caroline says, and the fact that she's not asking me what happened answers my earlier, unspoken question. "How did you get into that?"

I clamp my lips shut. Shrug. I'm searching frantically for a way to change the topic back to her, wondering if I might just claim a headache and go to bed early, but then I hear Mikaela speaking in my direction.

"You know, I was wondering the same thing! How did you start that podcasting thing, Theresa?"

Shit.

When I look around, the attention of the whole table is on me. Only Lena has averted her gaze, and for a moment, I wish, desperately, that she'd have less respect for my autonomy. That she'd step in the way she would have when we were kids, take me under her arm, and expertly shut it down.

"It's Tessa," I say, weakly.

Mikaela waves her hand at me, drinks from her glass of wine. It was fuller a minute ago, and she's got high spots of bright red on her immaculate cheekbones.

"Sure, sure," she says. "But seriously, podcasting! How did you get started with that? Did you study media science at university?"

I'm suddenly very grateful for the refill of my glass. I buy myself some time, gulping down wine without tasting it.

"I didn't do the whole university thing," I say. "It wasn't really for me."

"Oh," Mikaela says and smiles, "it's never too late to go back, you know. That's the beauty of higher education. You know my aunt went back to get a Ph.D. in French literature after she retired? She'll be done next spring!"

"Yeah, well, I don't think I'll do that," I say. "I've never really liked French literature. Too much sex and death for me. I prefer my novels bone dry."

No one laughs; Mikaela just looks confused, and a little bit annoyed. I want to sink deeper into my chair.

I should have just gone to bed.

Mikaela decides to skip right past it.

"You must have really loved it," she says, drawing a short, quick breath. The light in here is dimmed, and outside, the sun has fallen beneath the horizon, creating a sky so deep blue it's almost dark purple.

It has left Mikaela's pupils wide and black, like those of a shark smelling blood.

I try my best not to notice the lump in my throat. Try not to think about it, at all.

Be normal. Don't be so Tessa.

"I did," I say, feeling momentary pride at how sincere my voice sounds.

It's always easier to tell the truth, after all.

Mikaela leans forward across the table, resting her chin in her hand. She's overlined her lips just a little bit, and it's bled into the corners of her mouth.

"So how are you doing now, sweetie?" she asks. She reaches out with her other hand and puts it on mine. It's colder than I expected. Probably from holding the wineglass.

"It must be really hard."

I draw a short, sharp breath. Open my mouth to respond.

I have any number of platitudes lined up, ready to go. I've been practicing them in the mirror.

It's rough, but I'll get back on my feet.

I'm trying to view it as a transition, instead of a failure.

I'm taking responsibility for my actions, while hoping to move forward.

Any one of them will do, really. Anything to communicate that I'm okay, and that it's okay to ask me about it, and that I won't blow up, or melt down, or do anything outside the bounds of socially acceptable behavior.

But nothing comes out. Nothing at all. And I can feel all their eyes on me, watching me, waiting for something. Needing something from me. Something I can't give.

Little black spots are floating around the edges of my field of vision. When I look at Anneliese, it's like her face is distorting. She doesn't look like my oldest friend anymore. She looks like a stranger. Someone I knew once, who cared for me, once, but doesn't anymore.

Because how could she, after what I did?

I stand up so abruptly that I see out of the corner of my eye how Mikaela falls back in her chair.

"I'm sorry, I need some air," I say, in a voice so strangled it doesn't even sound like mine, and I stalk off toward the patio doors.

Ignoring the fact of my impractical high heels, ignoring the cold outside, ignoring the dark. The panic is stronger than all of that.

Someone calls my name.

I wish I could turn back. I really do.

But I can't stay in there.

Because suddenly that old, kindly face is flashing in front of my eyes, and I can hear his voice in my head.

Do you think it was my fault?

May 8, 2012

Matilda managed to pull her phone out of her purse and answered on the second ring. She'd finally folded and gotten an iPhone a couple of months ago, and she still wasn't used to it.

"This is Matilda," she said.

"God, Tilly, I hate your grown-up voice," Anna complained through the speaker. "It freaks me out. Can't you just look at the screen so you'll know it's me?"

"I just got out of a meeting," Matilda said. "I'm heading out to lunch. You're lucky I even picked up."

"Yeah, yeah, I know, you're very important," Anna said. Matilda knew, without seeing her face, that she was rolling her eyes.

As she exited the building, Matilda was met with a gust of wind, carrying the twin smells of spring and exhaust fumes. Winter had finally released its deathly grip last week, and central Stockholm had been struck by a frenzy. Despite the low temperatures, still closer to freezing than to comfort, the sidewalks outside the myriad restaurants had filled with rickety tables and chairs in an instant, the people eating huddled in jackets and blankets and frothing at the mouth at the very chance to eat lunch outside in the sunshine.

Still, Matilda envied them. She had less than thirty minutes for lunch today, and after the bout of nausea had passed around ten, she'd been ravenous. She'd have to pick something up and eat it in her office.

"Listen, I'm not going to take up too much of your precious time," Anna said. "Have you talked to Evelina lately?"

"I don't think so," Matilda said. "Why?"

"Well, we're coming up on the trip," Anna said. "I'm trying to iron out the last details, and she won't call me back."

"That's just Evelina," Matilda pointed out. "Have you tried texting her?"

"Of course I've tried texting her," Anna said. "That's the first thing I did. She didn't even respond to the group email." Anna paused.

"I was really proud of that group email, too," she added. "It had a sign-up sheet and everything."

"I loved the email," Matilda reassured her, stopping at a busy crosswalk, waiting for the light to change. "It was beautiful. It had real gravitas."

"Thanks," Anna said. "Anyway, could you take over Evelina-wrangling duties for a while? I don't know what's going on with her, but she might pick up if you're the one calling."

"If you're going by order of closeness, vis-à-vis the friendship, I think Linnea would be your best bet," Matilda said.

Anna responded, "I don't feel like talking to Linnea right now."

The light changed to green, but Matilda stayed on the sidewalk.

"What happened?" she asked. "Did you guys get in a fight?"

This was so typically Anna. Of course she would have gotten into a fight about something stupid with Linnea, just days before the trip, making everything infinitely more complicated than it had to be.

Then, a second later, Matilda felt bad. That wasn't fair. Anna wasn't like that. She was opinionated, sure, but she didn't start fights for no reason.

"No, but, you know . . . I don't know," Anna said.

"What's wrong?" Matilda insisted. "Come on. Tell me."

"I saw Linnea on Sigrid's Facebook," Anna finally admitted. "Apparently they had drinks together."

Matilda swallowed.

"You don't think they are . . . ?" she started, unsure of how to finish the sentence.

"No, Jesus. Of course not. Linnea has always stayed firmly in the hetero part of the Kinsey scale. I mean, how long has she been with that hunky boyfriend of hers now, three or four years?" Anna sighed.

"If there ever was a reason to date a man, it would be that he could cook. That's the only reason I'm jealous of Linnea.

"It feels uncomfortable. I don't mean to sound like a child, but, like . . . Linnea is supposed to be my friend, you know? I thought it was implied that you don't hang out with your friend's ex just a couple of weeks after they broke up."

Matilda didn't know what to say to that. She agreed.

"Or, if you're going to, at least have the sense not to let it get posted to fucking Facebook," Anna added.

"I'll talk to Evelina," Matilda said. "I'll get ahold of her and sort everything out. I promise."

"Thank you," Anna said.

"Do you want to talk about it?" Matilda asked.

A quick look at her watch revealed that she had less than twenty minutes left to go of her much too short lunch break, but she didn't feel in a position to not ask the question.

This was Anna, after all. It was unusual for Anna to admit the slightest sign of vulnerability.

She wasn't even sure if she meant whether Anna wanted to talk about Linnea, or about Sigrid, or just about how she was feeling in general.

"No," Anna said. "We'll save it. For the trip."

Matilda felt herself smile.

"Yeah," she said, as a lump formed in her throat. "We've got a lot to talk about."

CHAPTER 11

April 14, 2022

I stop once I can no longer see the hotel when I turn around, once I've walked far enough along the shoreline that the trees blur the outline of the high, bright walls. I sit down on the sorry excuse for a beach, listen to the sound of the waves gently hitting the shore. Try to catch my breath.

My cardio's gone to absolute shit.

I clench my jaw, feeling the sorrow and shame pulsating, red and raw.

Try not to think about it.

Try not to think about his face.

Try not to think about his voice.

Try not to think about what I did, or what I could have done differently, or what's been lost.

I know I shouldn't be reading what they are saying about me. Shouldn't be googling myself, shouldn't be reading the articles. But it would take superhuman strength to stay away from it all. When we're kids, our parents all tell us not to pick at scabs, but show me the child who's ever managed to stay away from one as big and juicy as this one.

Of course I'm picking at it. Of course I'm reading.

Lying whore.

Insensitive freak.

She's nothing more than a vulture.

Ugly bitch.

Someone should teach her a lesson.

I'm not scared. Or at least that's what I tell myself. Feels better to be angry than to be scared. It's not like any of those anonymous people think about it for more than a couple of seconds, anyway.

I'm not important enough to get murdered. I haven't done anything that would really rile the dangerous ones up, like be an attractive woman talking about sexism, or criticizing a video game. I'm just a sad bisexual podcaster who fucked up so bad it really hurt someone one time, nothing more than a temporary diversion, someone to be pissed at for five minutes before moving on to something else.

You shouldn't have come here.

Do you really think this is going to fix anything?

I'm not crying anymore, at least. Instead, my eyes feel dry, staring unblinking out over the black waves.

The breeze lifts a few strands of hair from my shoulders, deposits them gently over my face. I don't bother pushing them out of the way.

Some part of me always knew I would end up here. Not on Isle Blind, not at Baltic Vinyasa, but here. It was always a sandcastle. It didn't start out that way, but I always knew, deep down, that it couldn't last.

The cold damp of the beach has started soaking through the seat of my dress. It's a deceptive sort of chill; it didn't feel that bad when I stalked out of the hotel, but it's seeping in under my skin now, settling against my bones like smoke.

Crunch.

I sit up straighter, look around.

It sounded like someone walking over the rocks.

The bright nights of summer haven't arrived yet, and the bits of the night sky peeking through the cloud cover are a deep, blackened blue. My eyes have adjusted to the dark as much as they can, but I'm still half blind. When I stand and turn around to look, all I see is the gnarled silhouettes of the trees, the shimmering lights of the hotel in the distance.

They look like a lure, from here. Something to trick travelers into making the journey out to this spot, leaving the safety and comfort of civilization behind for the promise of something beautiful and un-known.

Only to find themselves stuck, in the cold and the silence. On a little rock barely sticking out of the frigid sea.

This island, that rose through the depths only to peek above the surface. How long will it be before the water swallows it again?

Have the waves come closer while I have been standing here?

I take an involuntary step back, the rocks moving unsteadily under my feet, and my throat feels like it's going to close.

I feel so very vulnerable, suddenly. So aware of how fragile I am. How quickly skin and bone can break. How difficult it would be to run on this beach, if I needed to. How fast the breath would leave my lungs. How swiftly my blood would wash away from the rocks beneath me. Just a few short hours of waves rocking gently in over the shore, and there would be no trace of me anymore.

She was murdered. Right?

I call out, my voice so high and reedy it nearly blows away on the light breeze.

"Hello?"

No one responds.

For a few seconds, I stand there, straining to listen. I'm shaking, my skin prickling with fear.

Crunch.

That sound again. Closer now.

Her silhouette separates out from the trees, and for a long, slippery second, I see Matilda Sperling. See her short, dark hair, that gleaming smile that's stared out at me from the computer screen for dozens or hundreds of hours.

The ghost of a woman ten years gone.

But then she comes closer, and I recognize Caroline.

I breathe out hard, through the nose.

"You scared me," I tell her, as she walks toward me, hands in her pockets.

My thoughts still have a ragged edge to them. Chemicals in the blood don't go away just because reality has set in.

"I thought someone should check on you," Caroline says simply.

I look away, not wanting to hold her gaze. I'm suddenly aware of how cold I am, but when I stare up at the hotel, it looks less inviting than the sparse woods. It's all harsh, white angles, yellow light spilling out and breaking up the soothing dark.

"I'm . . . fine," I say and turn back. "But thank you. It was really nice of you to come check on me."

Embarrassment, both from what happened at dinner and from my wild imagination just now, is making my cheeks feel hot and my tongue uncomfortable in my mouth.

This time, it's Caroline's turn to stay silent. Her short hair is mussed from the wind, and her face is unreadable behind the cat eye glasses.

"Is there anything you want to talk about?" Caroline finally asks.

The tension feels like physical pain, like an ache in my very skull. I can feel it in my teeth, and I'm almost worried she'll be able to smell it coming off me.

The desperation, and the shame, and the exhaustion.

"I'm just . . . ," I start, trying to find the words, trying to prevent the truth from spilling out of me.

I'm so sick of holding it all in.

Would it not be such a sweet relief, to let it all go? To let someone else carry it, just for a little while?

"I know you've had a rough few months," Caroline offers, and a small laugh escapes my lips.

"You could say that," I say, and suddenly, horribly, I'm close to tears.

Caroline is quiet. She just looks at me with that clear, steady gaze I recognize all too well from the days when I could still afford to go to therapy.

I draw a deep breath, trying to force it into my lungs, convince them to expand past the crushing weight on my chest.

"Everything I had worked for, it all . . . went away. In an instant. All it took was one mistake. One bad decision. And it's not just about me, either, you know. People took what happened and made it bigger, made it mean more than it did, and they ran with it. It hurt people. Colleagues of mine. Friends."

Friends who won't take my calls anymore. Friends who've publicly disavowed me.

"I'm trying, you know," I say. "I don't want to mess this up for you guys. Or for Anneliese. I want to have fun. I want to *be* fun. But it's . . . hard. And I'm worried that . . ."

I can feel the words sticking in my throat.

There is something in the way Caroline is looking at me. Maybe it's the muted lighting, but for a moment, I feel like I can see traces of the girl I knew once, hiding just behind the polished exterior she wears now.

If I told them—if I was honest, and open, and all those things you're told to be, without any regard for the potential consequences—would they back away from me, as well? Just like all those supposed friends did, once it all came out?

I may not have seen Anneliese much these last few years. And I may not have seen Mikaela and Caroline since high school. But they have a piece of my heart, nevertheless, in the way that only people who knew you while you were in the process of becoming can. Had we met as adults, they would have intimidated me. Annoyed me, and frustrated me, even.

But I will always know them as the girls they were. I will always see what they were before they got their degrees, and their partners, and their apartments; before they figured out how to do their hair and dress for their body types. I know their awkward, hesitant inner selves, just as they know mine.

And I can't bear the thought of losing them. Even what little our relationships have dwindled to.

So I can't tell Caroline the truth. There is too much at stake.

"I guess it's just challenging, with what happened," I say, instead. "You know, I'm trying to rebuild my career. Doing the best I can. If I could just figure out what happened to them, maybe I could . . . do something good. Give something back."

I'm rambling, trying to paper over the cracks.

"Who are you talking about?" Caroline asks.

"What do you mean?" I ask her.

"You said 'if I could just figure out what happened to them,'" Caroline quotes me. "Who are they?"

"The Nacka Four," I say.

The moment the words have left my mouth and become reality, I immediately regret them.

"That sounds familiar," Caroline says, and I feel a fine sweat breaking on my forehead.

She can't bring it up. Not to Anneliese, not to Lena. Especially not to Irene.

Not until I've had a chance to talk to her myself. Explain to her what I'm trying to do, so that she'll understand. So that she won't think what everyone else thought.

Vulture.

"Don't—" I start, but I don't know what I'm supposed to say.

Caroline tilts her head to the side.

"I just . . . I don't want the others to . . . just, please don't tell them what I told you," I say. "I don't want to make this whole weekend about me."

A shitty attempt at damage control.

Caroline smiles.

"Well," she said. "Not storming off in the middle of dinner might help with that goal."

"Are you allowed to say that?" I ask. "You're a therapist."

"You're not exactly paying me," Caroline says.

She sighs and turns half around.

"Come on," she says. "Let's head back. I'm really excited about sunrise yoga tomorrow morning, I haven't had time to do that in ages. I want to get to bed early so we're in decent shape tomorrow. I think Mikaela has a pretty packed schedule planned for us."

She starts walking, and I catch up to her in a couple of steps.

I want to ask her again not to tell them, but the words catch in my throat.

What the fuck have I just done?

CHAPTER 12

April 15, 2022

I wake with a dry mouth and a pounding head. The stress of last night has seemingly latched on to my scalp like an evil little spider, digging its claws into my skull and pumping venom directly into my brain.

It's still dark outside, so I turn on the lights to check the time. Two minutes past three in the morning. The breeze coming through the window I opened before falling asleep is chillier now than it was, enough to make my face feel cold and numb.

When Caroline and I got back to the hotel, the dining room was quiet and empty, the candles blown out and the mess on the table gone as though it had never been there in the first place. There was something spooky about it. For a second it felt like the whole dinner had never happened, or like it had taken place years earlier; the dining room was so devoid of life that it looked abandoned.

The thought sent a shiver up the nape of my neck, but when I turned to Caroline to say something about it, take the edge off with a joke, she was already heading for the stairs. I waited a few seconds before making my way up to my room, spent the next couple of hours staring at the ceiling and wishing fervently that I had my phone before falling into a gossamer-thin, confused sleep.

I roll out of bed, still wearing my worn, oversize Tokio Hotel T-shirt—the same thing I've slept in since I was fourteen, the faces of the band members nothing more than smudges at this point—and the boxer shorts I'd stolen from a hookup back in the day. The sound of the calm sea from the open window is the only sound I can hear, and the chill is making me break out in goose pimples, but I try to soldier on.

I need painkillers, and I don't have any, but I'm pretty sure that Lena will have brought some.

She used to get regular migraines; not so much anymore, since she got the Botox treatment a few years ago. Most of the time, she just jokes that it was an excellent excuse to get the little commas between her eyebrows fixed without anyone accusing her of being a bad feminist. But I know she still gets them sometimes, and she's too well-organized not to have planned for an emergency.

As I open the door and step out into the corridor, I wince at the feeling of the cold floor against my bare feet.

The house is almost freakishly quiet. I imagine that at some point in the future, the hotel will be full of guests, and the atmosphere will be different. Homey and intimate. The perfect setting for a boutique vacation with family or close friends.

But right now, it feels almost . . . skeletal. Lifeless. No staff, and hardly any guests. It's too perfect, with no signs of wear and tear, as though the hotel is not meant for human occupants at all.

In the near dark, everything is painted in shades of white and gray. It's like I've stepped into an old photograph, one that's been leeched of all color by the years.

I walk to Lena's room as quickly as I can, raise my hand to knock, and feel a hand on my shoulder.

I yelp and am about to scream at full volume when I hear a familiar voice.

"Tessa, it's me."

When I turn, I see Irene.

She's in a lovely little fuzzy pajama set, an oyster-pink tank top and matching shorts, the kind of thing you'd see someone wearing on Instagram but never in real life. Actually, Mikaela would probably love it.

"I'm sorry," Irene says. "I didn't mean to startle you."

Her hair is pulled back in a tight ponytail, and her face is free of makeup. Without the pearlescent powder and the brown mascara, her lashes are pale and her nose a little shiny. It makes her look less perfect, though no less pretty; *more human* might be the words I'm looking for.

"What are you doing up?" I ask her. Realizing I might be about to wake up half the wedding party, I decide to modulate my voice.

"I couldn't sleep," Irene says. "Insomnia. It hits me a couple of times a month."

"I'm sorry," I say, and Irene smiles.

"Not your fault," she says. "What are you doing up?"

"I woke up with a headache," I say. "I didn't bring any painkillers. I figured Lena might have some."

Irene smiles, but there is something sad about her eyes, the way they tilt downward.

"I'm guessing she's the older sister?" she says, and I nod.

"Let's not wake her up," she continues. "I have some painkillers in my room. Come on, you can have a couple."

Irene looks over her shoulder, and I say, with some hesitation:

"That's, uh, really kind of you, but . . . it's . . . I don't know how to put this, exactly, but I'm not sure natural medicine is going to do it in this case."

Irene guffaws.

"Don't worry," she says. "This is the proper, chemical kind. Nothing natural at all about these pills. They will make that headache their bitch."

Irene's room is smaller than the guest rooms. It's in the basement, at the far end of the hallway where I found the kitchen, and less perfectly turned out than the room I'm staying in. The window looks out over the sea, and as it's open, there's a not unpleasant smell of brackish water in the room.

"Hang on," Irene says, opening the door to the bathroom. "I'll get them for you."

I look around as I hear her rooting around in the cabinet, take note of the small navy sofa, the fluffy white rug by the bed, and the colorful painting on the wall. It's comprised of blocks of primary colors, blue and green and yellow, creating a vaguely humanoid shape. It's the kind of painting where you can't tell if it's the result of a kindergarten art class or worth millions, but I like it.

"Here," Irene says, right behind my back, and I jump again.

She's smiling as I turn around.

"Sorry," she says again. "I'll try to make my walk louder. Can't go around scaring the guests."

She's holding a glass of water and two white pills, and I accept them gratefully. The throbbing in my head has quieted, but not nearly enough.

"I like your painting," I say, before swallowing the pills with a gulp of water.

The only light in the room is coming from a small brass lamp on the bedside table; a book is lying next to it, with the kind of gently cheerful cover that indicates it's about the power of the self.

But even in the soft lighting I can see her face change.

"Thank you," she says, looking at the picture on the wall.

"Who's the artist?" I say.

"My sister painted it," Irene says. "It was one of those sip-and-paint classes. We took it together. She messed up her lemons, so she painted over it and called it an abstract masterpiece. I laughed at her, so she gave it to me for Christmas."

Irene clears her throat and looks away.

I realize I'm squeezing the glass so hard I'm running the risk of breaking it.

It's now or never.

"Your sister Matilda?" I ask.

Irene's eyes widen.

"Yes," she says. "Did Lena . . . ?"

"Lena didn't say anything," I say. "I . . . well, you know that Lena and I grew up in the same area as you and Matilda?"

Irene nods slowly.

"I . . ." I don't know how to say this. Don't know how to express it in a way that doesn't risk upsetting her.

". . . well, Matilda actually used to babysit us. Me and Lena, I mean. When Matilda disappeared, I was . . . sorry to hear what had happened."

I can see Irene's jaw clenching.

"The 'Nacka Four,'" she says softly. "That's what they called them. Such a silly name." There's a deep vein of bitterness running through the last sentence, a window into something much deeper and more painful than the words themselves convey.

"It was," I say, feeling how very dry my mouth is despite the water I just drank. "It always seemed reductive to me. And the way they wrote about them in the papers, making them out to be a bunch of silly girls, taking a boat out for a joyride, despite Anna having worked as a boating instructor . . . It never sat right with me."

Irene exhales hard through her nostrils.

"No," she says. "Me neither."

I put the glass down carefully on the windowsill.

"How come you built the hotel here?" I ask her.

I've been wondering about it, ever since I made the connection, way back when Mikaela emailed us all about the hotel.

I don't believe in the supernatural; I'm simply not optimistic enough. And of course there was a practical explanation. The families of the four women who disappeared knew one another socially, and one of them owned Isle Blind. If Irene was looking for a place in the archipelago, it would have made sense for her to have remembered Isle Blind, to have approached a family friend about buying the island, as opposed to looking at the open market. No one in the investigation ever seemed to think that Isle Blind had anything to do with the case, after all. Irene would have had no reason to believe the island was anything but a prime piece of real estate, perfect for her new business venture.

But part of me couldn't help but wonder if she'd felt something. Some kind of pull. A connection to the place.

Irene has crossed her arms, and she's looking out the window.

"Well," she says, and her voice sounds just a little bit strangled. She clears her throat.

"Tilly loved the archipelago," she says. "I've always felt closest to her, out here."

When she finally turns back to me, I can see that her eyes have gone a little red. She's smiling, but it's a smile I recognize; I've performed it myself, many times.

It's not an expression of joy. It's a kind of armor.

I'm smiling. Don't worry about me.

I feel a strange pull, right under my ribs.

"Have you ever . . ."

God, I'm not sure I can do it.

Now that I'm standing here, talking to Irene, it's suddenly all so real.

Matilda Sperling wasn't just a fictional character, someone who went missing in order to give me something to obsess about. She was Irene's sister. One day she was there, and the next day she wasn't, and she never came back. There was never a body, never a headstone. Just a gaping, ragged hole in the middle of Irene's life that could never fill in, never fade and heal with time.

But, then again, isn't that why I want to do this?

If something happened to Lena—the thought is almost too painful to bear, enough to make my knees buckle—and someone knew something, or thought they knew something . . . I would want to know.

I would have to know.

"I know Anna's father owned Isle Blind," I say. "At the time. You bought it from him. Right?"

"Right," Irene says. There's a wariness to her voice now.

"When I was reading about the case, I kept wondering if they were going here," I say. "On their trips. Every year. Isle Blind. It would have been perfect. Completely abandoned. So far out no one would be able to hear them, or disturb them."

Or find them.

The words I'm not saying hang in the air between us.

I have no idea what Irene is thinking.

To be honest, I'm not so sure what I am thinking.

Is she going to yell at me? Throw me out of the hotel, ask me to take the dinghy to the next island over and wait for a ride?

"I told the police at the time," she finally says. "Over and over again. Matilda never would have gotten into a boat while drunk. We had a boat, growing up. Our dad taught us both to drive it when we each turned twelve."

When she looks into my eyes, hers are glistening with tears. She smiles through them, and it looks gritted and painful.

"The police wouldn't listen," she says. "They thought they were just a bunch of stupid girls making bad decisions."

"They never looked at Isle Blind," I say, heart pounding. "They never really looked at all. But if I could look around, if I could find something . . . we might be able to drum up some attention for the case. If I could find anything, anything at all, it might be enough to get people to pay attention. If you would help me."

Irene looks at me, quietly, for what feels like a very long time. I don't know what she is searching for; I'm hoping she will find it.

"I don't think you will find anything," she finally says. "Not after ten years. But . . . I appreciate you wanting to try." She sighs, and it makes her sound much older than she is.

"I'm glad someone remembers my sister," she says, barely any louder than a whisper.

CHAPTER 13

April 15, 2022

Jesus Christ, I can't believe there are people who actually enjoy this.

Actually, I don't believe there are. I don't believe there are people who genuinely like the taste of green juice and kombucha, who take joy in getting up at five in the morning, or who get their kicks from sweating out made-up toxins by exercising in saunas. I think runner's high is a myth and sunrise yoga is a scam, and I'd give my left foot to go back to sleep.

The leggings squeeze my midsection, and as I make my way down the stairs, I'm already cursing my sports bra. I only brought two of them, thinking that the yoga I remembered wasn't a very strenuous activity and that I'd get at least three or four wears out of each pair.

Sadly, the session we partook in yesterday wasn't the yoga I remembered.

My whole body aches, and my joints feel like they are creaking. I ended up washing the sweat out of the first sports bra in the sink, but it's not dry yet, and so I've had to resort to the bright orange one I bought on sale years ago in a post–New Year's fit of athletic inspiration. I used it once, threw it in the back of my closet, and am only now remembering that the reason I never used it again wasn't just my general lack of interest in exercise but the fact that it's the single itchiest garment ever constructed.

Irene is standing at the bottom of the stairs, sipping something that looks like green tea out of a tall glass with a metal straw.

"Good morning," she says, and I manage to force my face into something resembling a smile.

"Barely morning yet," I say, and she laughs quietly. But kindly.

"I think you're going to enjoy yourself, once we get started," Irene says. Her voice is slightly hushed, probably for the sake of the ambience. Then she asks:

"Did you manage to fall back asleep? Did the pills help?"

"They did," I say.

They had, in fact, helped. Not with the sleep, but with the headache. I might have been able to fall back asleep if I hadn't known I only had about an hour and a half before I had to get up for sunrise yoga, but I still got to close my eyes for a while, and I'm grateful.

"I think I managed to get another hour and a half or so," I say.

Despite Irene's similar lack of sleep, she looks great, fresh and energetic. Her eyes are clear, her thick hair flowing down to her clavicles, and she's wearing a fitted, dove-gray cashmere set. Perfect for yoga on a cold morning.

Maybe all that clean living does have an effect, after all.

"Anneliese is already out on the patio," Irene says. "You can grab a mat and just sit down and take in the morning. We'll start in a little bit."

I look at her, searching for any sign of the conversation we shared last night, and she gives me a small nod, a closed smile; a look directed out at the patio tells me that any follow-up conversation is one she does not want to have while any of the others are listening.

It makes me feel something. Something good. Like she trusts me.

The sunlight on the patio hits me like a slap in the face. It's reflecting off the sea, creating a million glinting stars. I'm not usually one to be taken in by the beauty of nature, but it's impossible to resist, and I stop in place for a second just to take it in.

I find myself drawing a deep breath, like a film cliché of a woman rediscovering herself. If only reality were as simple as a '90s movie about girl power and self-empowerment.

"Hey, Tessa," Anneliese says, and I'm broken out of my temporary spell. She's already sitting on a mat, her back straight and her curly hair in a thick braid. She's smarter than I am; she brought a pair of sunglasses with her and has a thick shawl wound around her shoulders. It's only when I see the shawl that I notice the sunlight, while pretty, holds very little warmth.

"Hey, you," I say, looking around for one of the mats. Anneliese points, and I see them neatly rolled up and stacked on top of one another by the door. I grab one and look around, wondering if I should leave room next to her, and then realize how ridiculous it would be seeing as we're the only two here.

I sit down next to Anneliese, look at her, and smile.

"Wow," I say. "This is really gorgeous."

"Oh, come on," Anneliese says and laughs. "You hate this."

"No!" I protest. "It's stunning. I'm almost never up this early. Actually, the only time I've ever been up before six in the morning is if I haven't gotten to bed yet."

"God," Anneliese sighs, and then she smiles again. Lips closed this time. "I can't remember the last time I did that."

Actually, I can't, either. All I know is that it must have been in the Before times. But I don't say that. I'd rather have her think I still have some semblance of a social life; would rather she think of me as someone enjoying a life of partying, happily stuck in arrested development, than as someone who doesn't even have that anymore.

"But hey," Anneliese adds and punches my arm lightly, "you're first! That's impressive! Getting out of bed must have been a struggle."

"Hey now," I say, rolling my eyes. "Do I look tired to you?"

"Yes," Anneliese says, and I snort with laughter.

Her lips are pulled into a smile.

"I missed this," she says. "I never laugh with other people the way I laugh with you."

"I'm easy to laugh at," I say, and now Anneliese frowns.

"Don't say that," she says. "Don't put yourself down like that."

"Sorry," I say.

"You don't have to apologize," Anneliese says, and stretches. "Not to me, at least. But sometimes I think you carry around too much guilt."

"I thought we all did," I say. "Isn't that just part of being an adult?"

"It doesn't have to be," Anneliese says. "The truth is, we're human. Sometimes we do fucked-up things. You can't keep mulling over every bad action you've ever taken, trying to trace the outcome of every single thing you've ever said or done. Just . . . try to look forward." I can feel her looking at me through the sunglasses.

"There's a lot to look forward to," she says.

And I ache, because I know that Anneliese is right, as long as you're Anneliese. As long as you're protected by a thick layer of beauty, and talent, and charm; as long as you have a loving family and an adoring fiancé to fall back on.

As long as you've never done anything bad enough to warrant actual consequences.

When I drop my eyes I notice her hands are balled up in tight fists. The engagement ring, an over-the-top number with a giant emerald surrounded by diamonds, very impractical, very Anneliese, looks like it's cutting into the tender flesh below her knuckle.

"Anneliese—" I start to say, but I'm interrupted by Mikaela's voice behind our backs.

"Good morning, ladies!" she chirps, and the moment is lost.

I turn a bit, see Mikaela in fitted black Lycra, taut abs peeking out from between her cropped shirt and her fitted shorts. She's carrying her own yoga mat and puts it down on the other side of Anneliese.

"You really can't buy this kind of view, can you?"

"Isn't that exactly what Irene has done?"

I turn slightly, seeing Natalie putting her mat down behind Anneliese. She's wearing an enigmatic smile, her hair pulled back in a loose French braid, the faint smattering of freckles over the bridge of her nose and the slash of pink lipstick on her lips failing to disguise the dark circles under her eyes.

"Hey, sweetie," Anneliese says, her voice brimming with sympathy. "Rough night? I could hear you tossing and turning when I got up to pee."

Natalie's smile doesn't falter.

"I never sleep well in new places," she says. "But it's okay. I'll have an extra cup of coffee."

Anneliese turns to me and Mikaela.

"You used to have trouble sleeping when you were pregnant with Milo, right, Mikaela?"

Mikaela nods enthusiastically.

"Yes, it was a nightmare," she says to Natalie. "I was taking so many herbs I swear I started peeing green. Green!"

Anneliese catches my eye and smiles.

I've always been impressed with her ability to do that. Natalie might be the odd one out in the group, but she won't be for long. Anneliese has always had a knack for that. Building bridges. Connecting people.

Irene comes around and takes her place facing us by the edge of the patio.

"We'll get started as soon as the others join us," Irene says. "Hopefully they will be here soon. We don't want to lose the last of the early-morning sun. The first rays of the day have powerful healing capabilities. Breathing them in can lower your cortisol and center your chi."

Her posture is perfect, and her face is serene.

"Let's prepare for today with some deep breathing," Irene says. She closes her eyes and demonstrates by breathing in deep, her chest rising dramatically and then falling.

I reluctantly attempt to do the same, but just as I'm about to close my eyes, I see something. Out in the water.

"Oh, there you are!" Irene says, and I sense the others opening their eyes again, turning around. "We are just about to start."

"Sorry I'm late." I hear my sister's voice behind me.

But I'm not listening.

There's something out there. Drifting. A shape that isn't a wave, a shadow breaking through the shimmer of the sunlight on the surface.

At first, I took it for a sunspot, but it's too tangible for that. And it's moving.

"Did you run into Caroline on your way down?" I hear Natalie asking.

"No," Lena says. "I thought I was the last one."

I get to my feet, walk up to the edge of the patio, try to shield my eyes from the sun as I peer out over the water.

"What are you doing, Theresa?" Mikaela asks.

I don't respond.

I can feel the grinding fear from yesterday returning. My breath shortening, my abdominal muscles clenching.

You're all alone out here. No way to escape. No way to run.

It feels like the wind is whispering to me.

Out there, on the waves, is the dinghy. The one Irene showed us, telling us it was our way off the island, in case we needed it.

In case we needed to get away.

CELL PHONE RECORDS OF PHONE NUMBER ENDING IN 1220
May 4, 2012

09:11—Missed call—phone number ending in 9813

09:13—Missed call—phone number ending in 9813

09:16—Incoming call—phone number ending in 9813 (13 minutes)

11:13—Incoming text message—phone number ending in 9797:

"hey sweetie, do you want me to pick anything up from ikea? sis
  going there after work and asked if I wanted to tag along"

12:39—Outgoing call—phone number ending in 9501 (7 minutes)

12:51—Outgoing text message—phone number ending in 9501:

"Apartment looks perfect. Great location. Would love to have a look
  at it this weekend. Get back to me as soon as possible."

12:52—Outgoing text message—phone number ending in 9501:

"On second thought, it might be better to stick to email for all further communication. Don't want to spoil the surprise!"

13:06—Incoming text message—phone number ending in 9501:

"I should be able to arrange for the current owners to let you see the
  place Saturday."

13:07—Incoming text message—phone number ending in 9501:

"Sorry, just saw your last text. Copy that. I'll send you the rest of the
  information via email."

16:49—Outgoing text message—phone number ending in 9797:

"Sorry ab. the late response! I was stuck in meetings all day. Do you
  want dinner, or are you going to gorge yourself on meatballs?"

16:51—Incoming text message—phone number ending in 9797:

"def. gorge myself on meatballs. see you later. love you!"

16:52—Missed call—phone number ending in 9813

16:53—Missed call—phone number ending in 9813

16:55—Missed call—phone number ending in 9813

16:56—Missed call—phone number ending in 9813

16:57—Missed call—phone number ending in 9813

16:58—Outgoing text message—phone number ending in 9813:

"Stop fucking calling me. I meant what I said this morning. You
  need to stop this."

CHAPTER 14

April 15, 2022

I rene is off and running down toward the water, and I follow her, the rocks biting into the bare soles of my feet, my mouth tasting like iron and dehydration. The sun is stinging my eyes, and some part of me is hoping that I made a mistake, or that it's some other boat, that it's drifted over from the next island and that our one and only way off the island hasn't just disappeared out of reach.

Irene is faster than I am, in much better shape, and she reaches the pier before me. I see the emptiness where the dinghy used to be, see her covering her eyes with her hand, and suddenly I wish I hadn't followed, since I know neither what to do nor what to say to make it better.

"Jesus," I say, once again looking around, hoping my eyes are fooling me. Hoping, stupidly, that this is some kind of prank the rest of them are playing on me, that this is some kind of cruel punishment for my outburst during dinner last night.

But the others are still up on the patio. When I turn, I can see them gathered at the railing, talking and pointing.

"Well," I hear Irene say, and I turn back to her. "That's not ideal."

"What happened?" I ask her. "Did someone cut it loose?"

"No, of course not," Irene says, with what sounds like surprise.

"Adam must have forgotten to secure it properly when he took it over to Möja yesterday morning." Her mouth twists into something small and angry, and she turns to look at the pier again.

"I told him over and over again to be careful," she says. "I must have showed him that knot six or seven times." She sighs and rubs her eyes.

"Adam took it?" My voice is shaking.

Irene doesn't look as scared and upset as I feel. She mostly looks distracted, and annoyed, the way one would be when an employee has messed up.

It should be calming me down, but instead the sinking feeling in my stomach sinks ever deeper.

"Yeah, he went over and picked up some supplies," she says, a shrill note of irritation running through her words. "I was hoping he'd be able to pop over to Harö today. We're low on ginger for the ice water. I guess we're going to have to make do without it."

Adam. The cook.

She was murdered. Right?

The look in his eyes, when I asked him about Matilda.

The expression on his face, when I saw him through the kitchen door.

That must have been just a few hours before the dinghy got loose.

Or was cut loose.

"Do you think we need to call someone?" I ask her, doing my best to sound practical. Like I'm not freaking out.

"Get them to come, I don't know, pick it up and bring it back?"

"Yeah, I'll call my guy," Irene says. "I'm sure he can pick it up for us. Or maybe the waves will bring it back in to shore. The currents are weird around here. I think it has something to do with climate change."

Irene turns back to the pier for a second before sighing and starting the walk back up to the hotel. I follow her, my hands balled up into fists and my mouth dry.

The little animal part of my brain is screaming at me, and I'm doing my best not to listen to it. It's telling me that I'm in danger, that this is strange, and wrong, and that I need to flee before it's too late.

But I know better than to listen to it. It's all those hours spent thinking about Isle Blind, all those hours wondering if Matilda Sperling spent her last few hours here. If this was where she died. What her last, gasping moments were like.

I've spent years thinking about Isle Blind as a dangerous place. That doesn't mean that it's true. Not now, and not for me. Just because the chef seemed a little strange yesterday doesn't mean that he's violent. I've slept with plenty of people in the service industry. Most chefs are more than a little strange.

To distract myself, I grasp on to the last thing Irene said.

"I didn't know there were currents around here," I say. "Are they dangerous?"

"Not really," Irene says. "You can swim just fine. It's a bit further out that it gets tricky. As long as you stay close to the beach you should be good."

"I think it might be too cold to swim," I say, and Irene shakes her head.

"No, no," she says. "It's actually very good for you. The cold water has amazing rejuvenating powers. You should look into taking regular ice baths. It's a beautiful feeling. It's like you can *feel* the negative energies leaving your system. Incredibly cleansing. It lengthens your telomeres, too."

"Oh," I say, because contradicting her seems rude.

Irene looks over her shoulder at me, slows down, and smiles.

"We're fine," she tells me. "Don't worry. I know that what we talked about last night—well, it might have primed you to be a little skittish. I know that it had me thinking that, well . . . when I saw the boat out there, I got scared. But let's not overreact. It's a dinghy. We'll have it back and tied safely to the pier in no time. I promise."

I draw a deep breath, nod, and follow Irene up the stairs.

"How did it go?" Natalie asks. "Was the boat there?" Her eyes are so big and wide they seem completely devoid of expression. Natalie, at least, it seems, is not worried.

"No," Irene says with an apologetic lilt to her voice. "The one drifting is definitely ours, sadly. So I hope you girls don't make it through all the booze tonight. I mean, worst-case scenario I can call Ivar, the captain of the boat that brought you here, and ask him to pick something up. But using the private ferry like an UberEats will add substantially to the bill."

She laughs, and Natalie and Anneliese laugh with her. But I see Mikaela frowning.

"Does that mean we're stuck here?" she asks. "I mean, not that I wanted to leave, or anything like that. But in case of emergency. I just mean if something were to happen to my boys. It's not that I don't trust my husband, but when boys get sick they want their mom."

Irene shakes her head.

"No, not at all," she says. "Even if Ivar couldn't make it for whatever reason, there are private boating companies that can come pick you up if something happens. I've got them all on speed dial. We had to make use of one of them when one of the builders fell and broke his ankle, and they were here within the hour. I don't even use the dinghy that much; it's too small to be practical for transportation. So far, it's just been the cook, Adam, using it to pop over to Möja or Harö for special ingredients."

She smiles, and Mikaela visibly relaxes.

"Okay," Irene says, and walks over to the yoga mat. She beckons me over to mine, and I reluctantly sit down.

"Let's get this party going, huh?" She smiles at the group.

As Irene starts leading the group through a chant that probably isn't supposed to sound as ominous as it does, it dawns on me that Caroline still hasn't come down.

I feel a little stab of a guilty conscience. She must have overslept, thanks to coming after me, despite the fact that she was so excited for the sunrise yoga.

I'll have to apologize to her when she wakes up.

CHAPTER 15

April 15, 2022

I've just finished my post-yoga shower, having luxuriated in the rain shower under the excellent water pressure for far longer than I should have and letting the hot water wash the ache out of my poor tortured and stretched-out muscles. Hoping it would do the same thing for my mind.

But when I get out and grab a lush heather-gray towel, the bathroom window is positioned perfectly for me to look right at the dinghy.

It looks slightly further out now. The currents Irene was talking about must be pulling it away from us.

I shouldn't let it bother me so much. Just because this island might have been the scene of a violent crime ten years ago doesn't mean that the blood has lingered in the stone.

But I'm having a hard time letting it go. The unease is making me jittery and nervous.

I manage to find a shirt that looks borderline suitable and pull it on, pair it with jeans that stopped being fashionable when the teens started roasting them on TikTok, and open the door to head out to the hallway. I'm taken aback when I see Anneliese and Natalie standing there speaking quietly to each other, heads close together and faces worried.

"Hey," I say. "Is everything okay?"

Anneliese looks up at me.

"Oh," she says. "Tessa."

She sounds disappointed to see me, and I try not to take it to heart.

"What's up?" I ask, and Anneliese looks at the closed door to her left.

"Nothing, I was just . . . I was thinking that maybe Caroline was with you," she says.

"What do you mean?" I ask, and Anneliese colors.

". . . I was thinking that she'd maybe, you know, slept in," Anneliese says. "In your room."

It takes me a couple of seconds to catch up.

"Jesus!" I say. "She didn't!"

"It's just that she didn't come down to yoga, and I haven't seen her," Anneliese says. "She went after you last night, and then, I thought, when you came back, maybe . . ." She lets the silence speak for the rest.

"No," I say. "As far as I know, Caroline went back to her own room." My voice wavers a bit, and I can feel my heart thumping painfully in my chest.

"Wait," I say. "So no one has seen her all morning?"

Natalie shakes her head.

"I thought she just . . . overslept," I say.

Anneliese shakes her head. She's biting her lip, and not in the cute way she used to back in school to get the boys' attention; this is hard enough to look painful.

"Caro never oversleeps," she says, quietly. "Not really. She's very punctual. This isn't like her at all."

"I'm sure she's fine," Natalie says, putting her hand on Anneliese's shoulder. "We shouldn't bother her. Maybe she's just not feeling good. I got food poisoning once and I was out cold for like twenty-four hours."

Anneliese shakes her head.

"No, I want to check on her," she says. "If she's sick, she might need something."

"We should see how she's doing," I agree.

My thoughts are running so fast they are getting tangled and unwieldy.

I think about the conversation we had last night, Caroline and I, out on the beach. The words flowing out of me, unstoppable.

Who are they?

The Nacka Four.

The hallway suddenly feels too small, the air too thick.

I knock on the door, so hard it makes my knuckles hurt, and I raise my voice.

"Caroline?" I say. "It's Tessa. And Anneliese, and Natalie. We just want to know that you're okay. Are you there?"

Nothing.

I look back at the other two. Put my hand on the door handle.

Anneliese nods, and I push it down.

"Caroline, I'm coming in," I say, and I open the door.

As I step into it, I'm staring at a copy of my own room. The same stark-white walls, the same rough, natural fibers, the same black-and-white photographs. The only thing that's different is the view; the window in Caroline's room overlooks the lonely little pier.

It's empty. The bed is neatly made, hospital corners still intact. No one has slept in it.

"But . . ." I hear confusion in Anneliese's voice as she takes in the room. "Where is she?"

"Maybe she remade it this morning," Natalie says. "She probably got up while we were at yoga and took a walk, or something. She just might not have felt up for yoga."

"You think she's been walking around this tiny island for two and a half hours?" I say. I don't mean to sound cruel, but it seems I have failed; Anneliese looks at me with a shocked expression.

"I'm sorry," I say, immediately. "I didn't mean to . . . I'm sorry."

"Her bags are still here," Anneliese says.

"Why wouldn't they be?" Natalie asks.

"I don't know," Anneliese says. "I just meant she couldn't have left, or anything like that."

"Well, I think we would have known if she had taken off," I say. "She would have told us."

"She couldn't have," Anneliese says. "With the dinghy drifting."

She looks shocked at her own words, and I see her swallowing, the muscles in her slender neck straining.

"Anneliese . . . ," I say, and I reach out for her, but Anneliese just shakes her head slowly.

"Where could she have gone?" she asks, her voice small and soft.

I take a second, longer look around the room. Anneliese is right; the sleek black bag I saw Caroline hauling onto the boat is still here. As is her purse. But . . .

I step up to the closet and open it. Nothing. A quick look under the bed reveals nothing's there, either.

"Her jacket is gone," I say.

"What jacket?" Anneliese asks.

"You know, that leather blazer she was wearing," I say. "She had it on last night. And her shoes aren't here, either."

"Okay," Anneliese says. "So . . ." She looks at me, expectantly.

"So she probably got dressed and left the room expecting to be going outside but knowing she'd be back soon," I say.

Natalie clears her throat.

"I still think she might have gone for a walk," she says, trying to soothe, reassure. "Maybe she's been walking around for a couple of hours. Sometimes I do that. You can lose track of time when you're in nature. Once I went out to shoot some pictures of the woods around my house just to test out my new lens, and when I got back it turned out that I'd been out there for more than four hours. It wouldn't be the craziest thing ever."

I look at Anneliese. She's biting the inside of her cheek, seeming deep in thought. Troubled.

It should feel validating, that someone else is sensing the same wrongness that I am, that I'm not alone in it, but instead it scares me.

Because if I'm not the only one, if I'm not, as Lena put it, being overly Tessa about it, then that means that something might be very wrong.

That the dinghy, and the island, and Caroline might be the first few snowflakes of an avalanche.

We're on Isle Blind, after all. In a hotel run by the sister of the woman who may have gotten murdered here ten years ago.

Who's to say that the person who did it hasn't come back to finish the job?

I open my mouth, but then I hear Mikaela's voice from downstairs. "Anneliese? I think you should see this!"

CHAPTER 16

April 15, 2022

Mikaela is standing at the bottom of the stairs, holding a note. Anneliese, being the first one down, grabs it from her hand and scans it.

I see her shoulders relaxing, though the set of her face is still tense.

"Is that from Caroline?" Natalie asks.

Mikaela's the one to answer.

"Yeah," she says. "I found it taped to the front door. I was down on the beach seeing if I could find some seashells. I saw it on my way back."

I reach out for the note, and after a beat, Anneliese hands it to me.

Ladies,

I'm so sorry to have to take off like this. I got an emergency message on my smartwatch (yes, I kept it—I apologize, Irene, my patients need to be able to reach me). One of my patients is in crisis, and so I had to grab a ferry to the mainland. I used the landline to order a transport earlier this morning.

I didn't want to wake any of you up and take away from your beauty sleep. I would have texted, but since none of you have your phones at the moment, I thought a note would be best, in the spirit of the weekend.

I'll be back tonight, or tomorrow at the latest. Don't let this slow the festivities down, and make sure you drink enough to make up for my absence tonight.

Love, Caroline

"So," I say, looking up. "A work emergency."

I try to believe it as I'm saying it. It's perfectly believable, after all. But the words have a sour taste, and I can't help but look down, read the note again, searching for something that isn't there. I hand it back to Anneliese.

"I guess it can't be helped," Anneliese says, trying to sound chipper. "And she says she'll be back tonight."

"No, come on," Mikaela cuts in. "She could have at least told us in person. And, honestly, Anneliese, sometimes you have to prioritize in life. What, is she the only therapist in Stockholm?"

Natalie frowns.

"I mean, if it's an emergency . . . ," she says, but Mikaela shakes her head.

"No, this was a shitty thing to do," she says. "Four days is not a long time to be gone. This weekend is supposed to be about Anneliese. And it's been *meticulously* planned. Now the dynamic is completely wrong!"

Natalie puts an arm around Anneliese's shoulders.

"She'll be back soon enough," she says. "The rest of us will take care of you in the meantime. Won't we, Tessa?"

Natalie looks at me with those big eyes, and I nod.

"Of course we will," I say.

Mikaela, not to be outdone, threads her arm through Anneliese's.

"Yeah," she says. "With all the mimosas and meditation I've got planned, you'll hardly notice she's gone until she's back!"

Anneliese smiles. It's a tight one, but it looks real.

"True," she says. "And I have to say, mimosas and meditation sound really good right about now. I think that was enough excitement for one morning. First the dinghy, and now Caroline doing a runner. I could use some cava and orange juice."

"Irene said that brunch is almost ready," Mikaela says. "She told me twenty-five minutes, and that was twenty minutes ago. I was just about to come get you all when I found the note."

"It's just a shame that Caroline has to miss it," Anneliese says.

"I'll take lots of pictures," Natalie promises. "So that she can take in the full glory of the brunch after she's back." She smiles, and I can see what drew Anneliese to her now; she's got that same optimism, the same urge to make the best of any situation, to suppress any negativity by sheer force of will.

"Good," Mikaela says. "Show her what she's been missing." Her smile is decidedly more pissed off than Natalie's, but no less real.

Anneliese puts the note down on the driftwood hallway table and follows Mikaela and Natalie out to the dining room, where Irene's muted voice greets them.

I can hear the siren song of organic croissants and cloudberry jam calling me, but I stop, almost against my will, and pick up the note.

Study it.

I woke up at three A.M. I didn't get back to my room until slightly before four. And then I woke up again when my alarm went off, at five thirty, for sunrise yoga.

I don't really think I fell asleep properly between those two points in time. I slid into that gray state between waking and slumbering, sure, but when the alarm rang, I had no sensation of waking.

So . . . wouldn't I have heard, if not Caroline walking around, at least the boat arriving outside?

My window was open, after all. I remember the sound of the wind. The smell of it.

The silence.

Quickly, I stick the note in my pocket before making my way out to brunch.

May 9, 2012

"Do you want a beer?" Irene asked, and Matilda shook her head. "No, I'm good," she said. "I'm fine with a Coke."

Irene turned to the fridge, and Matilda silently panicked for a moment. Could she have soda, or was that bad? Was that one of those things she wasn't supposed to drink? She knew about alcohol and cigarettes, but wasn't there something about caffeine, too?

There was just so much she didn't know.

"I'm sorry, I'm all out," Irene said, her hand on her hip. "Is orange juice okay?"

"Orange juice is fine," Matilda said. Feeling relieved, and just a bit disappointed.

She'd really wanted that soda.

No, actually, she'd really wanted that beer.

Irene's apartment was small, but much nicer than Matilda's; Irene had always been better at that stuff, at the homemaking. When Matilda had moved in with Carl, she had done her best, but it had all ended up looking a bit haphazard.

Carl loved it, though. No wonder, given where he'd been living before they had gotten a place together. Bare walls, hand-me-down furniture donated by various relatives, and a bathroom that smelled like mildew and body spray.

"Here," Irene said and put a glass of orange juice down in front of Matilda. She'd gotten a beer for herself, and Matilda eyed it jealously as Irene put the bottle against her lips and took a deep first sip. She could almost imagine that cold, fresh taste, the sour and bitter mingling on the tongue, signaling the end to a long and draining day.

"Thank you," Matilda said, and picked up her own, disappointing glass of orange juice.

Irene put the beer down and said:

"So, what's up?"

"What do you mean?" Matilda asked quickly.

Too quickly.

Irene started undoing the long braid her hair had been done up in. She'd apparently left work at three and gone straight to the gym, hadn't bothered to shower yet; as a real estate agent her hours were more flexible than Matilda's, something Matilda frequently envied her.

"You said you didn't feel like going out," Irene said. "You don't want a beer. You're staring at me in a really weird way. Clearly there's something you want to talk about."

"There's nothing," Matilda said, knowing she didn't sound very convincing, hoping Irene would just let it slide. "I'm just tired. Long day at work."

Irene studied her as her quick, nimble fingers worked at freeing her long, dark hair. She was still wearing a gray sports bra and matching leggings, showing her toned midriff.

Matilda hadn't had time to work out in ages. She hadn't had time to do much of anything for herself in a very long time. Every four months or so, she promised herself she would pull back a bit, try to do less for a while, carve out some space for herself, but somehow things kept coming up, small emergencies everywhere, none of which ever seemed to matter, in the end.

She'd gotten into HR because she'd studied psychology at university, and it had seemed less stressful, and significantly less heartbreaking, than working in the public health system. But somehow, that cushy, well-paid job that had seemed so good on paper, and that she was constantly told she excelled at, had started feeling like it was eating her alive. Hollowing her out, bit by bit. Sometimes, when she was sitting in a meeting talking about the next multinational leadership development program, she could hear a buzzing sound in her ears, like she was stuck in an invisible web, being slowly digested while still droning on about how to improve the employee experience without raising wages.

She never had time for the things she enjoyed anymore. There were times when she thought she didn't even remember what she enjoyed, or if she had ever enjoyed anything, really. She kept trying to make space for something else in her life, something that wasn't Carl, and wasn't work, and that space just never materialized. The mild, numbing exhaustion seemed to have settled in her very bones.

And how would it ever let up, with a baby?

Matilda felt her eyes filling with tears, and she quickly looked down at her glass, hoping to hide them.

But of course Irene saw it.

She'd never been able to hide anything from Irene.

"Oh God, Tilly, what's wrong? What happened?"

She felt, more than heard, Irene sliding her chair back from the table, coming around, putting her arm around Matilda's shoulders. Felt her sister's long hair falling across Matilda's own back, as though it belonged to her. Felt the earthy smell of drying sweat as Irene leaned in closer.

"Come on, Tilly." She heard Irene's voice, the undercurrent of worry. "Talk to me."

"I'm pregnant," Matilda wheezed out.

It was easier to say it without looking at Irene. Easier to try out the words, to feel the shape of them.

Irene was quiet.

Matilda sniffled and looked up at her sister, who was staring at her, her eyes wide and shocked.

"Really?" Irene asked.

Matilda nodded.

"Six weeks," Matilda said. "I think."

Irene's arm was still around her shoulders. Matilda could see every individual freckle on her cheeks, and found comfort in knowing they mirrored her own. She could see the beginning of crow's-feet at the corners of Irene's eyes, where they crinkled when she smiled, and knew that her own would start to come in, in exactly the same place, in just a couple of years, just as they had for her sister.

"Have you told Carl?" Irene asked her.

"Of course I've told Carl," Matilda said.

"And are you . . . happy about it?" Irene asked, the hesitation written all over her face.

It was the doubt that did it.

Matilda nodded.

"Of course I'm happy about it," she said, with as much conviction as she could muster. "And Carl is thrilled."

"I didn't even think you wanted kids," Irene said, and Matilda wriggled her way out of her sister's grip.

"Well, I do now," she said, forcefully, hating herself for the lie and hoping she could will it into truth.

Irene nodded, slowly.

". . . okay," she said. "Okay. Well, in that case, that's really great news, right?"

"Right," Matilda said, staring her sister down. "Great news."

Irene smiled. It almost managed to look effortless.

"Well . . . fuck, Tilly! Congratulations! We should celebrate!"

She got the voice right, the thrilling happiness in it. But she made no move to hug Matilda again.

"Just say it, Reenie," Matilda said.

Irene shook her head.

"There's nothing to say," she said. "It's not what I thought you wanted, but you're allowed to change your mind. I'm really happy for you."

Matilda pressed her lips together and looked away, out the window. Let her eyes rest on the Stockholm skyline outside, the rows of turquoise and terra-cotta roofs seeming to go on forever, the overbright May-evening sunshine bathing it all in a golden glow.

"Yeah," she said. "I'm really happy, too."

"Have you told your friends?" Irene asked.

"Not yet," Matilda said, sipping her orange juice. It didn't taste right. The pulp stuck to her teeth.

"I'm going to tell them this weekend," she continued. "On the trip."

"You're still going on that?" Irene asked, and Matilda turned back.

"Of course I'm still going," she said. "I just won't drink."

"I just meant . . . ," Irene said. "What if something happened?"

"What could possibly happen?" Matilda asked. "It's just one night, with the four of us."

"But, I mean, if something were to go wrong with the . . . baby . . ." Irene hesitated on the last word.

"It'll be fine," Matilda said.

"You should at least tell someone where you're going," Irene said, and now they were back in familiar territory, that well-worn argument about the trip. "This whole secrecy thing is starting to feel a little childish."

Matilda stuck her tongue out at Irene, who rolled her eyes.

"Thanks. Not proving my point at all."

"You're just jealous," Matilda said.

Irene smiled. In the warm light from the window, with her hair loose across her shoulders, crouched down next to Matilda's chair on the floor, she looked, for a moment, just like an old picture of their mom Matilda had seen once.

She wanted to tell her, but the turmoil still seething in her chest wouldn't let her.

"Sure," Irene said, gently touching Matilda's cheek. "Always. You're the baby, after all."

CHAPTER 17

April 15, 2022

". . . so I shriek at her to get out and I turn to him and ask him who the fuck she is, and he says, 'Oh, it's okay, honey! This is my cousin!'"

The table erupts with laughter. Natalie has put her hand over her mouth in shock, but her shoulders are shaking; Mikaela is laughing so hard she's got tears in her eyes.

Anneliese shrugs with the casual nonchalance of the seasoned storyteller.

"As if that would make the fact that this woman was in our hotel room, naked except for a thong with a bunny tail on it, better," she finishes the story, and drains her fourth mimosa to punctuate her statement.

"God," Lena says. She wipes her eyes and shakes her head. "You broke up with him, right?"

"Well," Anneliese says. "After we got back. I didn't want to waste a free five-star hotel experience." She pauses.

"I did fuck the bellboy, though, so I'd call it above even."

The rest of us start laughing again. I can feel my head spinning a bit when I tilt my head back. The mimosas have more bite than you'd think, and they go down easy. Always a dangerous quality in a drink.

I reach for another mini blueberry scone, hoping it'll suck up some of the alcohol. When I bite down on it, I spray crumbs all over the table. If Irene had joined us for lunch, I might have felt embarrassed, but she's off trying to reach Ivar on the phone for help with the lost dinghy, something that has soothed my nerves enough to relax a bit.

"I can't believe the losers I dated before Samuel," Anneliese says, shaking her head. "You know, one of the nicest things about getting married is that I never have to date again. I love Samuel, and I'm excited about the rest of our lives together, but I might be even more excited about never having to go on another first date again."

"Oh, please," Mikaela interjects. "You used to be the Queen of Tinder! I remember you showing up to Pilates in some guy's shirt, smiling like the Cheshire Cat."

Anneliese smiles.

"Yeah, but isn't that what you have to do?" she says. "You make the best of the process, but no one actually enjoys dating. You're just playing the game as well as you can, hoping that you'll win sooner or later."

"I don't know if I agree with that," Mikaela says. "When you've been married as long as I have, you start to miss some of the excitement. I mean, you all know I adore Wilhelm. And I *love* my kids. Love, love, love. I wouldn't trade my life for anything in the world."

She's slurring her *s*'s a little bit. It seems I'm not the only one feeling the effect of the mimosas.

"But I can't deny that I miss being single once in a while," Mikaela continues. "Being untethered, being free to do whatever you want. I feel like I always have to put the needs of Wilhelm and the kids ahead of mine. Sometimes I think that I'd give anything to just have a few days to myself where I could just be . . . me."

Anneliese puts her hand over Mikaela's, squeezes it, and smiles.

"I think everyone feels that way sometimes," she says. "No matter where you are in life, you always wonder about the other side of the coin, right?"

Mikaela sets her gaze on Natalie and me at the far end of the table.

"I mean, let's ask our single gals," she says. "I know both of you guys are out there living it up, but you must wonder about the quiet domestic life sometimes, right?"

I see Natalie blinking.

"I don't date much," Natalie says, and her voice sounds steady. There isn't a trace of anger on her face. Either she's tougher than she looks, or she's very good at rolling with the punches.

"At least not right now," she continues. "I've just never been that into the dating scene. I met all of my exes sort of organically, through work or friends. The whole swiping culture isn't for me. If I meet someone, that's great, but it's not something I'm looking for actively."

"No, of course," Mikaela says. "I agree, I don't think I would have liked the whole Tinder thing, either. I'm glad I missed out on that. It seems so impersonal to me."

"Well," Annelise interjects. "You sure seemed like you enjoyed swiping on my phone back in my Tinder days."

"Well, what's a little swiping between friends?" Mikaela says, and they snicker, their heads tilted slightly toward each other.

Funny. I don't think I'd realized that Mikaela and Anneliese had stayed this close since high school. It almost makes me feel . . . not jealous, exactly. I've always known I'm not Anneliese's number one, and I never thought I had a wish to be.

Or maybe I just never thought it was within reach, so I didn't try.

"But what about you, Tessa?" Mikaela says. "You seem like you would have some stories!"

"I, uh, just went through a breakup not too long ago," I say. "So I don't really think I'm ready to get out there again."

"Oh, no!" Mikaela says. "I'm so sorry, that really sucks."

"It . . . does," I say, going for nonchalant, ending up sounding, even to myself, like I'm trying too hard.

"But, hey. That's life, right?" I attempt a chuckle.

"Wait," Anneliese says. She has put her glass down on the table. "I didn't even know you were seeing anyone!"

"Well," I say. "It wasn't really an official thing. We were seeing each other for a long time, but it was never, you know . . ."

I don't know how to explain what I had with Minna without sounding like a profoundly sad person. The only way to get away with it would be to make it sound breezy, like a mutually unattached thing, but I've already nixed that option for myself by calling it a breakup and saying it left me in bad enough shape to not want to meet anyone new.

"I've heard about that!" Mikaela says. "It's called a 'situationship,' right? A relationship that isn't really a relationship?"

Ouch. I don't love hearing whatever I had with Minna described that way. But I can't deny the accuracy of it, either.

"I came across it on TikTok," she says. "It's a whole thing now."

"That sounds very modern," Anneliese remarks. "I'm so conservative when it comes to dating. I mean, I didn't mind sleeping around a bit, but as soon as I started liking a guy, I had to know we were going somewhere. I told Samuel on our second date that I was looking to get married. I figured that if that scared him off, he wasn't right for me, anyway."

"I don't know," I say. "I don't think we were ever heading in that direction. We were working together, so . . . anyway. She was great, but we were never going to be anything serious."

"Oh," Mikaela says, and her tone is very different now.

Shit. I should have known better. Those damn mimosas have dulled my senses.

Of course Mikaela would be fascinated by a non-straight at her table. There's about a fifty-fifty chance that she's about to start talking about how she'd "love to date girls but couldn't imagine herself having sex with another woman."

"I didn't know you were gay," Mikaela says. "You weren't out in high school, right?"

". . . No, I wasn't," I say. "But I'm not gay, I'm bisexual."

Mikaela raises her eyebrows. It's a fraction of an inch, and it's only for a second, but it's enough.

"I see," she says.

"I've always been jealous of bisexual people," Mikaela continues, airily. "It seems so cool to have such a big dating pool. I would have loved to have a break from dating guys, back in the day."

I pull the corners of my mouth up in a rigid death-mask grin. Tell myself that she's just drunk, that she doesn't mean anything by it. Pretend that this isn't a conversation I've already had to suffer through a million times.

"Yeah," I say, voice cold, words chopped. "Sure was great. To be able to take a break from guys."

"So that's why you weren't in a real relationship?" Mikaela asks. "Because you didn't want to stick to just one woman?"

"That's not really how it works," I say, but she keeps talking over me.

"I don't know if I could do that," Mikaela says. "I'm sorry, I know it might not be politically correct, but I just don't understand how anyone could be okay with having their partner sleep with other people. Maybe I'm just old-fashioned that way. But there's just something kind of *icky* about it? I mean, sometimes I have a hard time having sex with Wilhelm thinking about all the germs that are being spread. I guess I'm kind of OCD." She laughs.

"I don't think that counts as OCD," I say. "I'm pretty sure that's a serious mental health condition."

Mikaela rolls her eyes.

"You know what I mean," she says.

Lena clears her throat. The whole table quiets down. It's always been a special skill of hers, that high-pitched little *hrm-hm*.

"Mikaela, I'm sure you don't mean to insult my sister by implying that her sexual orientation makes her unable to sustain a monogamous relationship if she so chooses," she says, her voice sharp as an icicle. "Dating doesn't get easier because you're part of a sexual minority, as I'm sure we all know."

Mikaela's cheeks turn pink under her highlighter.

"No, of course not," she says. "That's not what I meant."

"I know it wasn't," Lena says, her lips in a razor-thin smile. "You would never. It's just easy to slip up with these things."

"It is." Mikaela nods. "It's just hard to know what's okay to say these days. There are just so many words and stuff and I can never keep track of what's appropriate and what isn't."

I feel Lena's eyes on me as I draw a quick breath, but she gets ahead of me.

"Well, if there's one word I know is still okay, it's 'bride'!" she says, suddenly all excitement and smiles. "I want to hear about the proposal again, Anneliese. I just can't get over the fact that he *actually* managed to find your first car and restore it?"

As Anneliese launches into the story, and the table is once again enraptured, I catch Lena's eye and smile at her. She toasts me silently with her empty glass.

She's always had my back.

But side by side with that warm, safe feeling is the fact that one of the chairs around the table is empty.

Everyone else seems to have accepted the note as an explanation. No one else seems worried. We're all just having *such a great time*.

But then again, the others don't know what I know.

About the island.

About its possible history.

And I can't get rid of the feeling that there is something I'm missing.

CHAPTER 18

April 15, 2022

Brunch runs long, and when we finally get up from the table to, in accordance with Mikaela's orders, "drink some water, get sobered up, and get ready for the mindfulness hike," I've got less than half an hour before I'm supposed to show up for the walk in question.

I wait until the others have noisily ascended the stairs before walking back to the brunch table, where Irene is busy cleaning up, and I clear my throat.

She looks up at me, holding a stack of beautifully mismatched, though messy, plates, and smiles.

"Hey," she says. "What's up?"

"Did you get ahold of Ivar?" I ask her. My voice is shriller than I intended.

Irene nods, shifting the weight of the plates a bit.

"He's going to try to come by this evening," she says. "He's doing it for free, as a favor, so if he gets booked up he'll stop by tomorrow morning. The weather is supposed to be calm tonight, clear skies, so it shouldn't be a problem."

"You're not worried?" I ask her.

"Worried about what?" Irene asks. "The boat is fine."

That now-familiar little spike of panic shoots through me, and I tamp it down as well as I can.

"I just mean, if we needed the boat . . . ," I say.

Irene puts the plates down on the table, furrowing her brow.

"Are you feeling nervous?" she asks. Some of that soothing yoga teacher voice has crept back in.

"I just . . ." I can't sound hysterical, can't sound like I'm overreacting, or she might not listen to me. "I have a feeling that something might be going on."

"Like what?" Irene asks.

"Just . . . with the boat, and now Caroline leaving in the middle of the night . . . it feels odd, to me. Especially considering, well, what happened to your sister."

Irene becomes very still. Then she sighs.

"You think—what? That someone hurt Tilly and her friends, and that that person might have come back?" She sounds very brittle. I can't tell if it's fear, or anger, or something else.

"When you say it out loud, it sounds crazy," I say, trying to communicate that I know how I'm coming across. "But . . . if I had killed four women on a small island in the archipelago ten years ago, and if I then found out that the sister of one of the victims had bought the island, I might start feeling a bit nervous. I might get paranoid enough to want to do something about it."

Irene is biting her lip.

But then she shakes her head.

"I see why you're feeling a bit skittish," she says. "It's a lot to take in, at once. A lot of small things at once can pile up. But if there was someone on the island who wasn't supposed to be here, I think we would have noticed. It's not a very big place, after all. There's really nowhere to hide."

What she's saying makes sense. I just can't shake this itchy, maddening feeling.

When I look up, Irene's face has softened.

"Do you want to leave?" she asks me. "It seems this might all have become a bit too much for you."

I open my mouth, and she interrupts me.

"If you still want to look into Isle Blind and what might have happened, you can come back some other time. You are welcome whenever you want. We can walk around the island together, see if we can find . . . anything. And we can talk about it. See if there is anything to dig into. We won't be opening fully to the public for at least a couple of months, so there will be plenty of time. I can call a ferry for you to come pick you up sometime in the next two hours. I'm sure the others wouldn't mind. They care about you."

For a few seconds, I find myself speechless.

Because it holds such an appeal. Just leaving. Leaving this island and the horrible, humming tension I feel in the air, coursing through my system, that building sense of doom that has seemed to follow me since I first set foot on the shore.

But I can't leave. Not now. Not over some ridiculous, unformed hunch.

"No," I say. "You're right. I'm overreacting. I think it's just the stress of it all. I'll try to relax. I'm sorry I keep bothering you about it."

"You're not bothering me at all," Irene says, and I still see concern in her eyes, but her smile looks genuine. "Caring too much is better than not caring enough."

I hesitate, but I have to ask.

"About your sister," I begin to ask. "Do you know if she told anyone where she was going, that night? I read in the papers that they used to go out to the archipelago once a year, but no one ever mentioned where they'd go."

Irene shakes her head, sadly.

"No," she says, her voice heavier. "I asked her about it, just a few days before she left. She wouldn't tell me. It was part of the whole tradition of it all."

"Did she get in touch with you that night, at all?" I ask.

"No," Irene says. "I spent the night at our parents', that day. Our dad was a bit older than our mom, and I tried to make sure to see them at least once every two weeks. I remember that my mom asked me about Tilly, that night, and said that she'd seemed distant on the phone the day before, and I thought about checking in on her, but I never ended up following through on that."

I can see Irene's jaw clenching, hear how her voice hitches.

"I'm sorry," I tell her, and Irene closes her eyes briefly, shakes her head, and smiles. When she opens them, she picks up the plates and says:

"How about this: what if we agree to keep an eye out, for the rest of the day. Both of us. If we see something strange, or if we hear something, we'll tell the other one, and we can look into it. Just to feel safe. And if you change your mind, and decide that you want to leave after all, or if we see something and decide that we all have to get out of here, I'll get Ivar here in less than thirty minutes. No matter the upcharge. Does that sound good?"

I exhale. It's less than I'd hoped for, but, then again, I don't know what I had hoped for. For her to convince me I'm wrong? For her to join me in my discomfort?

"Sounds good," I echo back.

CHAPTER 19

April 15, 2022

The low-grade nausea in my stomach has been roiling gently for the better part of an hour. I'm not sure the acidity of the orange juice and the alcohol in the champagne are getting along with my stomach lining. Should have had more of those mini scones.

The afternoon activity is apparently called a "mindfulness hike." In my mind, hikes are associated with climbing uphill while wearing sweat-wicking clothes and eating copious amounts of unsalted nuts, but this is nothing like that. We're all taking oddly small, slow steps, while—as instructed by Irene—"breathing in for four heartbeats, holding our breath for six, and letting out all the breath in our lungs for eight." The first time I tried, it just made me dizzy, so I'm silently, secretively breathing normally and trying to stave off the boredom by letting my thoughts run wild.

I've fallen to the back of the pack so my duplicitous breathing won't be discovered, but now and again one of the others will turn their head to look out over the water, their expression impossibly peaceful.

Enough to make me jealous.

Irene made it very clear we were not supposed to talk while on the hike, so as to focus on "breathing in nature and feeling the movement of energy in our bodies."

And I tried. I actually did. But the rumbling in my stomach and all the leftover feelings from brunch have made it impossible.

When Lena took over and managed the situation, it felt good. But now I can't help but hear the conversation in my head, again and again.

So hard to know what's okay to say these days.

I could never.

Just . . . icky.

I don't know how I wasn't prepared for this. I didn't come out in high school for a reason, after all. For a long time, I had even managed to convince myself that it didn't matter much. I was still attracted to men, after all. I had crushes on guys, fell in love with guys, enjoyed dick as much as the next straight girl. Just because I'd occasionally fall in lust with a beautiful redhead on the subway didn't mean I had to do anything about it.

It just seemed easier.

Because I *knew* back then that my bisexuality wouldn't fly. Everything I had ever seen on TV told me that bisexuals were exactly what Mikaela described: slutty, untrustworthy, and slightly gross. Good for a three-way but not much more. Definitely not girlfriend material. How could you ever trust someone like that, someone who couldn't even make up their mind about which gender they preferred?

The upper-class neighborhood where we grew up was an odd amalgamation of open-minded and conservative. It was, and still is, so violently white that they had to put the lone Pakistani kid in our grade on the school website four times to make it look even a little bit diverse. Kamran made it out like he didn't care, and maybe he didn't. Or maybe he had to say that. Maybe acknowledging it would have made it worse.

So I pushed it down, and I never talked about my sexuality with anyone.

I knew when I entered puberty, and it took me ten years to actually act on my same-sex attraction. The solution to my self-imposed repression turned out to be a gorgeous soft butch named Malina, seven years my senior, who bought me shots of Fernet-Branca and then brought me home. What fascinated me wasn't her slightly androgynous brand of beauty but how open, and out, and relaxed she seemed.

Not just in her sexuality. But with everything.

I never saw her again after that night. Isn't that so often the case with people who change your life for the better? Meanwhile, the ones who change you for the worse are the ones who stick around. Both in your life and in your mind.

I wish I could say that Malina made me less ashamed of myself. But she didn't. Neither did any of the ones who came after her. Not really. I'm still ashamed. The lessons I learned as a teenager have stuck to my bones like smoke clings to your hair. Every time someone asks about who I'm seeing, who I'm dating, I have to push that little voice away, the one that whispers:

Wouldn't it be easier to just lie?

Wouldn't it be easier to just stop?

Do you really want to make everyone uncomfortable?

And then I do it anyway, because I have to. And then, today, Mikaela was sitting there, and it was like no time at all had passed since we were teenagers. Like she was still the beautiful, perfect, *normal* one, and I was Anneliese's little project, the weird girl Mikaela could make fun of, gently and politely, enough to sting but not to call out, for fear of looking hysterical. Fear of making things *awkward*.

"Hey," Natalie whispers to me, and I twitch as I'm pulled out of my thoughts. I didn't notice she'd fallen behind to join me.

"How's your mindful breathing going?" she asks me, so quietly that I might have to try my hand at lipreading if she goes any lower.

"I don't know," I whisper back. "I don't think I've gotten the hang of it yet."

"I think Irene is cheating," Natalie says. "I swear I saw her breathing normally. She's faking it."

I snort, cover it up with a cough. A quick look ahead indicates that the others haven't heard me. We're on our third lap around the island, and it occurs to me that Irene never actually told us how long we'd be doing the mindful hike. It feels like it's been going on for hours, and I don't have a watch.

"Hey, I just wanted to say, it was really shitty what Mikaela said at lunch," Natalie whispers to me. "I'm going to talk to her later. It wasn't okay."

"Oh," I say, startled. "That's . . . really nice of you. But you don't have to do that. She was drunk, it happens."

"No, it doesn't," Natalie says. "I know I'm kind of new to the group, and Mikaela seems nice and all, but that whole schtick she's doing, the clueless rich lady-of-the-manor thing, it's ridiculous and it sucks. I hope you don't mind me saying, but I don't think she actually feels that way. She seems like one of those people who sometimes get so caught up in themselves that they forget that other people have feelings."

She's still speaking quietly, but I'm anxious that the others will hear her. Anxious for her, mostly, anxious that Mikaela will hear her and get angry. But either the others are so caught up with their mindfulness that they aren't paying attention to the whispering at the back, or the crunching from the rocks under our feet is enough to drown out her voice.

"Yeah, it wasn't great," I admit. "But I'm used to it."

"I actually . . . ," Natalie starts saying, but then stops. Her voice grows even quieter.

"I was wondering," Natalie breathes. "When did you realize?"

"When did I realize what?" I ask. My mouth feels dry. I should have had some water with those mimosas.

"Just . . ." Natalie has turned to look out over the water. Our walk has slowed to a crawl, and the others are getting farther and farther away.

"I don't know, when I was younger . . . I didn't think about it much, it just seemed like one of those things, you know? You're young, you want to experiment. That's what people say. Right? But I've been wondering lately if it might not have been just a phase," she continues.

"Ladies!"

Irene's voice has never been less welcome. She's stopped out at the far end of the isle, the one that faces unending, steel-gray water.

"Let's take a stop here."

"Oh, wow, we're further behind than I thought," Natalie says. "Do you think it's okay to walk normally now?"

That thoughtful, nervous look she bore just a second ago is gone, and she's back to looking fresh and perky, like butter wouldn't melt in her mouth.

"I . . . yeah, I think so," I say.

She speeds up and I fall into her new speed, but my heart is beating faster than would be explained by the sudden change in pace.

I don't have time to dwell, however. We reach Irene and the rest of the group in what seems like seconds. They've gathered on the shore. Lena is standing so close to the water that an occasional brave wave nearly touches her flawless pearly-pink sneakers.

"How do we feel?" Irene asks.

A murmur rises from the group. "Brave." "Fully myself." "Strong." None of them is a word I associate with taking a very slow walk.

"Grounded," I hear Natalie saying by my side, and I curse myself for not thinking of that one. I sneak a peek at her, and the word that rises within me is *confused.*

"Good," Irene says, and smiles blissfully. "No feelings are out of bounds here. Mindfulness can allow us to feel things we've been pushing down. Existing fully in the moment and listening to our bodies lets us experience our thoughts and feelings as they arise. Don't be surprised if memories of things good or bad from our past start coming up in the hours to come." She breathes in, deep, and exhales slowly.

"Let's take a moment to just experience this place together," she says. "Look out over the water. Study the sky. If you want, you can pick up a few of the rocks and roll them between your fingers. Feel the smooth surfaces. Think about the water rolling them back and forth, back and forth, for thousands of years. Think about the continuity of time. Imagine yourselves as one of those stones. Life rolls us back and forth, smoothing out our rough edges and teaching us about ourselves. Sometimes, that process can be painful. But it's necessary for us to become the truest versions of ourselves."

To my surprise and horror, I find that I have a lump in my throat. I can't believe this stuff is working on me. It's so clichéd. Something I'd usually make fun of and laugh at.

But, goddamn it, something about her words strikes a chord,

whether I want them to or not. Something about being a rock in the water, about being pushed back and forth.

The rest of the group has gone quiet. Some of them have closed their eyes. The wind from this morning has quieted down, and the water has gone so still it looks slick as oil. If I dipped my hand into it, it seems as though the rest of me would glide in as well, so quick and easy I might not even feel it.

I can feel my chest rising and falling. It doesn't even feel like I'm doing it. It feels like a natural phenomenon, like I'm following my breath as opposed to trying to force air into my lungs.

When is the last time I breathed like this? For the past few months, my chest has felt constantly constricted. At night, I've woken up gasping so many times it's felt like someone is standing on it.

I close my eyes. I see his face.

This time, though, it feels different.

I can imagine every detail. It's all burned into the insides of my eyelids, every detail sharp and clear as glass. The strong nose, the heavy brow. How the skin sagged as though hanging loose off the skull. He had a birthmark to the right of his nose, and a faint patter of burst veins over his cheeks, the result of a life spent working outside.

In my mind, he's on the verge of tears, but they never fall. He didn't look like someone who'd ever cried much in his life. His words were slow and delivered with care; after every question he would take a moment to think, to weigh what he was about to say, to make sure it would come out the way he intended.

Afterward, I read that he'd had a stutter, growing up. I had managed to keep it together, up until that point. I don't know why that was the detail that made me come undone. That was the thing that broke me. Realizing that his way of speaking had been worked out over the course of a lifetime, a way of making sure he was understood as he wished to be understood.

I haven't been able to touch on that memory since the day I fell apart. But now, it's coming to me, whole and unbroken, and for some reason, I can see it clearly.

I hurt someone very badly. I caused harm to someone I never meant to hurt. I did that, and that is a true thing, and that is something I am going to have to live with for the rest of my life.

He did not deserve what I did, and the responsibility is fully mine.

I am the only one who can make amends.

I breathe in deep, again, and open my eyes. A quick breeze hits from the sea, and it smells like so many things. I haven't been able to pick them out until now. There's salty, and sweet, minerals mingling with the faint scent of fish and algae. So rich it forces me to close my eyes again for a moment.

When I open them, I look toward the others.

Mikaela's face is contorted in a frown, almost as though she's in pain. It's not the pretty, performative frown I've seen on her socials; this is real, tense and striking.

Irene's gaze is trained on the horizon. Her back is so straight it looks strained. Her eyes so empty she could be in a trance.

Anneliese has a faint smile on her lips, but her hands are balled into fists, squeezing so tight her long, slim nails must be pressing into her palms.

Natalie's face is smoothed out. Not a wrinkle or fold to be found. Her breathing is so slight her chest barely appears to be rising at all.

And Lena . . .

Lena is crying.

Her eyes are closed, and tears are running down her cheeks, leaving faint traces of brown mascara. She's not sobbing, not making a sound. Just those tears, ever falling, dripping onto the rocks below.

I want to speak. Want to say something. Want to comfort her, ask her what's wrong. But it looks so intensely private that interfering would feel wrong. I feel like I'm spying on something truly intimate, something my sister would never want me to see; I'd feel less out of sorts if I'd caught her having sex with Franz.

From the corner of my eye, I see Natalie bending down to the beach, picking up a few rocks, and enclosing them in her palm. Doing that seems better than watching Lena crying, so I do the same, feeling the slick surface of the wet stones against my skin. They are colder than I would have expected, and I feel the tips of my fingers going numb when I pick them up.

I do as Irene instructed, roll them between my fingers, focus on the image of water running over their edges. Three of them are so smooth they barely feel like stone at all.

The fourth, however, is different.

I look down at the stones in my hand, look closer. Three of them look normal, glistening slightly in the sun, grays and browns mingling with the glitter of fool's gold.

The fourth is white. Pale yellow and brown. It's bigger than the others, and has a weird shape, knobby and uneven with a hole running through the middle.

I raise it to my face.

And then I yelp, and I drop it just as quickly.

"Is something wrong?" Irene asks. When I look at her, I see traces of annoyance around her eyes, but her voice is all warm encouragement. The others have turned to look at me as well, most of them in varying stages of curiosity and irritation at being disturbed.

"I picked up some of the rocks, like you said, and one of them isn't—it's not a rock."

"What do you mean?" Irene asks. Now the annoyance is gone.

I look at her, wishing it was just the two of us, here on the beach. Wishing the others didn't have to hear what I'm about to say. But I have to tell her.

"I think . . . I think it's a vertebra. A piece of someone's spine."

CHAPTER 20

April 15, 2022

"**S**how me," Irene says.

All the yoga teacher Zen is gone from her voice now. I don't know what has taken its place, but it's harsh and immediate.

I pick it up and hand it over to Irene, and she takes it gingerly, holds it up to the sunlight.

The rest of the group has suddenly gone very quiet.

It's a different sort of quiet from a few minutes ago. This one has a charge running through it, as though the slightest movement could set us all off.

Irene has gone very pale as she brings the piece of bone closer to her face, and I find that I can't breathe, that my whole body seems to be in waiting. I'm actually mildly dizzy; it feels like the rocky beach is moving beneath my feet.

Then Irene looks at me, and she shakes her head. Just once.

"It's animal," she says. "Looks like something from a deer. They swim between the islands, sometimes, and occasionally they . . . drown." Her voice drops a bit on the last word, but she recovers quickly.

"How can you be so sure?" Natalie asks her, and Irene twitches, as if she, too, had forgotten about the others for a few seconds. She looks up at Natalie, and when she opens her mouth it takes her a couple of seconds to speak.

"I have a friend who makes jewelry out of bones," she finally says. She's still holding the piece of bone in her closed hand, and it's dropped to her side.

"She mostly uses bones from deer and wild boars," she continues. "They are smaller than human bones. I recognize it."

"God, that's disgusting." I hear Mikaela's voice from the far end of the group. "I hope she sterilizes them first."

Irene manages a smile.

"She does," she tells Mikaela. "Not to worry."

Irene looks back to me, and I don't know what it is that I'm reading in her eyes. If it's disappointment, or relief, or something else altogether.

"Do you mind if I keep it?" she asks me. "I could give it to that friend of mine. I'm sure she'd love to have it."

I nod.

"Sure," I say.

Irene turns back toward the group.

"I think it's time we make our way back to the house," Irene says. "We will walk back mindfully in the same manner we walked out and consider the thoughts and feelings that have come up during this exercise."

I see Irene's eyes sweeping across the expanse of the island before she starts walking. I wonder if she's looking for the same thing I am, or if she's just seeing the place she now calls home. The place where her sister might have died.

The whole way back, I see Irene squeezing the piece of bone tightly in her fist. And I wonder, again, if she's happy it turned out to be bone from a deer, or if it would have been some kind of solace, had it been human.

If it would have been a comfort to have had just one small piece of her sister back.

And I promise myself, promise her, quietly:

I will find something. I will do my best to bring you some kind of closure.

JOURNALOFTILLY85.LIVEJOURNAL.COM
May 9, 2012

Hello again.

I don't know if any of you are still around. I know it's been a while since I posted, but I felt like I needed to write some stuff down, and I remembered this page. It seemed nice to be able to shout into the void and to maybe have the void shout back.

I don't know where to start. I think last time I updated was something like 7 or 8 years ago. Last time I was here, I seem to still have been very into Sailor Moon crossover fic? Going over these old posts has been fun. I'm happy they are still there. There was stuff in there I don't even remember. It's funny how parts of your life can just slip away from you like that. I didn't have any recollection of having tried to get tickets to Green Day in Hamburg, for example. I don't even remember liking Green Day.

Sorry. I didn't mean for this to be such a ramble. It's just interesting, is all.

Since the last time I posted, I've gone to university, and gotten a proper grown-up job, and met a man. I mean, I've met several men. Back in the day when I used to hang out here all the time, I remember all of us lamenting the fact that none of us would ever get a boyfriend, that we'd have to buy a rickety old house in the countryside and create a convent for us ol' internet maids, buy tons of cats and chickens and keep each other company. But it happened anyway.

I don't wear the studded bracelets anymore. I actually wear blazers to work. And pumps. If any of you had told my teenage self that I would end up with an office and an assistant, I would have cursed you out and told you that I would never sell out like that, but then life happens. The years go by, and you turn into this other person, and then one day you realize that the person you used to be seems like a stranger.

Anyway. I thought you guys should know, if any of you see this, that I'm pregnant.

Writing it out, it doesn't seem real. Actually, none of it seems real. In theory, I know what's happening right now. I know that my uterus (it's such a disgusting word, isn't it? "Uterus." I don't know why, but it's always grossed me out) is busy constructing a new person inside of me. Pulling cells from all parts of my body to use for this new little stranger.

It's good news. It really is. On some level I must be excited too. It's the right time, with the right guy. In a weird way I ended up living the dream.

I remember being seventeen and wanting a big life. Like all of you. We all wanted something different, didn't we? Something that wasn't what our moms and dads wanted. Something that we built for ourselves, rules written by us, rich in something that wasn't money, a life that had some texture to it. So how did I fall into this? Did you do that, too? Did you keep making little decisions that didn't seem to matter at the time that all turned out to add up to the exact opposite of what we all dreamed of?

I hope there are still some of you out there who are actually doing the things we were going to do. Who are traveling and experiencing and living by yourselves and for yourselves.

I'm supposed to be excited, but somehow, this just feels like the final nail in the coffin. The end of the line. Once this baby is born, the person I was will be dead. I will be a mom, and a wife, and a professional, and that will be the rest of my life.

It's not that I don't like my life. It's just that it scares me, the fact that apparently, less than a decade ago, all I could think about was scraping together enough money to get the cheapest tickets possible to fly to Hamburg and scream my head off to Green Day, and now I can't even remember wanting it. Now I'm pricing hand-carved cribs and looking at fixer-uppers in the suburbs.

There has to be something wrong with me, right, that I'm more excited about an overnight trip this weekend than about having a child? But maybe that makes sense. The only experience I have with kids is babysitting the kids next door when I was a teenager. I have ten years of experience of doing this trip with my friends.

It's something we've always done just for us.

I really need that, right now. For someone or something to remind me of who I used to be. Maybe help me find who I want to be right now.

If you're still reading this, I'm sorry. I probably should have just written it in a diary. But this felt more natural, in a weird way. When I was a kid, this felt like a safe place. I don't know if it's sad or not that it still does.

<3

CHAPTER 21

April 15, 2022

After we get back, when everyone else heads to their rooms to get ready for the evening, I wait a few minutes and then take off downstairs to the basement.

The hallway seems different today. The smell of food cooking isn't as strong, and I can detect the scent of the new walls, freshly poured cement, the metallic burning from the fluorescent tubes in the ceiling.

My steps sound very loud against the floor. I remind myself that I'm not doing anything wrong, exactly; the worst I could be accused of is bothering the chef while he's preparing dinner, which can't be considered anything worse than rude.

So why do I feel so scared?

I knock on the door to the kitchen before I open it.

Adam is standing by the window, leaning out of it, and when he turns around, I'm surprised to see he's holding a cigarette.

"Fuck," he says, and, reflexively, I answer:

"It's just me."

Adam stubs the cigarette out on the windowsill and throws it out before shutting the small window. There is a tension in the way he's holding himself, and when he looks at me, he says:

"Listen, I would have gone outside, but I've got bread in the oven, okay? I didn't want to leave it."

"Don't worry," I say. "You can smoke as much as you want."

"Don't think Irene would be very happy," Adam says, and smiles, small and a bit crooked. It's unexpectedly charming.

"I won't tell if you won't," I say, and he nods.

"Thanks," he says.

Then, the very oddness of the fact that I'm down here seems to dawn on him, and he frowns.

"Did you need anything?"

"My sister was wondering if you had any mineral water," I say, the excuse I've prepared for my presence.

I'm sure Lena would appreciate a mineral water, actually, so it's not as though I'm lying. Not completely.

"Sure, I'll get you one," Adam says.

He's moving more easily now than he did yesterday, I notice, as he walks toward the fridge. I might have gotten lucky, catching him smoking in the kitchen; a small favor makes people relax, and a shared secret is even better.

"I spoke to Irene, earlier," I say, while he opens the door. "She's really impressed with the food."

"Oh, yeah?" Adam says, grabbing a bottle and closing the fridge. "That's good to hear."

"I was wondering," I say, as he hands me the tall, slim glass bottle of Vichy water. "I noticed your accent. You grew up in Stockholm, right?"

"Yeah," Adam says. "Same area as you did, I'm guessing. Lidingö, right?"

"Got it in one," I say, doing my best to sound relaxed. "How old are you? We might have been at school together. I was at Hersby."

Adam smiles again, and he leans against the counter with his arms crossed.

"I'm flattered," he says. "And, yes, I did go to Hersby. But you're, what—twenty-nine, thirty? I've got to have at least eight years on you."

The back of my neck is tingling.

"Irene is around thirty-seven, thirty-eight, right? Is that how you guys know each other?"

Adam shakes his head.

"No, but our parents go way back," he says. "My mom heard Irene was looking for someone and let me know."

Ah, yes. The upper-class whisper network. It's how Anneliese ended up with her first job, too. Subtler than nepotism, more effective than trying to make it on your own.

"Have you worked with vegan food before this?" I ask.

"Not really," Adam says. "I've worked in a lot of different kitchens, but never just vegan food before."

"Which restaurants?" I ask. "I go out a lot. I'm just wondering if I've had the privilege of trying your food before, without knowing." I try to strike a flirty tone, and it seems as though I've succeeded, because his smile grows wider.

"Oh, I doubt it," he says. "I think I would have remembered if I'd seen a famous media personality in the dining room."

I feel myself growing very still.

"I liked your podcast, by the way," Adam says. "Sorry about what happened. I was disappointed when it ended."

"Yeah," I say, and my voice comes out smaller than intended. "Me, too."

"I've always been fascinated by true crime," Adam says, and now he unfolds his arms and takes a step toward me. "The research must be really hard."

"It is," I say, and I manage to sound blessedly normal. A small miracle.

"I'm impressed," Adam says. "I've never been good with that stuff. Details and logistics. I'm better with my hands. I guess that's why I ended up working with food." He's only a couple of feet away now, and he's still wearing that strangely charming smile, revealing a small dimple in his left cheek. This close, I can see that he's got a thin scar through his upper lip, pulling it slightly upward.

"Well, thank God for that," I say. "You're really good at it."

He laughs, and it's a very warm sound. My eyes catch at the knife rack behind him on the wall, the blades gleaming in the light of the sunny afternoon.

"I guess I should be getting back," I say. "I don't want to be underdressed. I hear dinner is going to be amazing."

"You can count on it," Adam says. Then he cocks his head and looks at me with curious intensity, and I freeze up.

"I look forward to seeing what you're going to wear," he says, with naked flirtation, and nausea and sudden, unwanted attraction swirl in my stomach.

"I'll do my best to surprise you," I say, as I back out the door, my sweaty hand grasping the glass bottle.

As I walk back up the stairs, I find that I'm short of breath.

I didn't go to the Hersby school. I went to the Viktor Rydberg school in central Stockholm, just like Lena did.

But Matilda went to Hersby.

Matilda, who would have been thirty-seven this year, if she hadn't disappeared.

Our parents go way back.

Adam's parents. And Irene's. And, by extension, Matilda's.

They all knew one another, back then.

Which makes it all the more strange that Adam said that Matilda had been murdered. Because, sure, he might have mixed up two crimes he had no relationship to.

But a family friend disappearing suddenly, without a trace, never to be found?

That's not the kind of thing you forget.

Especially not when you end up working for the missing woman's sister, years later.

My mom heard Irene was looking for someone and let me know.

Such a gentle-sounding coincidence. Such a lucky twist of fate.

Such an easy thing to lie about, too.

Did he hear about it through the grapevine, the way we've all heard about open jobs and available positions over the years?

Or did he hear about what Irene was planning to build, and where . . . and seek her out?

CHAPTER 22

April 15, 2022

"Never have I ever . . ." Mikaela draws out the final word, rolling the *r* for added effect.

". . . had a threesome!"

Shocked gasps and giggles emanate from the group. Mikaela looks around at us, eyebrows raised, before finally training her gaze on Anneliese.

Who snorts, and drinks from her cup.

Irene, sitting next to her, is quick to refill it. She managed to get out of playing the game by pointing out that she has to be sober enough to get dinner on the table, and I'm trying to follow her example, keep myself sober enough to be able to catch the moment when I can talk to her.

I've squeezed myself into one of the only mildly glitzy dresses I own for the predinner drinks, a sequined red number that I remember picking up in a vintage shop almost as a joke, and painted my face with liberal amounts of liquid eyeliner and red lipstick. The result is less impressive than I was hoping, more "lounge singer past her prime" than "up-and-coming jazz starlet," but it's the best I can do.

Natalie and Mikaela shout and laugh, and I use the moment to take a tiny, discreet sip from my own cup. I could just abstain, but the rules of teenage games run deep, and even I have my principles. I don't cheat in relationships, and I don't cheat at drinking games.

I'm not discreet enough, though, apparently, since Mikaela points at me with an immaculately manicured ballet-pink fingernail.

"I saw that!" she says. "Bad girl," she adds in a singsongy chirp.

It's actually quite the feat; if anyone else had said it, it would have been impossible not to make that sound at least a little bit flirty, but in Mikaela's mouth it becomes a sugary condemnation.

"Okay, spill," she says to Anneliese. "Who and where?"

The last rays of sunlight are spilling over the deck. The clouds that were dotting the sky earlier today have all disappeared. The table Irene has put out on the deck where we had sunrise yoga this morning is overflowing with flowers, pink and white, roses and lilies; only a little bit wilted, as they had to be brought out yesterday.

"Uh," Anneliese says, half laughing. "Well, it was at university. During my wild and rebellious phase." Her cheeks are powder-puff pink, her eyes shiny with drink and excitement. The tiara is back, perched on top of her springy curls, and Mikaela has draped a big pink sash across her chest which proclaims her the Bride-to-Be.

"And it was with my boyfriend at the time and one of our class-mates. That's all I'm going to say!"

"Wait, wait," Lena chimes in. She leans forward. "Which class-mate?"

"Oh, right!" Mikaela says. "You guys went to university together, I forgot! Yeah, tell us, Anneliese." She shoots a look at Lena and stage-whispers:

"And then you can tell us if they were cute or not."

"Well, I can tell you her boyfriend was *very* cute," Lena says, and Natalie wolf-whistles.

Impressive. And a little bit sexy.

Jesus, where did that thought come from?

"No, no," Anneliese says and waves it off. She clears her throat, and says:

"I'm the bride, and I say we move on."

"All right!" Mikaela says. "By order of the bride, we move on." She pauses. "To Tessa!"

"No," I groan, but I'm ignored.

"Come on, Tessa," Mikaela says. "Let us live through you. When, where, and with whom?"

"I really don't want to talk about it," I say and shake my head, but then I'm shocked by Lena piping up:

"It was five years ago, on a trip to Copenhagen. At a festival. That Danish guy named Klaes, right? And some girl with pierced nipples."

"What the *fuck*, Lena?" I exclaim, but I'm not really angry; to my own surprise, I'm laughing along with Lena, and when the others start cheering for me, my blush doesn't feel like one of embarrassment.

"What?" Lena asks, shrugging innocently. "I didn't know that was confidential information! And now you didn't have to talk about it!"

"I'm never telling you anything, ever again," I say, and Lena winks at me and toasts me with her glass of pink champagne.

"I'd like to add, for the record, that threesomes aren't my thing," I say, trying to be at least a little bit subtle about directing my comment at Mikaela. "I'd been dating that guy for a while, and he wanted to fuck this girl. I guess I thought I could hold on to him if we did it together. Pathetic, right? And it didn't work because he broke up with me two days later anyway."

Anneliese frowns.

"I'm sorry, babe," she says, and I shake my head.

"No, no," I respond. "Please. It was for the best. Taught me not to go along with what some guy wanted just so he'd like me."

"That's good," Irene interjects, and I start, surprised; she's barely spoken during the game. "I don't want to make myself sound ancient, but I'm a little older than the rest of you. And if I have learned anything, it's that a lot of men—not all, but many—will try to hold you back, if they perceive you as a threat. They will try to tell you what you should do, and what would be best for you, and project their needs and desires onto you. It's important to learn the difference between what you want and what others want for you."

She's smiling at me, as she's saying it, and I feel a surprising warmth blooming in my stomach.

"Yes," I tell her. "Exactly."

Mikaela takes the opportunity to break the moment.

"Was it in a tent? If you were at a festival?" Mikaela asks. "Wilhelm took me glamping once, but I just couldn't make myself have sex in a tent. It felt too exposed. I felt like I was going to end up with ants crawling up my hoo-hah, if you know what I mean."

"I don't think you can get ants in your vagina," Natalie says. "I mean, they would just get smothered to death, right?"

"God, that is so gross, Natalie," Mikaela says, shaking her head.

"I think you're right, for the record," I say to Natalie. "You've got your bug-genitalia-science figured out."

"Ew, ew, ew!" Mikaela says. "Stop it! No more of this. Moving on."

Natalie shrugs, but she shoots me a quick smile.

"Wait, I've got one," Irene says, and Mikaela cedes the stage to her.

"Never have I ever . . . ," Irene says, looking around the table for dramatic effect, before landing on Anneliese.

". . . broken the law!"

I look around the table. No one is drinking, but Anneliese is flushing a pretty pink, suppressing a giggle.

"I knew it!" Mikaela points accusingly at Anneliese.

"I feel like I was set up," Anneliese says, looking between Irene and Mikaela, but she doesn't look upset. "Did you tell her?" she asks Mikaela.

Mikaela shrugs extravagantly.

"That's between me and our gorgeous hostess," she says. "Now, come on. Spill!"

Anneliese rolls her eyes, smile still playing on her lips.

"Okay," she says. "I lied to the cops once. I gave someone an alibi."

Mikaela gasps dramatically, while Natalie raises her eyebrows.

"It wasn't that bad!" Anneliese protests, laughing a little. "I was young, okay? He was this cute older guy I had been hooking up with. I think he was dealing, because he always had cocaine, but when the cops called me, it turned out he was a suspect in a murder case!" She pumps her eyebrows and rolls her *r*, and laughs.

"Jesus, Anneliese!" Natalie exclaims, with what sounds like genuine shock. "That's horrible. I read something the other day about how a lot of white-collar guys are involved with the drug trade these days. They think it's harmless, and when they realize it isn't, it's already too late."

"Yeah, it wasn't great, honestly," Anneliese says. "I stopped seeing him, for what it's worth. I thought it was fun when it was just some occasional sex and coke, but I got freaked out when it became so real. It was my first real grown-up moment, in retrospect. I quit dating shitty guys after that." She pauses, and Mikaela inserts, her tone as dry as the sparkling wine:

"Did you?"

Anneliese rolls her eyes, laughs, and punches Mikaela lightly in the arm, stopping to admire her.

"Jesus, you've got some muscle tone on you," she says to Mikaela. "That felt like punching a wall!"

"It's the Krav Maga," Mikaela says, all modesty. "I do it for fitness."

"You didn't drink!" Lena points out. "You don't get a pass just because you're the bride, Anneliese."

"Fine, fine," Anneliese says, and empties the glass. She looks around the table and says:

"Okay, it's my turn to ask a question, I need a break. Never have I ever . . . cheated."

The last word is followed by silence.

Mikaela looks around the table, perfect eyebrows perched high on her forehead.

"Nobody?" she asks. "Come on, ladies. I don't believe that."

"Fine," Natalie says, and when I turn to look at her, she's downed half her drink. She wipes her mouth with the back of her hand, smearing her pink lipstick slightly, making her mouth look softly bruised.

"Oh," Mikaela says, staring at her.

Natalie smiles, tightly.

"Well, someone had to drink, right?" she says. "Or we never would have been able to move on from the question."

"Well, who did you cheat on?" Mikaela asks, more than a little bit confrontational.

"It only happened once," Natalie says. There's a tightness in the corners of her eyes, but she hides it well; her mouth is still smiling. "It was toward the end of my marriage. I already knew he was doing it. I'd started looking up divorce lawyers, but I was scared to actually pull the trigger. I'd started feeling crazy. Kept telling myself that I was just imagining it. You don't want to believe it, I guess, even when you know. So, one of the weddings I shot . . . I fucked the best man behind the church. At least I could be absolutely, one-hundred-percent sure that it was over that way."

Her voice is too light for the subject matter, her smile too playful. Her eyes suspiciously shiny. It sounds like she's telling a story about someone else, gossiping about a mutual acquaintance. Natalie doesn't look like someone who could do something like that. She's pure sugar and cream, her thick blond hair falling down her back, the blue off-the-shoulder dress and dainty silver jewelry making her look like the perfect ad for the oncoming Swedish summer.

But the tension is there, under the surface, running through the story like a wire. Taut enough to snap.

Anneliese reaches out over the table, grabs for Natalie's hand with her fingertips.

"I'm so sorry, sweetie," she says. "You're better off without him. You didn't deserve to be treated that way."

Natalie smiles, a quick, bright thing.

"Hey, it's all water under the bridge," she says. "We're here to celebrate this lovely new marriage! Anneliese and Samuel! Having been in a bad one, I can say for sure that you guys are the real deal."

She raises her glass, and Anneliese laughs, toasting her back, and I find myself marveling at how quickly Natalie has managed to turn the situation around.

Is this what it means to be socially gifted? Being able to read those around you clearly enough to intuit what they want from you and then providing it? Natalie seems to do it so deftly, playing off even her own pain as a footnote. No wonder people like having her at their weddings.

Where do you learn that kind of skill? Is it some innate thing, or something you pick up as you go along?

I only realize I'm staring at Natalie when she suddenly looks at me.

There's something in her eyes.

I refuse to allow myself to try to read into it.

Irene breaks the moment and says:

"Ladies, I'm sorry to have to leave just as the game is getting good, but I have to go down to the beach and prepare the surprise for tonight."

Mikaela boos, but Anneliese shushes her.

"Of course! Tell us if there is anything we can do to help."

Irene smiles at her.

"As our guest of honor, you're obligated to do nothing but sit here and drink as much champagne as you can stomach. I will call on one of your friends if I need a hand."

As Irene disappears down the stairs to the beach, I wait until she's out of sight, and then I whisper to Lena:

"I'm just going to go to the bathroom."

I can't let this opportunity go to waste.

CHAPTER 23

April 15, 2022

I sneak down the stairs, one step at a time, so as not to make a sound. I can still taste the remnants of the pink champagne, feel stray crumbs from the lavender cookies stuck in my teeth, the tart and the sweet and the sour lingering on my tongue. My pulse seems loud as thunder in my ears, my heart fluttering in my chest, so clear and overwrought that my fear seems to be announcing itself to the world.

I'm not scared of Irene catching me. If she did, she'd probably just admonish me gently for not just asking her for help, and then insist on calling me that ferry.

No, I'm scared of being alone down here, in the dark. Having told no one where I'd gone.

Would they notice, if I didn't come up to dinner? Or would they just think I'd passed out in my room, from too much sugar and too much wine, and leave me to sleep it off?

That's just Tessa. She overdid it. She'll be feeling it tomorrow.

Would they think it strange if they found yet another note tomorrow morning, telling them I, too, had gotten a boat back to the mainland?

Or will they even still be here, by then?

That's the fear that lets me override my own terror. That's letting me creep down the stairs, my fingertips scraping across the wall, listening for sounds from the kitchen.

I walk as quietly as I can past the kitchen door, ducking low so I can't be seen through the small window. The next door is on my right, and when I try the handle, it glides open.

I glimpse a desk with a laptop, and I glide in as quickly as I can, shut the door behind me. The low click feels like it's echoing through the hallway.

The last of the daylight has faded, the oncoming night announcing itself with a deep, full blue, casting strange, muted shadows in the room I've just entered.

There is a built-in bookshelf on the wall opposite the door, the shelves still mostly empty. The desk is small and neat, holding only the computer, a corded telephone, and a picture frame.

I walk around the desk and sit down, feel a stab of guilt, the wrongness of being in this room where I have not been invited. But I push it aside.

I'm doing it for Irene, after all. For all of them. To try to keep them safe.

I'm about to open the computer, a slim MacBook that probably costs more than the car I had to sell a couple of months ago, when the picture catches my eye. I pick it up and angle it toward the window, trying to catch as much of the lingering light as possible.

It's an old picture. It has the look of something snapped with a disposable camera, that bleached, blurred, and yellow-tinted look that seems to plague every picture from the early 2000s. It's a photograph of two young women, one with her arm around the other's shoulder. The one on the left, the one in the sundress, is laughing; the other one, the one with the German-style braids and the festival bracelets around her wrist, is squinting at the camera, her eyes crinkling at the corners.

I look closer.

The one on the left is Irene. Fifteen or so years younger, but still unmistakably herself. She's in a short red dress, early-aughts sideswept bangs nearly covering one eye, a knitted sweater thrown over her shoulders.

And there, next to her, is Matilda.

She looks so different here from the pictures I've seen online, the ones released to the papers. The thick eyeliner, the mild dotting of old acne scars over the cheeks, the slim, knobby wrists. Those piercing blue eyes.

She doesn't look like a tragic dead girl, here. She looks like a real person. Not just a character in a story.

I put the picture down, carefully, and stare at it for a long, hard second before waking the computer.

The main user account is password-protected, naturally, but there is another user simply titled "Staff," and when I click on that one the computer opens up. Excitement overtakes me, for a second, and I feel that oh-so-familiar buzzing, the pleasure of cracking something wide open.

I find myself smiling, but then, out of the corner of my eye, I see the picture once again, and my smile falters.

This isn't some side project I've undertaken. This isn't a theoretical someone, somewhere far away.

This is about Matilda, who smiled sweetly at the camera, side by side with her sister. It's about Irene, who I've only known for a few short days, but who I already feel oddly protective over.

And it's about me. About Lena. About all of us.

I get to business. I open the browser and try to go on Facebook, but it seems the internet is down.

I frown and look around for a modem, with the vague notion that I could try to restart it, but I can't find it.

There might be something in Adam's employee file. Irene must have some documentation on him. Even if I can't use it now, I can try to find a way back down here once the internet is back up.

I push the chair back and get down on the floor, start trying the drawers to find an employee file, a pay slip, anything that might get me more information on him. The first two drawers are empty, while the third reveals a small stash of snacks. A four-pack of Snickers bars, a couple of bags of jelly candies, and a pack of beef jerky.

I stop for a moment and smile. Even Irene can't keep to the whole locally sourced, organic, vegan diet full time, it seems.

The next drawer, the one closest to the floor, stops me in my tracks.

It's the phones. Our cell phones.

I reach out for mine, at the top of the pile, and hear:

"What are you doing in here?"

His voice is soft, but it shocks me so bad I bang my head on the table. After a couple of seconds, I manage to get to my feet, my head throbbing, as I back up until I feel the bookcase against my shoulder blades.

Adam is standing in the doorway, looking mildly bemused. He's taken off the leather apron, is barefoot in a pair of jeans and a white T-shirt.

In his left hand, casually hanging by his side, is a long, slim kitchen knife.

It's strange, how the sight of the small blade in his hand seems to suck the oxygen out of my lungs.

I put my hand to my head, staggering a bit where I stand, and Adam's brows knit together. He takes a step toward me, and I hold my hand up.

"Stop," I say, and my voice is shaking. Weak.

But he doesn't stop, and there is nowhere to go. Nowhere to run. He advances on me slowly, the knife catching the cold light of the clear night, and there is a sense of time slowing, becoming elastic; of my legs becoming heavy, locking me in place, as though this is all just a nightmare and reality has turned into something that might slip out of my grip.

He puts the knife on the table and raises his hand to my head.

"Let me see," he says.

Mutely, I do as he says, all the while keeping my eyes fixated on the knife.

He touches my scalp gingerly, and I hiss in pain. When his fingers come away, I see blood on his fingertips, little droplets like jewels.

"You hit your head pretty bad, huh?" he says. "I'm sorry I scared you."

He's standing too close. I still can't find the air to speak. In my nose is the faint smell of his body, of char and sugar and sweat.

"I thought you were Irene," he says. "I just had a couple of questions for her about where to put the new champagne coupes."

"What?" I finally manage to squeak out, and Adam takes a step back, finally allowing me to breathe.

He picks up the knife from the table again, and I freeze once more, but he doesn't seem to notice.

"We've still got some boxes to unpack," he says. "I've been cutting them open and sorting the new glasses. It's a little unwieldy using this one, but I seem to have misplaced my boning knife. Not like I had much use for it out here, though, with the vegan menu." He pauses. "Anyway, I figured I'd take care of it while you girls are partying. Make myself useful. Ingratiate myself with the new boss."

He smiles, the same charming smile from before.

But then it falters.

"What were you doing in here?" he asks, once more.

I say the first thing that comes to mind.

"Don't tell Irene, but I was looking for my phone," I say. "I didn't want to break the phone ban, but . . ."

He laughs, shakes his head.

"God, that phone ban," he says. "I told her it'd be a bad idea." He pauses.

"Did you find them?"

I shake my head, automatically.

Adam winks at me. He manages to pull it off, too. I feel that odd mix of fear and desire come over me again, mixed with the wooziness from the bang on the head.

"You can make it for a couple more days," he says. "I believe in you."

He turns his head when there's a noise from the beach.

"I think it's time," he says. "You should probably get out there. Do any of the other girls know you snuck down here?" There is a glint in his eyes when he looks at me, when he lingers.

God, how I hate it when men call grown women "girls."

"My sister," I say, and swallow. "I told her."

"She might rat you out, you know," Adam says. "She seems pretty tight with my boss."

I squeeze out a weak laugh.

"I guess I have to hope she won't."

I'm still all too aware of the fact that he's in between me and the door, of the weight of his eyes on me.

But then he takes a step back, and says:

"I won't tell. It'll be our secret. Like the cigarette."

"Right," I say, tasting the adrenaline still humming through my body. "Like the cigarette."

I walk toward the door slowly, fearing that he will, at any second, change his mind; that he will move, all too quickly, and then the violence under the surface will reveal itself.

But instead, he just holds the door open for me as I walk out of the office.

"Do you want a Band-Aid for that?" he asks, so close to my ear that it sends goose bumps down my spine, as he closes the door behind us.

"No," I say, faintly. "I'm sure it's fine."

I start to walk toward the stairs, relief making my knees feel watery and weak, and I turn around to see that Adam has disappeared into the kitchen again before I stick my hand down my boot and fish out the cell phone I managed to push down the shaft of my ankle boot before standing up in the office.

When I activate the screen, I see that the phone has only got seven percent battery left. I'll have to get ahold of a charger. I've only got two bars. Not enough to call.

But enough to send a text.

I go to my contact list, find Caroline, and write her a message.

Caroline, if you're okay, please write me back ASAP. It's an emergency.

I hope, and I pray, that she texts me back. That I'm wrong about everything.

I've never wanted to be wrong so badly in my life.

CHAPTER 24

April 15, 2022

Dinner goes by in a blur. All I'm aware of is the phone hidden in my boot, the shape of it. The stillness of it.

Come on, Caroline. Just respond. Respond and let me know that you are all right. That you're with a patient, and that you'll be back in the morning, and that we're safe.

Please.

I can barely taste the food. Irene has explained it to us, I'm sure, but I didn't catch much more than the occasional "seasonal" or "environmentally conscious." There's oyster-mushroom cutlets, blue cheese presumably made from cashews and prayers, a honey vinaigrette that I can only assume has been created by unionized and fairly compensated bees. I'm sure it's wonderful, based on what the others are saying, but I don't manage to get more than a few bites down.

After the olive oil orange zest cake, Mikaela puts her fork down and clears her throat.

"So," she says, with the zeal of a cult leader. "Ladies. It's time for the surprise. We've put together a bonfire party on the beach!"

I follow them down onto the beach as if in a trance. At the sight of the fire, Anneliese whoops and envelops Mikaela in a bear hug;

Natalie snaps a couple of pictures before accepting a plastic cup full of champagne. I receive my own with numb fingers, my attention still focused on that maddeningly inert piece of metal shoved into my boot.

Someone turns on music on a portable speaker. My sister and Natalie start dancing. The sky above us is high, and dark, and full of stars; the waves crashing against the shore are steely gray, and they just keep coming, over and over again, as they have for hundreds of years. Carrying bits of debris in with them and depositing them, building the island, piece by piece.

When I look at the faces around the fire, none of them shows anything but drunkenness and glee. They are all holding plastic cups full of champagne, have all covered up their slinky, glittering dresses with chunky knitwear, but they all suddenly look so happy, so beautiful, so like picture-perfect young-ish women celebrating their friend's fast-approaching wedding that it doesn't quite look real.

They feel so far away from me, like we are living in different realities. As though I'm on the other side of a window, watching them through the glass. Because the feeling that has been haunting me ever since we arrived, the feeling of being hunted, stalked like an animal, is growing ever stronger.

And when I look at them, at my friends, I can see the faces of the other women I've gotten to know through the computer screen over the years superimposed over theirs.

Mikaela is laughing, and for a split second, she looks like Linnea Andersson. Beautiful Linnea, with her catlike eyes, who had just qualified as a dentist when she disappeared. She was described by her family as having a scar from a childhood bicycle accident on the inside of her arm. For the purposes of identification.

Lena turns over and whispers something to Natalie, and in the elegant line of her jaw, I see Evelina Banér. Evelina, whose family offered a reward in the hundreds of thousands for anyone who might be able to offer information that would lead to her being found. Her younger brother was only fifteen years old when she went missing; a few years ago, I found the website he created in her memory. It clearly hadn't been touched in years, but still, there it was, calling out into the void for his sister to return.

Natalie throws her hands up in the air and sings along to Destiny's Child, and, God, with that thick, blond hair, she could be Anna Wittenberg, brought back to life. Anna, whose Facebook page was still up, and still active; last I looked at it, I saw that her ex-girlfriend, Sigrid, was still writing on her wall, now and then. Writing that she missed her. Writing that she hoped she'd come back, someday. Like a diary, laid open.

And, my God, Irene. Of course she reminds me of Matilda, even as she's fifteen years older than her sister ever got to be. The shadows around her nose, the straight eyebrows, like inky slashes over her gleaming eyes.

They all look so happy. So carefree. And I wish I could join them, wish so badly that I could let go of the dark thoughts plaguing me, but my heart is caught in my throat, and my lungs feel like someone is standing on my chest.

How far away were we from where the Nacka Four spent their final hours? It could be here, on this very spot. Maybe they were dancing, like we are. Drinking, and laughing, not knowing that their lives were coming to an end. Not suspecting, even for a second, that something was lurking in the dark.

Unworried and unguarded.

Just like my friends.

Irene and Mikaela have carried chairs and benches over to the fire from the patio, and I sink down onto one of the benches, let my head hang down for a few seconds, try to breathe, even as my eyes are flickering around the beach, finding shapes in the shadows. The music has switched from Destiny's Child, to Rihanna, to Akon, and it all just feels like too much noise.

I can't think. I need to *think*.

"Mind if I sit?" I hear Mikaela's voice.

She sits down next to me on the bench without waiting for an answer, tapping her plastic cup against mine and drinking from it.

Her jacket is slim-fitting and elegant, her hair falling across her back in hypnotic spirals.

"You doing okay?" she asks. "Do you need a tactical puke?"

I shake my head.

"No," I say. "I'm just a little . . . overwhelmed."

A small smile is playing on Mikaela's lips.

"Yeah, when Anneliese gets going, she really gets going," she says. "Mark my words, one of us is going to be holding her hair back before the night is over."

I look over at Anneliese. She has managed to convince Irene to dance with her by the fire. Irene's a sexier dancer than I would have imagined, while Anneliese is all glowing cheeks and bouncing curls.

"I actually wanted to . . . ," Mikaela says, interrupts herself, and something about her tone manages to break through my burgeoning panic.

She sounds subdued, and unsure, neither of which are things I associate with Mikaela. Her face is a bit blurred, softened by the light from the bonfire.

"I feel like I made you mad, earlier," she says. "With the whole . . . bisexual thing."

She's spinning her cup between her fingers.

"I didn't mean to offend you, or whatever," Mikaela says, and she sounds mildly perturbed. "I just don't know much about that stuff, and sometimes I talk without thinking. But I didn't mean to make you feel like I was . . . like I wasn't taking you seriously, or something." She chances a look up at me, to judge my reaction.

It takes me a second to figure out what to say.

"Thank you," I finally manage.

"I just don't get it," Mikaela says, but then she continues:

"But I guess I don't have to get it. Right? If one of my sons told me that he liked both girls and boys, I'd want him to know that his mom was okay with it. I guess I don't have to understand everything to just . . . accept it."

"Yeah," I say. "I guess not."

Mikaela leans her head against my shoulder for a second.

"I'm glad you came, Tessa," she says. "I know Anneliese is really happy you're here. She didn't want to nag you, but she was really upset thinking you might not come."

"I'm glad I'm here."

That part is true. I am glad I'm here.

If it means I can help them, in some way.

If me being so very, very Tessa might end up keeping them all safe.

"I wasn't so sure Irene joining in on the partying was a good idea at first, but I like her," Mikaela says. She sounds thoughtful.

"Me, too," I say.

"I wasn't wild about her sister," Mikaela adds, the fire reflecting in her eyes, making her smudged black makeup look like ashes. "But Irene is nice. Nicer than I expected."

". . . her sister?" I say.

Mikaela seems not to notice the sudden weight in my voice.

"You know," Mikaela says. "Matilda Sperling? She went missing a few years ago. Really sad and all, but still, that doesn't take away from the fact that she was kind of rude. Caro lived in the same building as her. I ran into her in the elevator a few times. She always just seemed sort of, I don't know, mean."

"Wait," I say, trying to catch up, make the facts of it all make sense.

But Mikaela has lost interest.

"All right, enough sappy shit," Mikaela says and stands up. "I'm going to get some more champagne, do you want any?"

"Mikaela, wait," I say, but she's already danced off, in the direction of Anneliese and the bonfire.

Caroline lived in the same building as Matilda Sperling?

I stand up off the bench, the beach seeming to tilt slightly under my feet, and look around. Irene and Anneliese are still by the fire, Mikaela is kneeling by the cooler, Lena is fiddling with the speaker.

And Natalie is nowhere to be seen.

"Where's Natalie?" I ask, raising my voice over the music to the point of straining it.

No one seems to hear me. They are all in their own little world.

I stumble over to Lena and grab her by the shoulder.

She looks up at me.

"Where is Natalie?" I ask her.

Lena stands up, brushing the dirt off her knees.

"She just went to pee," she says. "Or throw up, I'm not sure. Something. She went over there, by the trees."

She points to the far side of the island.

"By herself?" I ask, but Lena has already turned away from me.

I look up. Along the beach.

I can feel my pulse fluttering in my chest.

Natalie is out there, by herself. Separated from the group. Drunk, and alone, in the dark.

So easy to surprise. Quickly, and quietly, before any one of us would notice.

"Natalie!"

I don't even think before I set off after her. The others don't seem to notice as I leave.

After a few short steps, I start running.

Central Stockholm Police Department
Swedish Police Service
Adult Missing Person Certification
Date Report Filed: 2020–09–14
Name of Missing Person: Carl von Thurn
Birth Date of Missing Person: 1985–02–26
Age at Disappearance: 35
Gender: Male

Appearance: 181 centimeters, slim build, short dark hair, hazel eyes, glasses with black frames. Small mole to the left of nose. Wears an antique gold watch on left wrist. No tattoos or piercings. Scar from appendix removal on right side of abdomen.

Date of Last Sighting: Isabella von Thurn, sister, claims to have last spoken to Carl von Thurn Monday 2020–09–07. Says her brother sounded normal on the phone, though possibly somewhat subdued. Brought up his fiancée, missing and presumed dead eight years previously, several times. After that, no contact between Carl von Thurn and sister. Employer Swedish National Bank states Carl von Thurn has not come in since Thursday 2020–09–10.

AMENDMENT—2020–09–18
Phone records show no calls made from cell phone belonging to Carl von Thurn with the number +46724001220 after 14:46 2020–09–10.

The owner of the Lidingö Marina, Herman Thorsson, confirms Carl von Thurn took his boat out the afternoon of Thursday 2020–09–10. Car belonging to Carl von Thurn, a black Toyota Prius with the license plate CRBÅ9010, found in marina parking lot.

AMENDMENT—2020–09–24
Isabella von Thurn states she received a letter signed by Carl von Thurn in the mail Wednesday 2020–09–23. Letter transcribed below.

Bella,

I'm so sorry for all of this. I didn't mean to worry you. I just couldn't do it anymore.

I miss Matilda with all my heart. All I want is to be with her.

Tell Mom and Dad I love them.

Carl

Isabella von Thurn confirms writing and signature match those of her brother.

CHAPTER 25

April 15, 2022

I take off along the beach, slipping on the rocks, eyes searching wildly for Natalie.

The wind has quieted down, the water soft and smooth as black silk. In the deep, dark blue of the spring night, it looks sinister, all the color gone out of it. As though it's hungry.

The cold air seems to be making its way in under my clothes, and I shiver, which soon turns into my teeth chattering. Far away from the heat of the fire, the deep-seated cold of the Baltic Sea has taken over, chasing the temporary warmth of day away.

It feels like we're on an alien planet. Like I'm about to run out of oxygen. I find myself taking deep, gulping breaths, trying to fill my lungs, trying to keep myself grounded.

"Natalie!"

I call her name again, but the night seems to swallow it. I can't see her. It's like she has disappeared completely.

Like the island is picking us off, one by one.

It feels like Isle Blind has a mind of its own. That the trees are fingers, stretching toward us, slowly but surely. Waiting to drag us down to the water, down to the ancient, rocky floor of the ocean, where we will rest as so many victims of Isle Blind have before.

How many ships have run aground here through the years? How many lives have ended? How many people have left their bones beneath Isle Blind, to turn white and wither in the cold, brackish water, until their names left the memories of the living?

This is a place where blood has been spilled. I can feel it, in the small, primal part of my brain that predates consciousness, the frightened mammal that resides inside of me.

I know when I am being hunted, with the instinct of prey. I can feel it in the prickling of my scalp, the shortness of my breath.

As I walk toward the point where the shore turns, a shape takes form in the dark. Low and squat against the water, banging softly against the pebbled beach with every gentle push of the waves.

I feel a sudden, ridiculous swell of hope.

The dinghy. It has floated back to shore. Just like Irene said it might.

We're not stranded here, after all.

Maybe it's all going to be all right. We're halfway through the night, and nothing has happened. Maybe there really is a good explanation for Caroline's note. Maybe she's going to be back tomorrow morning, just in time for brunch.

Maybe Adam is just a chef, and Caroline just happened to have an apartment in the same building as Matilda, and this is all nothing more than a bachelorette party.

Maybe I will wake up tomorrow with a clear head, and start to make some kind of plan for the future.

Maybe I'll even talk to the others about it. Ask for their help. And maybe they will offer it.

I'm almost at the dinghy now. It keeps bumping up against the shore, still half afloat.

There is something at the bottom of the boat. A pile of life jackets, or blankets.

The rocking motion of the boat looks so soothing. Maybe I will lie down in it, for just a couple of seconds. Look up at the stars, gently rocked by the slow waves.

I stop just by the boat, and the smile that's started forming on my face freezes.

The whisper that comes over my lips doesn't sound like me.
"Caroline?"

May 10, 2012

> Evie, can you please pick up or text me back? Need to know if
> you're good to bring the food.

Matilda stared at her phone while waiting for the elevator to arrive,
biting her lip and wondering if she should add something.

She could see that Evelina had read the text, thanks to the iPhone.
Carl had been on her to get one ever since they started dating, had
talked about all the neat little functions that would make her life easier.

But so far, all it was doing was showing her that her friend was
reading her texts and not responding. Almost like it was taunting her.

She'd tried to call Evelina twice yesterday without getting any
kind of response, and with all the other things she still had to take
care of, she really didn't have time for this. She was working over-
time to keep her emotions in check, keep everything running while
her life was changing around her, and having to wrangle Evelina into
just answering her goddamn phone was not something she was taking pleasure in.

Matilda hesitated, and then she added:

> Is something going on? This isn't like you.

Then she sighed, erased what she'd just written, and sent the first
part.

She was supposed to have left half an hour ago. She was going to be late for work.

Matilda barely had the mental space to wonder whether or not anything was going on with Evelina. Between Carl sending her listings for houses every five minutes, and Anna's breakup with Sigrid, which was clearly bothering her, and Irene getting on her case about visiting their dad more often, and Max on her team underperforming for the second quarter in a row, meaning that she might have to let him go, she barely had enough time to puke up her breakfast in the morning.

This really wasn't like Evelina, though. Evelina had always been the type A overachiever in the group, diligent and eager to show her worth.

Anna had once told her that she thought Evelina had a chip on her shoulder, a hidden dark side. Some deep well of insecurity. But Matilda didn't agree with that. Evelina was just . . . nice. Sweet. Surprisingly funny, after a couple of drinks.

Definitely not someone who'd go off the radar completely two days before their annual trip together.

She would have been worried, but she'd seen Evelina post on Facebook just yesterday, pictures from her mother's sixtieth the week before. Clearly, she was well enough to flood the feed with photographs of her shockingly big and seemingly happy family.

Why was it that she wouldn't pick up her phone?

The elevator doors opened, and Matilda was surprised to see a young woman she didn't recognize in there. She looked to be in her late teens or early twenties, casually stunning with long, thick ringlets of hair and a somewhat haughty expression on her face.

Her eyes widened when she saw Matilda. Maybe she hadn't expected to see someone waiting for the elevator, maybe she was up to something and wasn't expecting to see an adult at all.

"Oh," she said and exited the elevator. "Sorry."

"No worries," Matilda said.

As the elevator doors closed, she could still see the girl looking at her, with a faintly troubled look.

Probably promising herself she'd never turn into a drawn, hassled-looking near-thirtysomething wearing a rumpled suit.

In fairness, Matilda had never thought she would at that age, either.

She was thrown out of that line of thought when her phone buzzed in her hand, and she quickly looked down.

I'm sorry. I'm not sure I'm coming this time.

CHAPTER 26

April 15, 2022

"Caroline, get up," I hear someone saying, as though it's coming from very far away. It's a child's prayer, a voice so small it's begging for the sweet relief of denial.

I can't feel my hands. The tears have started falling again, but they, too, feel alien, and freezing.

This isn't right. This can't be happening.

Caroline is lying in the boat, on her side. That enviable dark blond bob is covering her face. She's got her leather blazer on, but only one boot; the other foot is bare, a shocking, blazing white in the dark.

The indifferent sliver of moon above is shining down mercilessly, and my eyes have long since adapted to the dark.

I am registering the details even as my mind refuses to take them in.

How her arm is slung across her body at an angle, twisting her body.

How there are three ragged holes punched in the dinghy, right over the waterline.

How the floor of the boat is covered in water much too dark to just be water.

I know what is happening. I just can't accept it.

It has all been theoretical, up until now. Not a game so much as an uneasy puzzle, pieces not fitting together, a sense of something not being quite right.

But all this time, the world as it is has seemed to be working against the whirring of my mind. The beauty and normality of my surroundings, the carefree joy of my friends have all been trying to tear me away from what I thought I could sense.

This can't be happening.

The voice in my head is so calm, so rational that it's near impossible not to give in to it. Not to agree.

I see, as though in a dream, how my body takes one more step, until my knees press against the side of the dinghy, until I feel the cold metal digging into the bare skin of my legs.

I see how I lean down into the boat and sweep the hair from her face.

I have seen pictures of dead bodies before. I have seen how the human body can be twisted and destroyed, and I have managed to harden myself against the sight, over time, to see the remains of someone who used to be human as an object, a point of study.

I guess that I, on some level, thought I would be too desensitized to react if I was ever to see a real corpse, that the violence and ruin would seem as two-dimensional to me in real life as the crime scene photos I used to hunt down on the internet.

But it's not. It's different.

This isn't Caroline. This is the parts of her left behind. Her cheek is covered in dried blood, thick and copious, cracking where it has baked under the April sun. The right lens of her cat eye glasses is cracked and splintered, and there is no eye left behind it. Only shards of glass, blood, and viscera, black on black in the cold light of the moon.

The long, slim knife is buried almost to the hilt in her eye socket, the handle sticking out like a grotesque accessory, a proud piece of decoration.

There are bumps in the pockets of her blazer. I don't need to check. Rocks, to weigh down the body.

Two of the toenails on her naked foot have been torn off.

Her throat is naked meat and caked blood. In the midst of the mess of gore, that necklace I noticed and coveted still glints.

It was made up. It was all made up. It was paranoia. I'm safe here. I'm supposed to be safe. This isn't real. This isn't happening. This can't be happening, because if it is . . .

But then the smell hits me.

I've read about people smelling death, read the descriptions of old meat, iron, and fear, but it doesn't compare.

I bend at the waist, and I puke into the cold, brackish water, the sound of the boat still thudding rhythmically against the shore beating in my ears.

May 10, 2012

"**W**hat do you mean you're not coming?" Matilda whisper-shouted into her phone.

Her office wasn't as soundproofed as she would have liked, and the big windows and lack of working air-conditioning made it unbearably hot in the spring and summer, meaning she was sweating and uncomfortable as well as stressed and angry.

Evelina was quiet on the other end of the line. She had finally picked up the third time Matilda had called her, but despite the connection she still wasn't saying much.

"I'm just really stressed right now," Evelina said. "I don't know if I will be much fun."

She did sound stressed. More so than usual. Evelina always had what appeared like a near-inhuman number of balls in the air, but usually she also seemed to thrive on the multitasking. This was the first time Matilda had heard her like this, her voice choked and uncomfortable.

Matilda shrugged out of her blazer one-handed and unbuttoned the top button of her shirt, which was straining over her chest, all while keeping the phone pressed against her ear.

"Is everything all right?" she asked, concern leaking through the anger. "Did something happen with Anna?"

"No, nothing like that," Evelina said. She sounded out of breath, and Matilda could hear the ambient sounds of the gym in the background.

Evelina always went for a workout over lunch. She'd been doing it since they were teenagers. Linnea always made fun of her for it, in a way that seemed designed more to hurt than as friendly teasing, but Matilda had always admired her dedication.

"Just . . . please, Evie," Matilda said, feeling absurd tears welling up. She didn't know if it was the hormones that were making her so overly sensitive, or if she was just feeling overwhelmed.

"We don't know how long we'll be able to keep doing the trip. Sooner or later, people are going to start having kids, and moving away for good, and it'll all be different. We might not get many more trips. I just don't want you to miss what might be one of the last ones."

Matilda could hear Evelina's quiet, controlled breathing, the faint sound of pop music blaring over gym speakers.

"I mean, let's be honest," she added. "I haven't seen you in months. You had to miss the last dinner we all did together, and even that was, what, in February? Just . . . move something around. Make it work. You're good at that."

Matilda knew she was being selfish. Whatever was going on with Evelina, it might be bigger and worse and more difficult than what she was dealing with.

But there was simply too much change going on right now for Matilda to be able to bear it for Evelina not to come on the trip.

She needed her there. She needed all of them.

"Okay," Evelina said, softly. "I'll take care of it. I'll be there."

Matilda felt her face splitting in a huge smile, the joy swift and the relief great.

"Yes!" she exclaimed, and laughed. "Thank you. Thank you for letting me bully you."

"You've never bullied me," Evelina said, and her voice sounded sad.

"I'm sorry," Matilda said. "I'm just kidding."

"No, no," Evelina said. "Don't worry about it." There was a short pause.

"I'm excited to see you," she said. Her voice sounded all wrong. Heavy with some unspoken feeling.

"We have a lot to talk about."

"Evie," Matilda said, knowing something was wrong, knowing

there was some question she wasn't asking, some nuance she wasn't picking up on. She noticed, vaguely, that she had brought her hand to her throat.

"What . . ."

A click.

Evelina had already hung up the phone.

CHAPTER 27

April 16, 2022

I stumble away from the dinghy, up the beach, away from the water.

Caroline is dead. She never left the island. She never wrote that note.

Someone stabbed her in the throat, dragged her thrashing, dying body into the dinghy, and then drove the knife into her eye through her glasses to finish the job. They punched holes in the boat hoping it would sink and take her body with it, and then they pushed it out to sea, before writing a note explaining her absence to lull the rest of us into a false sense of security.

I need to run, but my legs aren't cooperating. My knees feel like jelly. My body is shaking, and I'm vaguely aware that my teeth are chattering.

Shock.

The image of Caroline's body is burned into my retinas. That naked foot, those torn-off toenails.

She fought. And hard. It had to have happened quickly, and taken her by surprise, or we would have heard her scream. The person who killed her must have slit her throat to prevent her from calling out.

She must have kicked when she couldn't scream, when blood was pouring down her throat and down her chest. Kicked and thrashed and tried desperately to escape, her voice stolen, her life trickling away, until the killer stopped it with brutal efficiency.

I stop, falling to my knees on the moss-covered stone, my shins going instantly cold from contact with the deep chill in the bedrock.

I want to curl up in a ball, close my eyes, and sob. I want to sit here, on the beach, in the shadow of the trees, and wait until someone comes to get me. Someone who will fix everything. A real adult. Someone who will know what to do.

Someone who will save me.

Someone who will save all of us.

But no one is coming. There is just me.

The wind is cool against my bare thighs. I imagine myself seen from afar, a small figure crouched on the cliffside, drunk and scared and very alone. Red sequins appearing black in the dark of night. Hair mussed, face covered in tears.

So vulnerable.

Is the killer still there, watching me? Ready to keep going, to do it again before we realize we are being hunted?

Pure, animal fear rushes in, and I scramble up onto my feet, look around with wild eyes, feeling the terror settling in like something thick and viscous.

My breath is coming hard, fast and ragged. If I don't manage to calm myself, I'm going to pass out from hyperventilation.

I close my eyes. I bite down on my tongue, hard and sudden. The pain blooms behind my eyelids, the taste of iron fills my mouth, and nausea swirls in my stomach.

I lean over and retch again, expelling nothing but a long, thin strand of saliva. I spit viciously onto the rocks, trying to get the taste out of my mouth, the image out of my head.

Something is digging into my ankle.

The phone.

God. The cell phone. I still have it. I can use it. I can call the police. I will call the police, and they will send someone. A boat. A helicopter. They will send someone, and they will come get us. They will get us away from this place, get us back to reality, back to a place where things like this don't happen.

We never should have come here. I felt it, from the very start, the very moment I set foot on Isle Blind. I knew something was wrong. But I didn't speak up. I didn't say anything, because I didn't trust myself. Didn't trust my instinct. Didn't want to cause a fuss. Didn't want to make things *weird*.

My fingers feel thick and unwieldy as I struggle to pull the phone out of my boot, and I nearly drop it on the rocks below, but finally I have it in my hands. As I activate the screen, it lights up with shocking brightness in the dark. Showing my cracked screen, a battery that's on one percent, and a message.

Not from Caroline. It was never going to be from Caroline.

Instead, it reads, with clear and dramatic cruelty:

Hi, Theresa,

This is Madeleine from Larssen & Larssen. I've been assigned to take on your account.

I've received word that the family of Harald Sturesson has decided to move forward with the lawsuit.

If you still wish to have our firm represent you, please transfer an initial sum of 20 000 kr to the same account as last time.

We should try to make an appointment as soon as possible to discuss a possible strategy to deal with the upcoming trial.

I reach to swipe it away, to call for help, and the phone dies in my hand.

For a second, I stare at it. Then an alien, hysterical laugh escapes my lips, low and throaty, as I feel something begin to shatter in my mind.

This is it, then.

Maybe I've finally gotten the punishment I've been waiting for. Ever since that day.

CHAPTER 28

August 7, 2021

The gentle rocking of the train should have been soothing, but the nausea that had been following me since I'd boarded the train that morning was only intensifying. I had picked up a pack of gum at the train station hoping it would help, but instead, it kept getting stuck in my teeth, my mouth filling, again and again, with saliva.

I told myself it was just nerves. This was the biggest break I'd ever gotten, after all.

The last few months had been a slow spiral of anxiety. That first dizzying year of explosive growth was far behind me. We had been holding steady for a while, Minna getting increasingly more frustrated with the lack of growth, me desperately trying to hold on to the fact that the numbers were, at least, not dipping.

But then they had started to. Dip, I mean. Just a little bit, at first. Then faster. A trickle that might turn into a stream.

Everyone had told me it was normal. When I had brought it up in conversation, friends and colleagues had assured me that everyone went through rough patches, that my listeners were loyal, that *The Witching Hour* was an institution.

I hadn't liked the sound of that. I had been itching for someone to tell me the truth. And Minna had, because of course it would be her; for as long as I had known her, she had never been one to mince words.

"You need something big, babe. Attention spans are only getting shorter. I've told you a million times. If you're not growing, you're dying."

The thought had become an obsession. Something big. Something that would catapult me back to where I had been, when I had felt untouchable, when it had seemed like everything in my life, every failure, every humiliation, had been leading up to this.

The Svante Sturesson case was certainly that.

It had rocked the nation.

A teenage boy who had murdered three of his friends at a sleepover, offering no real motive and showing no remorse. The tragedy and brutality of it had proved especially titillating to the general public. He'd drugged the soda with sleeping pills he'd taken from his father's medicine cabinet, and then beat them to death with various . . . instruments.

The relatively short punishment doled out by the court, as mandated by law due to his youth, had provoked outrage. Politicians both liberal and conservative had raged against the case in the papers for months, suggesting harsher punishments for young offenders was necessary, blaming drugs, video games, and porn for the crime. Standard stuff, really.

After more than three years of doing the podcast I still hadn't covered the case, despite dozens of requests every week. There just wasn't enough to go on to make it a satisfying story. No narrative arc, so to speak. Without a motive there was nothing that would let me spin a tale. The crime had come as a complete surprise to everyone. The boy had been described by teachers and classmates as quiet and friendly, neither smarter nor dumber than your average sixteen-year-old. His closest friends might have been able to shed some light on the situation, but he had beaten them to death.

No leads, no story.

When my numbers had started dipping, I had begun to obsess over it. If I could uncover something in the case, something no one had found before, it would be a coup. It might be more than that. It might bring me the attention of the general press. Some recognition for the value of true crime.

Some respect. Finally.

No one had ever managed to interview the boy's father, Harald. He had never agreed to speak on the record. There were only two known photographs of him, both from the trial. If I could get him to talk, it would be the solution to all my problems.

It had taken weeks of digging to find an address. He'd moved, after what happened.

I had started sending him letters. Heartfelt, handwritten letters about wanting to hear his side of the story, wanting to represent the human side of his son, wanting to let people know that Harald wasn't a monster, or a bad father, or a murderer by proxy.

Whenever I had thought about giving up, whenever I considered whether or not this was the right thing to do, I just dug my feet in and wrote another letter. After a while, I stopped believing it would work.

And then, one day, he responded.

I cried so hard from the joy and relief, my throat was too sore to record the next day. But no one was upset with me. I tried to keep a tight lid on it, but I had to let Minna and my agent in on what was going on, and my agent sent me flowers. The card read: "I always knew you were destined for greatness!"

As the train pulled into the station—so small and rural it was barely more than a cement platform, overgrown and empty—I stood up, slinging my bag of recording equipment over my shoulder. It felt heavier than usual.

For a moment, I just stood there. Unable to move.

The nausea was growing, turning me dizzy.

The train would be turning around soon. Going back to Stockholm.

I could just sit back down. I could call Harald Sturesson and apologize. Come up with some reason for why I hadn't been able to make it. I could go back to my apartment, dig through my files, and find something else that might revive the dying heart of my passion project.

I heard Minna's voice in my head.

It's all up to you, babe. If you want to be a star, you have to shine."

My mouth tasting like metal, I departed the train.

The pictures I had seen "both" showed a tall man with a receding hairline and a slight potbelly. An average, forgettable face with a nice smile. He just looked like a dad in the pictures. He could have been anyone. Any tired, middle-aged man trying to get through the day in time to pick his kid up from school.

But when he opened the door, that average dad was gone.

He was still tall, but his back was bent. Those broad shoulders were slumped inward, as though his chest had collapsed in on itself. The potbelly was gone, withered away, along with the apple cheeks; his face was weathered, the wrinkles like cracks in granite.

"You must be Theresa." There was a polite smile on his lips, gentle and automatic, but no joy in his voice.

"Yes. Hello. Thank you so much for having me." When he shook my hand, his palm was cool and dry.

The house was small, and anonymous, the walls painted landlord white and the furniture utilitarian to the point of being punishing. There were no photographs anywhere, no art; no curtains by the windows.

He invited me to sit down by the kitchen table, which showed little sign of use, while preparing coffee for the both of us. The house smelled faintly of antiseptic soap, like a hospital waiting room. There was a small plate of store-bought cookies on the table, and as he put my cup in front of me, he looked at them with a small frown between his heavy eyebrows.

"I'm sorry. They might be a bit stale. Things go stale very fast up here."

I shook my head, smiling, and put a chocolate cookie in my mouth. Between mouthfuls of crumbs I said:

"No, thank you so much. I hope you didn't buy them for my sake. They are lovely."

He didn't respond. He just sat down, hugging his steaming cup between his hands. His cuticles were ragged and raw; there was a little bead of blood next to his thumbnail.

I could feel my breaths growing shorter. There was something about his stooped figure, this man who had once been so tall, that reminded me of my own father, despite the fact that they looked nothing alike; despite the fact that they had nothing in common.

If I had done something truly horrible, would I have wanted someone to seek my parents out, the way I had sought Harald Sturesson out?

I shook the thought off, as best I could, and brought my portable recording device up on the table. I set it down next to the coffee cups. When I turned it on, Harald twitched at the sound of it, a harsh, pained movement. I saw his lips growing paler, a muscle cramping by his jaw.

"Is it okay if we begin?" I asked him, and in that moment, I hated how my voice sounded. So soft, and so forgiving. Manipulative.

But he had asked me to come. He had invited me here.

"Sure," he said, not looking me in the eyes.

It went slow, at first. I asked him to tell me about Svante. What he had been like, as a child. What the experience of raising a young boy as a single father had entailed.

His answers were short, the traces of his Northern Swedish accent turning his voice into a soft staccato.

I felt myself begin to sweat.

Numbers started to flash before my eyes.

I had been losing, on average, sixty-four subscribers a day in the last month. Two months ago, it had been thirty-seven. If it kept going at that pace . . .

I had just bought an apartment, with a mortgage I could barely afford. I had been so proud when the real-estate agent had given me the keys. I had invited Lena over and bought a magnum bottle of Veuve Clicquot.

On an impulse, I reached over the table and put my hand on Harald's. I squeezed it, carefully, and looked him in the eyes as I said:

"I wanted to let you know that . . . I'm so sorry about what happened. It must be so hard. I don't have children, but I can't imagine what it must feel like. How lonely it must be."

Harald slowly looked from his hand to my face. I didn't know what he saw, in my eyes, in that moment. Maybe it was nothing more complicated than sincerity.

Because I meant it. I had read about the life he had led, before Svante had decided to kill his friends, seemingly based on nothing more than a whim, something broken deep inside his mind that he'd managed to conceal from everyone around him until it was too late.

I had read what people had written, about Svante, and about Harald. How they had claimed, again and again, that his father must, to some degree, be held responsible. That he should have seen something. Understood something. Done something.

"Thank you," Harald said, quietly. His voice had grown soft, and his shoulders slumped.

"You don't have to talk about Svante, if you don't want to," I told him. "I want to understand what you went through. If you want something taken out, later, all you have to do is ask me. I want you to feel like you can tell your side of the story. Even if that means just getting to tell the world about the boy you loved, before he did what he did. That's still real. That can still mean something."

Harald drew a deep, shuddering breath. When he began to speak, his voice cracked.

"He was such a curious boy," he said. "Always asking questions. I used to love answering those questions, when he was little. When I didn't know the answer, I would take him to the library, and we would find the answer together. Sure, sometimes the subjects he was interested in were a little strange, but I didn't want to hold him back. I worried, you see. I worried that I wouldn't be enough for him. So I tried to give him any answer he wanted."

I was still holding his hand when he whispered:

"Even when he asked me about the sleeping pills."

After I came home, I stayed up editing for thirty-six hours, running on black coffee and the Adderall Minna had slipped me for occasions like this one. My head buzzing, my pulse pounding in my fingertips, I cut the interview together with bits and pieces from the police statements and the trials. Made sound bites out of paragraphs.

The last thing to do was record my voice-over.

I tried to steady my voice, but the excitement was hard to conceal. I slapped myself lightly in the face a couple of times, but every time I started the recording and leaned close to the microphone, my throat seemed to close up.

I kept seeing Harald's face. That anonymous little house, deep in the woods. The deafening silence that seemed to emanate from the very walls.

I had told him I could cut anything out, if he wanted me to. I had told him to trust me.

My phone buzzed in my pocket, and I pulled it out.

Babe! Will the episode be ready by 6am tomorrow? I had a little chat with Radio 105.6 and they want to do a bit with you to promote your big scoop in case we can drop the episode in time for the morning commuters. A couple of morning shows are interested, too. I'm so proud of you.

My head was pounding. My lips were so dry they were beginning to crack.

I wrote back:

omg. so exciting. i'll have it to you in two hours.

When I put the phone back in my pocket, I cleared my throat, started the recording again, and leaned forward, my lips almost touching the microphone.

"At seven past seven P.M., on the seventeenth of February, 2016, Alfons Nordin had just finished taking a begrudging shower, urged on by his mother, when the doorbell rang. His mother and father, Kim and Niklas, were just heading out for the evening, as they were celebrating their anniversary in a small, three-star hotel in a neighboring town. Kim Nordin opened the door to find her son's oldest friend, Svante

Sturesson, standing outside, having arrived early for the sleepover Alfons had planned with his three best friends. They were going to play video games, eat junk food, and enjoy the kind of freedom you can only feel when you are sixteen years old and your parents are out of town.

"He smiled and greeted her politely. Later, Kim would recall that he had asked her several questions about when they would be back. She did not, at the time, take notice of his overnight bag. It was an Adidas bag, bought for him by his father on his fourteenth birthday. Inside was Svante's favorite gray hoodie, a fresh pair of underwear, a phone charger, a half-empty bottle of prescription sleeping pills, and a hammer.

"By the time Kim and Niklas Nordin returned home, their son Alfons and his two friends Hjalmar and Martin would all be dead. But why did Svante Sturesson, described by all as a sweet, shy boy, decide to brutally beat his friends to death?

"Did something happen between the boys, that night? Or had dark impulses been growing within Svante over the course of sixteen years? Today, I will take you on a journey through the psyche of a troubled young man. And, for the first time ever, we will hear from Svante's father, as he tells us about the last days before the murder . . . and the signs he might have missed.

"I'm Tessa Nilsson, and this . . . is *The Witching Hour.*"

The last thing I did, before I sent Minna the finished episode, was cut in a sound bite from Harald, right after the title.

"So I tried to give him every answer he wanted. Even when he asked me about the sleeping pills."

When I woke up Monday morning, I had received congratulatory texts from Minna, my agent, and our distributor.

When I woke up Tuesday morning, I had sixteen missed calls, too many texts to count, and a voicemail message from Minna. It was short and curt.

"Don't talk to anyone. Don't say a fucking word. And don't read the papers."

I didn't take her advice. I opened up the news aggregator on my phone, and three minutes later, I was heaving green bile into the toilet.

Harald Sturesson had listened to the episode, gone into his bathroom, and cut his wrists.

CHAPTER 29

April 16, 2022

I'm still laughing, head buried in my hands. The sound is echoing in my ears, sharp and broken, and it feels like the night is swirling around me.

I knew. I knew something would happen, sooner or later. I have spent the last nine months in a hellish state of waiting. Even as everything fell away, even as I found myself alone, and hated, and broke, I knew it wasn't enough.

I did something truly reprehensible. I spent so long trying to blame other people for my actions—blaming Minna, blaming my agent, even blaming Harald himself—but I knew, deep down, that it was my fault. My responsibility.

I was the one who kept pushing him to talk. I was the one who reached out to him, connected to him, and then cut his words to pieces in order to serve up a lurid narrative.

I told myself I was only telling the truth. But the truth is a many-layered thing, not fit for easy consumption. And so I transformed it into something light, and easy, and entertaining.

As I sit there, breath ragged and gasping, a small, cool voice speaks up in the back of my head.

Don't be so fucking self-centered, Tessa.

Somehow, it manages to cut through the noise in my head.

I draw a deep, painful breath, and stop laughing.

Not everything is about you.

Caroline didn't die as some sort of karmic punishment for you.

You have to tell the others. Before he gets them, too.

Adam is still here. And they don't know about him. They don't know about the Nacka Four, or about Caroline.

Get a fucking grip and fix this.

I open my eyes.

The beach is so still around me. The air feels heavy, loaded, like right before a storm, as though I can taste what's coming on my tongue.

I put my hands down onto the rocks below and push to my feet. Push my shoes off as I look around me.

The trees, twisted and battered, are black pencil strokes on the velvet canvas of the night.

Where is he now? Still in the house, waiting for us to come back, go to bed, so he can get to us, one by one, under the cover of the early-morning hours?

Or is he out here, picking us off one by one?

Natalie. She was out here. That's why I first came.

I have to get back. I have to tell them. If I can do nothing else, I can at least do that.

I start running, barefoot, pain beginning to pierce my side as the soles of my feet begin to ache. The bonfire seems a million miles away, but I have to get back.

I have to get to them before he does.

The image flashes by in my mind. Adam, standing in Irene's office, holding a knife up to the light.

He said he had been cutting up boxes.

He said he'd lost his boning knife.

And then he smiled, as though it were a joke.

I was right. I was right, this whole time.

Adam had something to do with the Nacka Four. He went to school with them. He knew them. Maybe he knew one of them in-timately.

For whatever reason, he decided to kill them. Out here, on Isle Blind, where no one could hear them scream.

When Irene bought the island, he decided to come out here and keep an eye on her. Make sure she didn't stumble over anything he didn't want her to find, that she wouldn't make any connections he didn't want her to make.

And now, one of us is dead.

Why her? Why Caroline?

She was smart. She was observant. I saw that, when she followed me out onto the beach that night. Just a few short hours before she was killed.

Maybe she saw something she wasn't supposed to. Maybe she noticed something the rest of us didn't. A look, or a word.

Whatever happened, I can't imagine he's going to let any of the rest of us leave the island alive.

Safer to do, once more, what he did ten years ago. Kill us all, and let the Baltic take us.

I have to warn the others. They don't even know they have reason to be scared. Right now, they are dancing around a shitty little speaker, feeling the surge of chemically induced happiness carry them ever higher. Feeling like they are going to live forever.

I have to get to them, before he gets to them. Before he gets to me.

There were so many other knives in that kitchen. So many other ways to kill a person. I can hear phantom steps behind me on the beach as I run, like a shadow approaching. Any moment now, he might grab me by the hair, my head snapping back, any strength I had left leaving me.

I have nothing to defend myself with. Nothing but teeth and nails, and now I've seen all too well all the good that does when you're up against someone far stronger, far more motivated, far more attuned to the idea of violence.

It's just me. Small, alone, and unarmed.

All I can do is run.

CHAPTER 30

How many times have I felt that prickling at the back of my neck? How many times have I been out on my own, walking at night, and felt that sudden fear? Grabbed my keys in my pocket just in case I'd need them for protection?

The terror of knowing there actually *is* someone here, someone who might be following me, someone who is ready to kill, is all-encompassing.

When I see the fire, my friends around it, a sob escapes my lips, and I try to run faster. I have never felt fear before this moment. I just didn't know it until now. Fear is not in the wondering if there might be someone stalking in the night; fear is in the knowing for sure, and suddenly seeing your own weakness writ clear.

"Tessa?"

I hear one of them calling my name, and I try to pick up the pace. If I can just get to them, I will be safe. If I can just get to the flock, to the fire, the bad thing won't be able to grab me, bite and tear.

"Tessa, what's wrong?"

I'm so close now. Not more than ten steps away. But the fear has taken over. I can't stop.

He's coming for you. Run.

A cold hand around my wrist, yanking me back, and a scream tears out of me.

"Tessa!"

My head snaps back with the sudden blow. My face is on fire. The shock temporarily makes my brain white out, and when I blink, Anneliese is staring at me, her hand covering her mouth. Mikaela is standing right behind her, her eyes wide and her mouth open.

Anneliese lets go of my wrist.

"I'm so sorry," she says, her voice shaking. "I didn't know what to do. Tessa, what's wrong?"

I shake my head, looking around, still trembling.

"Is everyone here?" I ask.

"We're all here," I hear a voice say, and I see Natalie approaching from the other side of the glowing remains of the fire, Lena and Irene clustered behind her, their faces very white in the light of the fire.

I take them all in, seeing that they are all here. Still here. No one else out walking on their own, waiting to be attacked, and the relief is sweet but temporary.

But I have to tell them.

"What happened?" Lena says. She's come closer, and now she pushes Anneliese aside, gently taking me by the shoulders. "Are you hurt?"

I want to tell her I'm okay, but I don't know how. None of us are okay.

"Tessa," Lena says, "tell me. Come on."

Her voice is so soothing, so familiar, and I want to give in to it. Let her take over and take care of me.

But I can't.

I look past her and at the others.

"The dinghy came back into shore," I say. "It floated back on the tide. And Caroline was in there."

Lena raises her eyebrows.

"Caroline?" she says. "No, she wasn't. Caroline went back to the city."

"Caroline never left," I say. "She's been in that dinghy all day. I found Caroline's body. She's been murdered."

CHAPTER 31

April 16, 2022

All that follows my words is silence. Even the music has stopped. There is nothing but the sound of the other five trying to comprehend what I have just said.

Lena is the first to react. She just shakes her head. She doesn't look upset. She just looks like she's refuting something she knows not to be true. The sky isn't green. Up is not down. Caroline's mutilated body is not lying further down the beach in the dinghy.

"No, she's not," Lena says, her face dismissive, her voice mildly annoyed.

She sounds like the classic older sister, admonishing me for making up stories.

"I don't know why you'd say that, Tessa, but Caroline left this morning. She left a note, remember?"

"Caroline didn't write that note, Lena," I say, putting as much emphasis on her name as I can muster. "Please. You have to listen to me, okay?"

"But, she—" Lena turns around, searching for support from the others. Irene is standing very still, and Anneliese is looking from Lena to me as though it's some sort of game, an exercise in debate, trying to decide whose argument holds more merit. Mikaela's right behind

Anneliese, her face unreadable, and Natalie has her hand up at her throat, grasping it, protecting it.

When Lena turns back to me, something in her eyes has slipped, just a little. I silently plead for it to be enough.

"I've thought something weird was going on for days now," I say, trying to hold Lena with my stare. "Ask Irene. I've talked to her about it."

I look to Irene, and Lena does, too. Lena is still holding on to my shoulders, but it feels more like it's for support now than anything else.

"Irene?" Lena says, a plea in her voice. Begging her to deny what I'm saying, to prove my reality false.

"Tessa thinks . . ." Irene's voice cracks, and she stops, draws a deep breath. "Yes, Tessa told me that she thought that my sister and her friends might have come to Isle Blind. Ten years ago. When they were supposed to have . . . gone missing."

When Lena turns back to me, I read betrayal written over her face.

"Why?" she asks me, and there are many questions hiding in her one.

Why didn't you tell me?

Why did you let us come here?

Why would you think that?

"One of Matilda's friend's dads owned the waters that Isle Blind was in. I think they were . . . well, the details don't matter. But I was worried that someone might have hurt Matilda and her friends, and that that person might have come back, now that Irene owns the island. I thought that the killer might have been worried about her discovering something. And I think . . ." I force myself to inhale, and Lena interrupts me.

"But that's . . . that's insane, Tessa. Tilly and her friends drowned."

The fear and the frustration threaten to overwhelm me, and I struggle to keep myself contained.

"Lena, Caroline is *dead*!"

All sounds seem to disappear, for just a fraction of a second, my words hanging in the air, as though the very pressure of them has pushed everything else aside.

"Are you sure you saw what you saw?" Mikaela asks, stepping forward. She doesn't look like herself, the shadows under her eyes making her look older, more hesitant.

"I'm sure," I spit out through gritted teeth, regretting it immediately when I see Mikaela recoil. I'm not helping my credibility.

"Where did you see the dinghy?" Lena asks.

"It's on the other side of the island," I say.

I need to get just one of them on my side. Need to get just one of them to believe me. To understand.

"I can show you," I tell them, desperation making my voice raw.

A part of me wishes it didn't have to come to this. I don't want them to have to see what I saw. They will never be able to unsee it.

But if that's what it takes . . .

Lena looks over her shoulder, makes eye contact with Anneliese, who has shrunk back, fear and confusion marring her delicate features.

Mikaela looks at me and seems to come to a decision.

"Okay," she says, as though trying to soothe a child. "How about you show us the dinghy, Tessa? Lena and me will come with you. You can show us . . . what you saw . . . and then we'll all decide what to do."

"No," I say. "We shouldn't split up. We're stronger together."

Mikaela takes a step toward me. It's clear she's trying to soothe me.

"Listen, it'll be quick," she says. "Okay? We'll come with you. We'll vouch for you, if you really did see what you think you saw."

I feel torn in two. Time is of the essence, but I can't just leave them here.

"I wish you would just believe me," I say, and I sound as pathetic as I feel.

Lena won't look me in the eyes. But Anneliese's nostrils are flaring, and I can see that her eyes are watering.

She does believe me. On some level, I know she does. Anneliese knows me. She knows I wouldn't make this up.

She just doesn't want to believe me.

She wants to believe that I've made a mistake, that her world hasn't changed in an instant, wants to believe that everything is safe and nothing bad could ever happen, not to her.

"Anneliese?" I say, and she manages a small, watery smile.

"Go with Mikaela and Lena, Tessa," she says. "Maybe it was just a trick of the shadows. It's easy to get scared in the dark."

I shift to Irene, who has sunk down on the bench by the dwindling fire.

"Irene, it's Adam," I say. "It has to be. He knew your sister and her friends. They went to school together. He approached you about the job."

"The chef?" Mikaela interrupts me, but I keep talking.

"He killed them. And now he's going to try to kill us. Please, we have to get out of here."

Irene is glassy-eyed and pale. She looks on the verge of passing out.

What would she feel, seeing Caroline lying there, knowing her sister fell victim to the same man ten years earlier?

And so I make my decision. If this is what I have to do to prove to them that we need to get off this island, I will.

"Okay," I say, trying to sound strong, trying to sound sure. "But Lena, please . . . stay here. And look out. Please. Stay together."

I stare at my sister, trying to put every ounce of conviction I possess into my voice.

"Please."

Lena looks me in the eyes, and with her mouth pulled into a thin line and her eyes overly bright, she nods.

If there is anyone I trust, it's Lena.

I hesitate, and then I reach down into my pocket and pull out my phone, hand it to Lena.

Her eyebrows fly up, as high as the micro-Botox will allow, and she stares at it.

"Where did you . . . ?"

I keep my gaze fastened on Irene.

"I'm sorry," I say. "I took it. I had to have it, in case something . . ." The rest of the sentence dies on my lips.

In case something were to happen.

"If we don't come back, and if you can't get to the other phones, see if you can find a place to charge it."

I look over to Mikaela and Natalie.

"Come on," I say, doing my best not to let the wild, manic nature of my fear shine through, chip away just a little more at my credibility.

"Let's go. We don't have much time."

CHAPTER 32

April 16, 2022

Mikaela and Natalie are behind me as we walk through the sparse woods. The carefree mood from earlier tonight has been replaced by a tense silence.

That soft, velvety feeling of the blue April night I felt earlier is gone. The island has turned into a twisted mirror version of itself. All I can see are the empty spaces in between trees, all the shadows where someone could be hiding. All I can see is the water acting as a border, encircling us, keeping us trapped like animals in a cage.

I'm sticking as close to the water as possible, my eyes drawn over and over again back to the fire, back to the house, in between the trees, trying to pick up on any movement, anything that might suggest that someone is watching us.

Was this always the plan, or was it an accident? Was this done out of necessity, or for the thrill of it, the joy of the hunt?

Maybe he got a taste for it, that night, ten years ago. Maybe he has just been waiting for another chance.

I don't know how he is planning to get away with this, yet again. But maybe I'm overthinking it. Maybe it will be as easy as putting all of us in the dinghy and sinking it, or setting fire to the hotel with us still inside.

Just a bunch of silly women, having a silly little party, getting too drunk and burning the place to the ground.

Maybe he would get away with it. Maybe not. In either case, if we don't manage to get away from him soon, I won't be around long enough to find out.

I jump when Natalie sidles up next to me. Her long hair has gotten tangled by the wind and the dancing, her eye makeup a little smeared around the corners. It gives her a near ghostly appearance in the dark.

"I don't think you're making it up," Natalie says. Her voice is quieter than mine, so subdued it's almost drowned out by Mikaela's whistling.

I just shake my head.

"I wish I was," I say. "Trust me. I wish so much that I was making this up, or hallucinating it. But it's real. I just . . . wish you could have trusted me." If only my voice hadn't betrayed me by breaking.

I understand that Natalie is trying to be kind. I even understand why they won't believe me. Would I have believed me, had our positions been reversed? If Mikaela had come running wild-eyed off the beach, screeching about finding a dead body, and if I hadn't taken notice of all the little things that seemed to add up to something sinister going on, would I have believed her, or would I have written it off as being a bad interaction between the sleep deprivation and alcohol and whatever else she might have in her system? We're all millennials, after all, which means there's a decent likelihood most of us are on antidepressants.

No, I would not have believed her.

Suddenly I understand why so many horror movies end with the whole cast dead. It's easy to judge when watching from the safe confines of your couch. But when it's actually happening, it's easier to write the danger off until it's too late.

We come round the edge of the isle. Not much further now.

I see it. I see the outline of the dinghy.

I stop.

Mikaela stops beside me.

"What's wrong?" she asks. There's something brittle about the way the words come out, as though her fervent denial has weakened out here, now that the dinghy is there in front of us, undeniably real.

I try to respond, but I can't.

My feet feel rooted to the ground. I look around, wanting not to find anything, but that feeling has come back, and it's stronger than it was.

Someone is watching us.

I see Mikaela steeling herself.

"Come on," she says.

I might be frozen to the spot, but Mikaela isn't. She starts walking with long, determined steps toward the shadowy outline of the boat. She looks so tall, so unafraid, perfectly at ease with herself and her image of the world as she strides across the beach, utterly convinced she's about to show me all my fears are for naught.

The nausea sinks in again, and my paralysis finally breaks. I start rushing after her, hearing Natalie following closely behind.

"Mikaela!" I say, a frantic stage whisper. "Wait!"

I don't know how to prepare her. I don't know how to warn her.

But she will not wait. She will not slow down. Challenging the world to prove her wrong.

There is a terrible inevitability to the way she's moving, and then she stops, and she is standing very still.

And through the terror, my heart breaks for her, a little bit, for having to see what I saw.

Mikaela is standing a few steps away from the dinghy. She's not saying anything. She doesn't have to. The change in the air is evidence enough on its own.

Natalie has stopped next to me. I hear her inhaling softly, and not releasing the breath.

For a moment, time has stopped.

I want Mikaela to turn around and look at us triumphantly, to raise her eyebrows and shake her head.

But she doesn't.

She just stands there, shoulders rigid, back to us. Staring into the boat.

"Oh, no," I hear Natalie saying, and there's not just shock in her voice, but denial. *No. Please don't.*

I steel myself, and I bridge the distance between me and Mikaela.

I don't look into the boat. I don't want to see her again. It's taking everything I've got not to break down, and if I have to look at her again, I won't be able to contain it.

I put my hand on Mikaela's shoulder and look at her, instead.

Her face is blank with shock. Tears are running silently down her cheeks. Her eyes are open wide, unblinking and empty, like a computer attempting to process and running into the same error over and over again, stuck in a loop.

"Mikaela," I say, but she's not responding.

"Oh, fuck," I hear Natalie saying next to me, her voice raw with shock. "Oh, fuck. Oh, *fuck*."

I turn my head. Natalie is backing away from the dinghy, hands over her mouth, head shaking.

"Natalie," I say, and my voice is suddenly sharp and clear. "Stop. Stay here. It's not safe. We have to stick together, okay? Come back."

She reacts, seemingly more to my tone than my words. But she stops walking away. That's the important thing.

I turn back to Mikaela.

"Hey," I say to her. "Look at me."

Mikaela meets my gaze.

"I know this is horrible," I say to her. "I know you're in shock. But we're in danger. We all are. You have to get it together right now."

She blinks. I'm not sure she's hearing me.

"You have to talk to me, Mikaela," I say. "I need to know you're listening to me."

"But . . . I don't . . ." She shakes her head, and I grab her by the shoulders.

"No," I say. "We don't have time for this. We need to get everyone, and we need to get out of here. Right now. Remember what I said earlier? This isn't safe."

"But Caroline left," Mikaela says, her voice thick and dazed. "She left, remember? I saw the note she wrote. She left and went into the city, and . . ."

"She didn't," I say, more forcefully now. My grip is too hard, I know that, but I don't know how to pull myself back. The more Mikaela pushes back against the truth, the harder I have to try to force the facts on her, because I don't know what else to do to make her understand. I don't know how to talk to her in a way that would get through to her.

The searing, painful irony of the fact that Caroline would have known what to say and how to say it hits me like a ton of bricks, and my knees feel like they are about to buckle, but I manage to resist.

"You think the chef . . . ?" Natalie asks, behind me, and when I turn it looks as though all color has been leeched from her face.

I release Mikaela.

"Yes, I do," I say. "And if he did this, and he finds out we found her, he might decide it's better that none of us make it off Isle Blind. So we need to focus right now. People panic in these situations."

I've read about it, so many times. People freeze in the face of death and violence. They don't want to believe it. They regress.

And they get killed.

"They split up," I continue, "or run off, or try to hide. It's the natural thing to want to do. When you get scared, you regress. You feel powerless. That's what he's counting on. He's counting on us to be too shocked and too frightened to see what is right in front of our eyes."

I look back to Mikaela. Some of the awareness has returned to her face. The wind has swept a few strands of dark hair across her eyes, but I feel like she's listening to me again.

Mikaela nods slowly. She looks at Natalie, and then down at Caroline, at the dark bundle at the bottom of the boat. Even catching sight of her out of the corner of my eye is enough to make me feel weak and woozy again, enough to make the tears prickle in my eyes.

"Oh, Caro," Mikaela says, almost too quietly to hear, but the sharpness of the grief in the words is all too clear. "You didn't even want to come."

I can't look at her. Can't listen to her sorrow. Have to focus on what needs to be done, or I will fold and fall and I won't get back up again.

Natalie is hugging herself tight, as if holding herself together, her mouth set in a pained grimace.

"So what do we do?" she asks me. "What are we supposed to—"

She breaks off in the middle of the sentence, straightens up, and looks around. When she seeks me out again, there's fear in her eyes.

"You don't know where he is," she says. "You think he might be . . ."

This time, there's a reason she leaves out the rest.

It's a belief that goes back to childhood.

If you don't speak the bad thing out loud, it won't come true.

"I don't know," I say. "But we need to stick together. We're stuck on this island with a fucking lunatic, but there's one of him and six of us. As long as we stick together, we should be okay. We just need to get everyone, get down to the basement, and call the cops on the landline. They will send someone. A boat, or a helicopter, or *something.*"

Natalie nods.

"Okay," she says. "Yeah. We should do that. But how . . . what do we do if he . . . ?"

I can see it on her face, see it as clearly as if I were feeling it myself. Images flashing through her mind. Of what knives and meat cleavers and pure, brute strength can do to flesh and bone. Of Caroline's broken face, splintered glass buried deep in her crushed eye socket.

Natalie wants me to say I have a plan. She wants me to say I can protect us, that I know some way of getting away. That if a man emerges from the trees with a knife in his hand intent on taking out the witnesses, I will be able to ward him off somehow.

I should know, after all. Out of everyone here, I should be the one best prepared for this situation.

I want to say to her that we can take him on together. That he can't fight off all three of us. But I've read too many accounts about what happens when people are faced with violence. I've felt it myself now, the shock permeating my body.

I don't want to lie to her.

"If we see him, Natalie," I say, swallowing, trying to draw from some kind of confidence or authority, pretending I'm not just as scared as she is.

"Then you run. Run as fast as you can, and don't look back."

CHAPTER 33

April 16, 2022

"We have to get back," I say. "Now. As soon as possible."
I turn to Mikaela.

"Come on," I say, and I try to take her by the arm, but she shakes me off.

"Wait," she says. "No. We can't just leave her here."

"Natalie is coming with us," I say, but then it dawns on me what she means, and I can feel my heart sinking.

"We have to bring her back," Mikaela says, and that's when I see she's started crying again. "We can't leave her here all alone."

"Mikaela . . . ," I say, and I want to be soft and gentle and caring, but we have left the others alone for too long, and the harsh prickling of adrenaline has started flooding my system again.

"We will come back for her later," I say, taking her arm again. "I promise. But we have to go."

"NO!" Mikaela says, and she tears out of my grip. "What the fuck is wrong with you? I know you don't give a fuck about Caro. You don't even know her. But we can't just leave her here. It's so dark. And cold. Caro hates the cold. She absolutely hates it. She would hate lying out here all alone."

I look around, eyes wide, scared that she will have attracted attention with her scream, but when I try to shush her, she pushes me in the chest and I stumble backward.

"Please, try to keep your voice down," I say to her, but this is clearly the wrong thing to say.

"Fuck you, Theresa," she says. "You've never liked Caroline. You've never liked any of us. How do we know it wasn't you who did it, huh? You've been sneaking around acting weird all weekend. You've always been obsessed with murders and weird shit. Maybe you snapped and decided to stage your own sick little murder and finally live out those fucked-up fantasies of yours."

She's panting, mouth open, eyes wide and furious. Tears still running down her cheeks.

I feel like I've been slapped.

"What now, Theresa?" Mikaela continues. "You're going to herd us into the house and then hunt us down one by one for sport? Or burn it all down? You've got nothing left to lose, right, so why not go out in a blaze of glory?"

I finally find my voice again.

"Are you out of your mind?" I ask, with equal parts fury and despair. "Why would I want to hurt Caroline? I'm the one trying to *save* you! You're the one trying to get us killed by shouting and refusing to get back to the rest of the group!"

"No," Mikaela says, shaking her head and backing away from me. "No, I'm onto your sick little game. You did this. Caroline went after you when you threw your little tantrum, and then no one saw her again. You did this. You killed her." Her voice starts to wobble.

"Look what you did. Look what you did to Caro."

I don't know what to say. I want to scream back. I want to cry. But there is no time to react to it.

Not when there are worse things around.

"You can't actually believe that," I say, but Mikaela's eyes are burning with panicked fury, even through the tears.

There is no way I'm going to get through to her.

"Mikaela," Natalie says and steps in between us.

Mikaela looks from her to me, and then back again.

"She's fucking crazy," she says. "She did this. She killed Caroline."

"I don't think she did, Mikaela," Natalie says. Her voice is low, soft and soothing. When she reaches out for Mikaela, the movement is slow and deliberate, as though approaching a skittish animal.

"It's the only thing that makes sense," Mikaela says, a bit more forcefully now. "She did it. She must have."

"I don't think you believe that," Natalie says. "I think you're scared, and sad, and I think you're really angry, too. I know you loved Caroline. I know you're shocked. I know you want it to be someone you can punish. But right now, you can't focus on that. Caroline wouldn't want you to do that. I think you know that."

"Caroline"—Mikaela inhales, almost sobbing—"Caroline wouldn't want to be *dead*. She didn't even want to come. She didn't even want to be here and now she's . . . now she's . . ."

"I know," Natalie says, and I hear her voice hitching, too. "But that's not Tessa's fault. She's just trying to help us. She's trying to help you, too. So I think we should listen to her right now, and get back, and get out of here."

Mikaela looks away, face still contorted with rage and sorrow.

"I'm not going to just leave her here," she says. Quieter now. Defeated.

"Caroline wouldn't want you to stay here and risk your life," Natalie says. "She'd want you to take care of yourself. Get yourself to safety. Make sure you got home to your kids."

Mikaela shakes her head, and miraculously, she laughs. A teary laugh, yes, but all the same.

"Caroline fucking hated my kids," she says. "She hated all kids."

Mikaela wipes her nose with the back of her hand, and then she looks over at me.

"I still don't fucking trust you," she says. "I'm not taking my eyes off you until the cops get here. But . . . yeah, let's get the others and get off this island."

I wait for a few seconds. For what, I don't know. But when she stays quiet, when Natalie turns and looks at me for confirmation, I nod.

"Okay," I say. "Let's go."

May 11, 2012

When Matilda opened the door to the apartment, she could smell meat and vegetables frying, hear the quiet sounds of jazz playing in the kitchen, and she felt the tension draining out of her shoulders.

"I'm home!" she yelled, kicking her shoes off by the door and dropping her bag on the floor.

Carl appeared, his cheeks reddened by the heat from the stove and his glasses slightly fogged up.

"Welcome home, darling!" he said, in a terrible attempt at a transatlantic accent, which made Matilda laugh. "How was work, dear? Launch any big projects?"

"It was a fucking zoo today," she said, following him into the kitchen to see rice boiling and beef and broccoli frying.

He'd lit a couple of candles, though the candleholders were mismatched, and the table was half set, only missing cutlery and napkins.

"I wanted to have it done by the time you got home, but the time got away from me," Carl said, pushing his glasses up his nose. "Sorry."

"No, this is lovely," Matilda said, and smiled. "Thank you."

"You're still okay with meat, right? I googled it, and apparently, it's important for you to get enough iron in this stage of the pregnancy."

The word made her stomach twist, but she didn't let it show. Or tried not to, at least.

"Meat is great," she said. "And it smells lovely."

"Sit down," Carl said. "I'll get you something to drink."

His stern, focused face made Matilda laugh, again, but she obediently sat down on the chair he pulled out from the table.

"You don't need to dote on me so much," she said, while he searched the fridge for the non-alcoholic wine they'd picked up a few days previously. "I'm not sick, you know."

"I know, I know," Carl said, pouring her a glass of fake wine that would only make Matilda long for real wine. But she still accepted it when he handed it to her.

It was all about the gesture, after all.

"So, seriously," Carl said. "How was your day?"

Matilda sipped from her glass, allowing herself a frown since he couldn't see her.

"Well, I finally got ahold of Evie," she said. "She seems really out of sorts about something. But I managed to convince her to move some stuff around and make it to the trip."

Carl took the pot full of rice off the burner and strained it in the sink. He called it "the pasta method," and insisted it resulted in the best and fluffiest rice. Matilda had never been able to tell the difference, but she wasn't about to argue.

Carl was all about things being done the right way. That was why he was so set on them getting married before the baby came.

She'd always suspected he'd gotten that from his dad. Matilda had been relieved when she'd met Carl's mom, who was a lovely, if somewhat subdued woman, having feared the stereotypical mother-in-law from hell. Carl's dad, on the other hand, was stern and withholding, demanding excellence from everyone around him to the degree that he seemed to live in a state of perpetual disappointment.

"I mean," Carl said, hesitantly. "Don't be mad, but are you sure it's a good idea for you to go?"

Matilda sighed, rubbed the spot above her left eyebrow that was always the first sign of a stress headache coming on.

"We've been over this," she said. "This might be my last chance to go on the trip. Before . . . you know."

Carl turned to look at her over his shoulder, shooting her a quick, somewhat strained smile.

"I know," he said. "I'm just worried. What if something were to happen?"

"You sound just like Irene," Matilda said.

"Oh, so your sister agrees with me on something," Carl said, shutting the stove off. "That's a first."

His tone was mild, but Matilda knew him well enough to see he was genuinely bothered, which surprised her.

"Carl, come on," she said, getting up from the chair. "It's just one night. We've done it a million times. And we'll all have our phones with us."

He still didn't seem placated.

She wrapped her arms around his waist from behind, resting her head between his shoulder blades. She could feel the tensed muscles in his back, like steel wires under his skin.

"Besides, Linnea's boyfriend is catering a private party at a swanky hotel just a couple of islands away," she added. "They've got a doctor on staff, in case of health emergencies. Worst-case scenario, he can come pick us up."

Carl muttered:

"Unless he's too off his head on coke to realize the phone is ringing."

"God, you're such a snob." Matilda laughed, to cover up her irritation.

She loved Carl, but he had some leftover classist ideas passed down from his parents.

Carl sighed, and Matilda loosened her grip.

"Come on," she said. "Let's eat. I don't want all this gorgeous food you made to get cold."

CHAPTER 34

April 16, 2022

Mikaela starts walking in the direction of the trees, quickly, as though she's trying to get away from me just as much as she's trying to get back to the others. I try not to let it hurt.

Natalie is keeping pace with me. She isn't talking; whether from shock or tiredness or grief, I can't be sure.

Finally, I can't stand it anymore, and I say:

"Thank you. For defending me."

I'm having to struggle not to lose sight of Mikaela entirely; she's got enough sinewy muscle to outlast me by three or four days, and I am exhausted.

"It's okay," Natalie responds, but she's not looking at me. "She didn't mean it, you know. She just . . ."

"I know," I say, quietly. "I'm sorry. I didn't want you guys to have to see the body."

"I know," Natalie says. "You tried to warn us."

There is no anger in her voice, but it still hits me like a punch to the gut.

For a few moments, she's silent, and then she says:

"You're sure it's the chef who did it?"

I duck under a low branch.

"I mean, it must be," I say. "Right?"

"But, I mean—you didn't actually *see* him killing Caroline, did you?"

"No," I say. "Of course not. If I'd seen it, I would have tried to help. I would have told the rest of you. I would have done . . . *something.*"

"Yeah," Natalie says. "Okay."

The silence is loaded. I look at her as we approach the part where the shore turns in on itself.

God, how I wish the sun would start rising over the horizon. I just want this night to end. I want daylight to return. The night seems as though it's been going on for hundreds of years, time stretching on indefinitely, like the bloody, chaotic assault will never cease.

"You don't actually believe that I . . . what Mikaela said?"

I can't even say it out loud.

"Of course not!" Natalie says, and her outrage seems genuine, but there is something there.

"Jesus," I say, unable to keep the hurt out of my voice.

"I don't," Natalie says. "I'm just scared. And I can't help but wonder that, if he didn't do it . . . then he's in danger, too. Right?"

I don't have a response for that.

I haven't allowed myself to entertain the idea.

Because if the threat is someone unknown, if someone really has managed to hide away on the island, then we have some kind of responsibility to Adam. To warn him, as well.

But the truth of the matter is that I am selfish. Too selfish, and too afraid. I want to protect the ones I care about more than I want to ensure the safety of someone who may or may not be out to hurt us.

We're about to come out through the trees, and I speed up, catch up to Mikaela, that same anxiety gripping me. The closer we get, the more I feel it. That need to get back, to be in a group, to huddle together against the danger.

But when we exit the sparse woods, when we can once again see the hotel and the beach, it is dark and quiet.

The fire has gone out. There are no figures, no silhouettes shifting against the dark blue of the sky in the distance.

We are alone on the shore.

I stop, trying to force my eyes to tell me something other than what I see. My heart gives a painful *thump* in my chest, and my eyes are drawn to the house.

It's gone dark.

Before, there were lights in the downstairs dining room, shining out through the patio doors. But the windows are black now, eyes staring blindly out at us. The patio doors still hang open.

They look like they are waiting for us. Inviting us in. It's like the house, jutting out from the side of the rocky side of Isle Blind, is communicating.

There is no one else out there. There is nowhere else to go.

"Where are they?" Natalie asks, and her voice is so strained it sounds childlike. Like she's begging.

"What did you do?" Mikaela asks me, pushing past me and looking around wildly, as though I've hidden the rest of us, like I'm playing a cruel little trick on them, playing on their frayed nerves for my own amusement.

"What the *fuck* could I have done, Mikaela?" I finally break. "I was with you the whole time!"

"But where have they gone?" She spins around, and now I see the fear. My own terror, mirrored on her face. "They said they weren't going anywhere. They said they would stay here. Where have they gone?"

"Maybe they went back to the house," Natalie says, in a small voice that scares me worse than Mikaela's outburst.

"Maybe they decided they were going to call the police anyway, and they went back."

"No," I say, shaking my head. "They didn't. Lena wouldn't do that. She wouldn't have said she'd stay and then have left."

Natalie stares at me, mute with shock.

"So . . . ," she says.

"He must have . . ." I swallow, and I scrunch my eyes shut, trying to will myself not to imagine it.

"They are still alive," I say, more to myself than to them. "They have to be. Right?"

They don't respond.

I open my eyes, and I start walking again. My legs feel numb. My mouth tastes like ashes. The shock and the fear have become too much. My whole being feels like it's moving on autopilot.

The embers in the fire have been stomped out; the black, twisted remains of the branches are all that are left. One of the chairs has been knocked over, the legs tilted upward, like a bug stuck helplessly on its back.

I can see the last of the ice melting in the cooler, the empty bottles strewn among the rocks.

Something is building in my chest. I can't allow it to escape.

If I start screaming now, I might never be able to stop.

"It looks like there was a fight," Mikaela says, her voice empty of intonation. She's reciting a fact. When I turn to look at her, she looks smaller, like she is folding around herself, trying to disappear.

"Yeah," I say. "I think there was."

Three against one. Sounds like good odds in theory. Great, even. But if he managed to sneak up on them, if he managed to take them by surprise, or if he just put a knife to somebody's throat—what then?

They didn't think they were in danger. They thought I was making it up. They all did. Of course they wouldn't have been paying attention. They would have kept drinking, kept talking, just waiting for us to come back. Maybe discussing what to do about me. Irene expressing mild concern, Anneliese blowing it off, Lena trying to vouch for me and saying that she was sure I would have come to my senses by morning.

And then . . . what?

A shadow in the night.

"He must have taken them to the house," I say. "We have to go after them. We have to save them."

"Are you insane?" Mikaela asks. "We can't do that. We have to get help."

She's pacing, back and forth, tiny, jittery steps.

"We have to take the dinghy," Mikaela says, her voice so high it's cracking. "We have to take the dinghy with Caroline's body and try to row away. Get help."

"We can't," I say. It's like I'm hearing myself talk from very far away. My words sound eerily calm.

"He cut holes in the boat. Caroline wasn't heavy enough, so it didn't sink. But if we got in it, it wouldn't get far. It would sink almost immediately."

"I could go in it," Mikaela says, stopping. "I could go and get help. I don't weigh much. It might hold me."

Natalie shakes her head.

"We'd have to . . ." Her voice catches. "We'd have to move Caroline's body out of the boat to do that."

This makes Mikaela flinch, and go quiet. I see, more than hear, how she draws a deep, shuddering breath.

"We can't stay here," Mikaela says. "And we can't go in there. We can't."

I look up at the hotel. At those dark windows, the patio doors standing wide and inviting.

"We have to," I say. "The cell phones are in there. The cell phones and the landline are the only way to contact the mainland."

An odd sound from Mikaela; when I look over at her, I realize it's a twisted imitation of a laugh.

"I guess you shouldn't have given the phone to Lena," she says.

Natalie looks over at me.

"Maybe they managed to call someone," she says. "Maybe the police are on their way."

I shake my head.

"It was out of battery," I say. I can barely bring myself to force the words out.

Mikaela looks away.

"We can't just wait here," I say, and I swallow. "We have to help them. If we can. Right?"

Natalie smooths back her hair from her face, her eyes seemingly drawn to the house against her will.

I understand the scared, hypnotized expression on her face. I feel it myself.

There is a sense of a choice that isn't even a choice.

"You're right," Mikaela says, and my head snaps in her direction, surprise overtaking me for a second.

She nods at me.

"We have to help them," she says. "We have to try. You said the cell phones were in Irene's office, right? And there's a landline."

She looks over at Natalie.

"Tessa is right," she says. "We can't count on them having had the time to use the cell. We have to call for help."

Natalie nods, and Mikaela looks to me, her face set in grim desperation.

"Come on," she says. "I'm going to get home to my babies."

CHAPTER 35

April 16, 2022

"The important thing is that we stay together. We stay within touching distance of one another. We have to stay as silent as possible."

I'm speaking so quietly it barely feels like the words are passing my lips, but Mikaela and Natalie nod. We are crouching at the foot of the stairs leading up to the patio. I've got a broken-off chair leg in my hand, the ridges digging into my palm. Mikaela is holding an empty champagne bottle by the neck, and Natalie has palmed one of the large, flat rocks from the beach.

It's not much. It's almost nothing. But it's all we've got.

"I don't know if the cell phones have any charge left, but the landline is in Irene's office in the basement," I say, lips hardly moving. "I was down there earlier. It's the first door on the right once we get down the stairs. We don't know where he's taken them. We need to get to the landline and call the cops first, before we try to go after the others."

"He could be doing anything to them," Mikaela interjects, hissing at me. "We don't have the time—"

"No, it's time you listen to me," I whisper back, as harshly as I can manage. "If we can get ahold of the cops, we can get them to send people. We're not trained for this. None of us have even been in a real fight before. Irene and Lena and Anneliese thought they could defend themselves, and obviously, they couldn't. What do you think happens if we try to storm in there and we fail? That guy Ivar isn't supposed to be back with the boat until Sunday morning. No one knows anything is wrong. We *need* to call for help before we do anything else. Understand?"

Mikaela presses her lips together, shadows like thumbprints under her eyes, but she nods.

"If he is in the basement"—I draw a deep breath, can't quite stop my voice from shaking—"I'm going to try to engage him. While I do that, you two run to Irene's office. Mikaela, you block the door while Natalie gets the phone. You are going to be really scared. You might freeze up. But try to focus on getting to the phone. First door on the right. Mikaela, hold the door. Natalie, dial the phone. That's all you need to remember."

They both nod.

I draw a deep gulp of air, trying to gather some strength from the cool, fresh wind, finding I can barely force it down into my lungs. One more.

The house is so quiet. Not a sound is escaping it, despite the open doors. It would be so easy to convince myself that we are the only people on the island. The only people in the world.

But he is waiting somewhere in there. Somewhere deep in that house is my sister, and my friend, and a man who has killed and will kill again.

I don't say anything. I just take the first step up the stairs.

Without the soft light from the candles, the white, eco-friendly bulbs in the ceiling, the dining room looks completely different. The stark, white walls seem to be glowing, and the monochromatic pictures on the walls look like they are moving, shapes in the corners of my eyes that appear to shift when I move my head.

I bite down hard to stop my teeth from chattering. My palms are wet with sweat, and I grip the chair leg harder, try to imagine swinging it at his head, the meaty crunch when it connects.

Could I do it? Could I act, if it came to that? I tried to sound tough, talking to Mikaela and Natalie, attempted to sound like I knew what I was doing, volunteering to take him on.

But when I saw Caroline's body, I froze. I threw up. I collapsed. And in here, listening for a creak from the floor above, for steps in the corridors, the fear seems like a living thing, a parasite that's taken hold of my body.

It's so easy talking about it, so easy claiming I'm going to throw myself on him like a wild animal, buy them some time, but no matter how much I tell myself that he's just a man, that I've got the element of surprise on my side, that I will do it to save my sister and my friends, the reality is that Adam has grown into the shape of a monster in my head.

He is the killer that's haunted my nightmares since I was a child. The beast I've been trying to prepare myself my whole life to face. And it has become abundantly clear to me that it wasn't enough. That it could never have been enough. That nothing could have prepared me for the reality of it all.

A creak behind me makes me spin around, heart pounding, but it's Mikaela. She's stepped on something, and I hold my hand out toward the other two, look around wildly, arms feeling numb, legs rooted to the floor. I hold my breath and listen.

Still nothing.

For a second, I doubt myself. My perception of the whole situation starts to slide away. Are they really in here? Could it possibly be this quiet if they were?

But he must have taken them here. It's the only scenario that makes sense. The island is too small for him to have taken them anywhere else. There is nowhere to go.

And someone must have turned the lights off.

I start walking again. We pass through the dining room. There isn't a trace of human movement in here. Nothing looks out of place. It's as though I'm looking at a photograph, a staged picture for the hotel website.

At the stairs, I stop again. Try to listen.

Nothing.

The hairs on the back of my neck are standing on end. There's something in the air, something like electricity, dangerous and unstable.

Mikaela makes a move toward the stairs, but I grab her by the upper arm, shake my head vigorously and silently. *No.*

Her face is a study in gray, naked fear. I don't know what is going on in her head. But I can feel it echoed in my own body, the need to run, to hide. To find a small space and squeeze myself inside it, close my eyes, begging the monster to go away. Praying to whoever is willing to listen. Wishing that when morning comes, the light will wash all of this away, and it will all have been a bad dream.

Natalie puts her free hand on Mikaela's shoulder, and standing behind her, she nods at me.

I turn and start down the stairs.

When I put my hand on the railing, the cold metal seems to burn my skin. Shrieking silently at me. Pulsing through my body.

Get out.

CHAPTER 36

April 16, 2022

The lights have all gone out here as well.

No sterile, fluorescent lighting coming from the ceiling. It's solid black, the kind of darkness you can only get in a small, confined space. The steps going down look as though they are leading into nothingness and oblivion.

If we go down there, we will be walking blind. Lambs to the slaughter. We won't have a chance to see him coming.

Any moment, I could feel cold steel meeting skin. Feel the cut before the pain. The warmth of blood flooding down my chest, smell the heavy iron, feel my heart pumping its last, panicked beats.

I won't even have time to realize I'm dying. The darkness will be the same, either way. Nowhere to run. Nowhere to hide. Not even a chance to try to fight. Not even a chance to fail.

I can't go down there. I can't.

I take a small step backward, but then I feel fingers encircling my wrist. I twitch, but when I look over my shoulder, I see Mikaela's face. Her hair is pushed back from her pale face, her makeup smeared down her cheeks from crying, but the fear I saw mere seconds ago has receded.

She holds my gaze.

I feel my own panic slipping away.

Mikaela lets go of me, and I walk down into the darkness.

After only two or three steps, I can no longer see where I'm going. I have to feel out the steps with my feet, have to trust my senses. I can smell the lingering scent of something burning. I refuse to allow myself to wonder what it is.

I can feel, more than hear, Mikaela and Natalie behind me. I don't know if I can actually hear them breathing, or if I'm imagining it in sync with my own, their steps just a beat behind mine.

What are they seeing, now that we can no longer see? What are they imagining? Is it as bad as the images I can barely keep at bay? Is it worse?

The next step feels different. Steadier and colder, somehow. I move my foot gently forward, scraping against the surface. It doesn't end.

We've made it down.

I take two more steps forward to leave them room and stand perfectly still. Listening.

Something brushes against my side. My arm shoots out to grab for it, and my fingers dig into soft, cool skin.

"It's me."

The whisper is so clear down here it might as well have been a scream. Mikaela.

I turn my head. I can't hear Natalie.

"Natalie?" I say.

Nothing.

I'm still holding on to Mikaela. I don't dare let go.

"Where did she go?" Mikaela's breath is hot against my ear. "She was right behind me."

Any moment now. Any moment, Natalie is going to respond. She was right behind us. She has to be right there. We would have heard if something had happened.

There. A shuffling sound. Something that sounds like a muffled moan. It's right behind us. Not more than a few steps away.

I hear Mikaela shrieking and jerking away, slipping out of my grip.

"Mikaela!"

Running. The sound of feet disappearing in the other direction.

And then I am alone.

I'm panting where I stand, my whole body tensed up, the darkness pressing down on me from all directions.

I don't breathe. I don't move. All I can hear is the loud pounding from my own pulse, so fast it sounds like fluttering, so quick it's making me dizzy.

I want to call out for them, but I can't let myself do that. If I call out, if I make a noise, then he will be able to hear me.

Slowly, I raise the chair leg, and I sweep it in front of me, focusing on the feeling of it in my hand. Try to feel if it's sticking on anything, sweeping against anything.

If I can locate him, get a sense of where he is . . .

But there is nothing there.

I am swimming in the void.

My eyes are useless down here, so I close them. My chest hurts with the effort not to breathe, and all I want is to inhale, to feel that sweet relief, but in this silence, any noise is a giveaway.

I'm standing two steps out from the bottom of the stairs. The kitchen wasn't far from the stairs, and the office was maybe two steps further down, the doors not quite facing each other.

Did the office door have a lock?

It wasn't locked when I got there, but that doesn't mean a lock doesn't exist.

I'm only going to get one chance. He already got Natalie. I don't know where Mikaela is. She might have found a door, found her way outside, kept running. I hope so. I hope that is the case, hope that she'll make her way to the dinghy, that she'll push Caroline's body out and that her low body weight will actually let the boat carry her away, despite the holes. I desperately hope she's made it away.

But I won't.

That part is perfectly clear to me.

Even if I can't save myself, I'm not going down without a fight. I will try to give the others a fighting chance, if they are still alive.

The fear and rage I'm carrying are making me want to lash out, bite and scratch and hit, and I will do just that.

I'm going to do my very best to make it to the office, to the phone, to call for help.

And if he gets me before that?

I'm going to do my best to hurt him as badly as I can. To inflict so much damage that it might buy the others enough time to get away.

I owe them that much. I owe myself that much.

My lungs are aching. My rib cage feels like it's going to explode. I need to exhale.

I hear the shuffling of feet. Whisper soft. Over by the stairs.

My heart gives a single, painful beat.

I exhale, and start running.

I let my fingers run against the wall to feel for the door as I run, and the whispering sound seems loud enough to fill the whole space. He must be hearing me.

I don't know how far behind he is. The hallway isn't very long. I don't have more than a couple of seconds.

There. A groove.

I throw my entire body against the wall, and there it is. I've found the door to the office, and I search frantically for the door handle, feeling it out with my hands, knowing that those hands and that knife can't be more than seconds away; if I don't find that handle now then this is where it ends, this is the end of the road, not only for me but for all of us.

I give a yelping sob when my hand touches metal, and I push down.

The door opens.

I fall through the door and immediately throw myself against it, pushing back on it, and it shuts just as a body collides with it from the other side.

I scream as I feel the door start to give and push as hard as I can, begging it to stay closed, to stay intact.

"Tessa!"

The sound of his voice almost makes me step back, the fury in it igniting the urge to run, to hide, but I manage to override it at the last second. My fingers search blindly for a lock, and when I find it, I push down on it.

He must have heard the click, because for a few seconds, there is silence.

"Open the door, Tessa," Adam says, his voice calmer now. Closer to the voice of the man I met in the kitchen.

I don't respond. My heart is beating so fast it feels as though it might explode in my chest, and I stay pressed up against the door, and it's as though I can actually feel him on the other side. As though the vibrations from his pulse are spreading through the wood itself.

"You don't understand, Tessa," Adam says, and when he pounds on the door again, a single time, I jump.

All I want is to get as far away from him as possible, but I can't leave the door. Not while he's there, on the other side.

"I know you think you know what's going on," he says, and there is something I can't quite decipher in the sound of his voice.

An attempt at understanding, perhaps. At trying to lull me into a false sense of security.

At appealing to whatever short-lived connection he thought we might have had.

"Let me in, and I'll explain it to you," he says.

I close my eyes, tears leaking down my cheeks, and I shake my head, even though he can't see me.

I don't know if it's minutes or seconds that pass.

But finally, I hear something that might be a sound of frustration.

Or a laugh.

"Fine," he says. "Try calling the cops. See how well that works out for you."

And then I hear his footsteps leaving, echoing down the hallway.

CHAPTER 37

April 16, 2022

I press my back to the door as I slide down onto the floor, unable to hold the sobs back as my body shakes. I can't fall apart now, I can't, I have to get to the landline, have to call the police, have to do what we came for, but, oh God.

Irene and Anneliese might already be gone. If not yet, then soon. And my sister . . . it's too painful to even think about, even now. A red-hot, glowing pain in the center of my body that is making me gasp for breath.

He left, for now. But he'll be back. Of that, I'm sure. He sounded certain that he's got all the time in the world.

If he can't get through the door, there are windows, after all. And even if I got out, what then?

There is no place that is safe on this island. It feels cursed, as though it has been waiting out here for us, to devour us whole.

I put my hand over my mouth to try to stop the thin, wailing sound working its way up my throat.

I have to keep going. I made it in here. I have to use the landline, have to call the police. Tell them what happened. Hope that they will make it in time, and pray that my call will be enough to ensure Adam can never hurt anyone else even if they don't.

I use the chair leg to help me get back up on my feet, look back at the door. It's quiet again. I don't hear anything outside. Maybe he's already gone outside, to go around, to break the windows and drag me out of here. But I don't need much time.

The dark isn't as dense in here; the moonlight has made its way inside, giving just enough illumination to let me make out the room.

Everything looks the same as it did. That same picture on the desk. That same high-end computer.

Jesus, what I wouldn't have given for a heavy paperweight right now. Or a letter opener. But why would Irene have a letter opener? The hotel is paper free. For the environment.

I should have known the environmentalist movement would end up being the death of me. It's what I get for not recycling. Karmic retribution.

The landline is sleek and old-fashioned. It doesn't look like salvation. It just looks like a half-forgotten phone you keep around because your one elderly aunt refuses to use your cell-phone number.

Right now, I can't remember ever seeing anything so beautiful.

I pick up the handset and press it against my ear. The moonlight isn't enough to let me make out the numbers, and my vision is blurry from the tears, but it doesn't matter. The keypad is big enough to make it easy.

I press the numbers. One, one, two.

I've never called the police before, but I know what is going to happen. Some comfortably middle-aged woman with a crisp, competent voice is going to answer.

This is 112 emergency response, how can I help you?

I'm going to sound hysterical, but they are used to that. They will know what to do. They will keep me on the line and keep me talking. Maybe, if I break the window and hide under the table, he will assume I've taken off. Maybe I can hide until they make it out here, until the boat or the helicopter or whatever it is they are going to send arrives and the police storm the building, until someone arrives to carry me out and put a blanket around my shoulders and give me something warm to drink and then it will all be over, it will finally all be over, and I won't have to try anymore. It will be safe.

But the voice doesn't arrive.

I put the handset down to reset the connection and pick it up once more. Just as I'm about to start punching the numbers again with shaking fingers, eyes trained on the window, expecting the hulking shadow of a man approaching in the distance coming to get me, I realize.

That low, persistent beep I remember from childhood, the one I used to hear every time I had to make a call when we were children and everything was easier, isn't there.

The phone isn't connected.

I can't believe it. There is no way the phone isn't working. I've been holding the landline up as our salvation, as the way we are going to get out of this, our one connection to the outside world.

The phone has to work. The phone has to work, or what was all this for?

I fall to my knees on the floor, wrench open the drawer with the cell phones, start trying to activate them one after the other. They are all dead. None of them have any battery.

I open the computer, try to force it to connect to the internet. It keeps flashing that sad little symbol at me, over and over again.

NETWORK NOT FOUND.

My breath is coming in deep gulps. I push the monitor off the table, hear it crashing onto the floor, and then I pick up the handset again, press it so hard against the side of my head that it hurts, and I still hear nothing but dead air.

I hear myself screaming with frustration, see myself smashing the handset down, again and again, feel the plastic starting to give in, but it's like I'm watching myself from far away. Like some other Tessa is doing this, some other Tessa is losing her mind, while I float silently away.

So that's it, then.

There is no way out.

It's over.

We will just be yet another scary story. A case for a podcast. In a year or so, someone will be sitting in a recording studio—maybe even the same one where I used to record *The Witching Hour*—reading the script they've written about six women going out to an island for a bachelorette party, not knowing they were never going to return.

They will describe all of us in sweeping terms, adding little details for texture, in the same way I used to do. They'll mention Mikaela's kids and Lena's volunteer work, maybe throw something in about the tragic disappearance of Irene's sister, just enough to work the listener's tear ducts. If they really want to twist the proverbial knife, they might try to get an interview with a close relative. Anneliese's Samuel, probably.

And then they will get into the gory details of it. They will linger over the autopsy reports, go over the timeline of the murders. They will hold enough back so as to not be accused of murder porn but tell the listeners more than enough to tickle the part of them that enjoys the vicarious thrills.

We will be gone, all of us, reduced to nothing but what the pod-casters and documentarians will mine for content.

Like I did.

I wish I could appreciate the dramatic irony in that. But there is nothing left in me. Nothing left to do but to wait for the inevitable.

All I can do is hope that it will be quick.

Still, my entire body stiffens when I hear quiet steps approaching in the hallway outside the door. I close my eyes, draw ragged breaths tasting of horror, try to think of something good. A happy memory. Try to find a place to go while he breaks down the door.

I think about Anneliese, on the beach, just a few hours ago. That happy, relaxed smile on her face. Dancing and laughing, creating her own light, the way she always has. I think about Mikaela, apologizing for her thoughtless comments, despite the fact that she's never, as long as I've known her, wanted to apologize for anything.

I think about Lena when we were kids, so little I can't place the memory, patiently helping me hold the crayon between my fingers, tracing the paper with my hand until I'd drawn a big, green splodge that looked like nothing at all.

I think about Lena, nine months ago, the day after the news broke and everything crumbled, showing up outside my door and ringing the bell until I let her in and just holding me, crying for me until I felt I could cry.

There is a knock on the door. I tense up. Does he expect me to open the door for him and let him in? Or is that just the first one, the one that comes before the splintering of the wood?

"Tessa! Tessa, you have to let me in!"

A low, hysterical whisper, muffled by the wood. It's a voice I know.

"Come on, Tessa, please, we don't have a lot of time."

I scramble to my feet, see the door handle twitching as someone is trying to tug at it from the other side of the door.

"Irene?" I say, voice shaking.

"Please, Tessa," she says, and her voice sounds broken, thick with exhaustion and tears. "I don't know if he noticed I'm gone yet or not. If he sees me, he'll . . . please, please, open the door, Tessa."

I walk up to the door. I put my hand out, but I hesitate.

"Are you alone?" I ask.

"Jesus, yes!" she says, and she sounds so different, that calm, Zen-like quality completely gone. "There is no one here with me. He tied us up. I think he left to go after Mikaela. He might already have found her. Please, just open the door."

I don't want to open that door. I am too scared of what might be on the other side.

But I can't leave her out there.

I reach out to the lock.

CHAPTER 38

April 16, 2022

"Irene," I say once she's inside, finding it hard to form the words. "How did you get away? Did he get Natalie? Are Lena and Anneliese . . . are they . . ."

I can't say it. I can't make myself say it.

Irene shakes her head. She's staring off into space, her lips pale. I can see her chest moving in short, explosive bursts. One of the straps on her dress has torn, and she's got scratches on her cheek, deep and bloody, that have only begun to crust over.

"He's got them tied up," she says. "Upstairs. Your sister, and Anneliese, and Natalie. He left to go after Mikaela. I tensed my wrists when he was tying me up. I said I'd run for help."

She sounds like she's talking about someone else. Telling a story from long ago.

I swallow the metallic taste of terror, force myself to hear what she's saying.

"So it's just the others upstairs, right now," I say, slowly, wanting to pull back from where I'm going but knowing I have to say it. "We could . . . if we could get them free, if we could surprise him when he comes back . . ."

I hate how weak I sound, wish I could sound stronger, more like a leader, more like someone who believes this might have a chance of succeeding.

Irene stands up from her chair. She stares at me, a severe, solemn expression on her face, her features reduced to harsh lines by the cold moonlight streaming in the window.

"I don't want to know what he might do if he gets back," she says. "But I agree. I won't let what happened to my sister happen to your girls, as well."

Standing behind the desk, Irene resembles nothing so much as the final girl in a horror film. With her tousled dark hair, the scratches on her face, the torn dress, and her determined, stoic expression, she looks like she might have gone through hell and survived what no one else could, the only one strong and fit and iron-willed enough to loosen her restraints and flee.

I'm praying that's true. I'm praying she's up for being the hero. Because I've tried, given it my all, and found myself wanting.

"Okay," I say.

She walks around the desk and grabs my hands, firmly. I wince as she pushes my fingers together, as the not-yet-scabbed-over cuts on my fingers send shooting pains up my hands and arms, but I don't yank them away.

"You didn't do anything wrong, Tessa," Irene says, and when she looks into my eyes, I can almost bring myself to believe her. "You tried your best, but you couldn't have stopped any of this. It's not your fault. I promise you that. Can you try to believe that? It doesn't matter what you noticed or didn't notice. None of this is on you."

I'm all cried out, too exhausted to expel more emotion, but I still feel my eyes welling up, and I nod.

"Yeah," I say. "Okay. I believe you."

"Now," Irene says, and lets go of my hands. When she stretches to her full height, she seems to be towering over me.

"Let's go finish this."

May 12, 2012

Matilda zippered her bag and took a step back, admiring her own work. The morning sun shining through the window spoke of clear skies, and she was hoping it would last.

It felt like a good sign for the trip. She'd woken up this morning with no nausea to speak of, and everyone had texted, confirming that they were ready to go.

Linnea had mentioned that her boyfriend was throwing a bit of a tantrum, wanting her to come with him to the big, swanky event he was cooking for, but she'd assured Matilda that she'd talked him down.

It was almost time to leave.

Matilda picked up her bag and went out into the living room, where Carl was sitting at his computer, still in his pajama bottoms and with two empty cups of coffee next to the laptop on the table. He had headphones in, and when she leaned over to kiss him on the head, he started.

He pulled the headphones out and turned his face up, smiling at her.

"Hi," he said. "Do you want to go out for brunch somewhere?"

"I don't have time," Matilda said. "Maybe a late brunch tomorrow, when I get back? I won't be hungover, so I should be in decent shape after a shower."

Carl's face clouded over, and he turned around in his chair.

"Matilda, I . . . I just . . ." He sighed. "I really don't have a good feeling about this."

Matilda sighed.

She didn't want to have to deal with whatever it was Carl had gotten in his head. Not again. Not today.

But she had to be a good partner. Had to listen. Had to empathize.

They were about to take a really big step together, after all. What did it say about her, if she didn't listen to his concerns?

"What is it?" she asked.

"You know I love your friends," Carl said. He looked smaller, sitting down on that chair; it was easy to forget he was almost half a head taller than she.

Maybe it should have been making her feel caring. Maternal.

All it did was make her feel like he was trying to play on her feelings, and for a brief second, it made her dislike him. Quite intensely.

It wasn't a comfortable feeling.

"I mean, Anna and Linnea are both great," he said. "But Evelina . . . I don't know. The way she's been acting lately . . . she seems a bit unstable."

"Unstable?" Matilda sputtered.

"I just don't think you're seeing her clearly, Matilda," Carl said, standing up, pushing his fingers through his hair. He sounded short, too angry for what the situation deserved.

"It's just because you've known her for so long. And I get it. But don't you think it's time to grow up? We're having a baby, for Chrissake."

"Grow up?" Matilda repeated.

She could hardly believe what she was hearing.

Carl's eyes were shot through with red, and his nose looked irritated. Maybe he was coming down with a cold; maybe that's why he was acting so weird.

But that was no excuse.

"Don't overreact," Carl said, rolling his eyes. "I'm just telling you the truth about her, okay? I've never liked her. She's not right in the head. She makes things up. And I think she's jealous of you. She's never liked that you've got what she wants."

He was speaking quicker than usual. She'd noticed he'd started doing that, lately. Attributed it to stress. He kept swinging between being overly loving and being tetchy, and argumentative, about small things that she kept letting go, kept letting slide, because they didn't matter, fundamentally, and wasn't that just part of a relationship?

But this was a step too far.

"What the fuck are you talking about, Carl?" Matilda burst out. "And why are you bringing this up now?"

"Because I was worried that you'd be like this!" Carl yelled, startling her.

She took a step back from him, eyes wide, and her hand went to her stomach.

Carl's face fell.

"Hey, no, wait," he said, holding his hands up.

She could see him making a conscious effort to lower his voice.

"I'm just trying to look out for you, Matilda," he said. "Because let's face it, you're not always great about taking care of yourself, are you?"

He took a small step in her direction, and Matilda fought against the urge to back away from him further.

"And it's not just about you, anymore," he said, voice even softer, his lips glistening. They were too red, somehow.

"You have to think about the both of you. About the kind of people we want around our child. And Evelina isn't that. God, if she found out you were pregnant . . . I don't even want to imagine what she might do."

Bile was rising in her throat. Matilda swallowed, again and again.

"What, you think she's going to hurt me?" Matilda laughed, small and brittle, because that was what you did, right?

What else could she do, with how he was acting, but laugh? Laugh, and hope it would make the sudden fear and disgust recede?

"Not necessarily," he said. "But . . . I wish you wouldn't go."

Matilda drew a deep breath through her nostrils, and forced her lips into a smile, hating herself just a little bit for it.

"Listen," she said. "I hear what you're saying. How about this: I promise not to tell them about the pregnancy. Okay?"

She could feel something in the air, between them. Something ugly and unnameable.

Carl nodded.

He suddenly drew her in for a hug, squeezing her so tight she could barely breathe, burying his nose in her hair.

"I'm going to miss you," he said, and Matilda could smell a faint odor of sour sweat coming off him.

"It's just twenty-four hours," she said. "I'll be back tomorrow."

CHAPTER 39

April 16, 2022

Stepping back out into the corridor feels like falling back asleep and reentering the nightmare you've only just managed to escape. That compact darkness triggers something in me, but then Irene hits a light switch, and the basement is flooded with light.

I turn around and whisper furiously:

"What are you doing?"

"If he's down here, I would rather know," Irene says. "I'd prefer to see him and know where he is, rather than be taken by surprise."

There's no arguing with the look on her face, so I let it go. And I can't deny it lowers my heart rate, seeing that wide, empty space, knowing nothing can hide in the shadows.

Irene takes the lead, walking quickly toward the stairs. Her steps are so quiet it's disconcerting; it makes her sound like she's not even there. It must be something she picked up in yoga, the ability to move without making a sound.

I'm guessing she never imagined she'd be using it for this.

She stops and waits for me at the stairs before looking up, nodding at me, and then going up quickly.

The second floor is still dark and quiet. Irene looks around, seems to listen for something; she tilts her head upward, eyes trained on the ceiling, and then appears to determine that it's safe to proceed. She takes us around the corner, sticking close to the wall, but when we get to the stairs she hesitates.

I motion to her, put my lips close to her ear. Catch a whiff of sweat and old perfume, a minerally scent, like powder, and something sharp and acrid. Fear.

"What's wrong?"

Irene looks at me. She looks like she's struggling with something.

"If we go up there . . . ," she says. She seems to catch herself, and then she continues:

"I mean, if he's up there, we don't know how things are going to work out. I'm going to do my best, but it's not going to be safe. Maybe you should try another way. Maybe you should run out and see if you can get that dinghy to float. Take it. Try to get to the nearest island and get help."

Her words are so soft they are barely more than a whisper.

I shake my head.

"I'm not going to let you do this on your own," I respond. "I'm with you, Irene. We'll do it together. Okay?"

She's searching for something in my face. What it is, I don't know. But then she nods, and she smiles a heartbreaking little smile.

"Okay," she says.

I realize I'm happy I'm here with her. That she's the one who came and got me. If there is anyone who can pull this off, this insane, impossible rescue, it's her.

She's already survived losing a sister. She's rebuilt herself.

She got captured by a crazy killer, and she managed to escape, and she's still going to go back in with me to get the others.

I might not believe that I can do this, but I believe Irene might be able to.

"Let's go," I say, and when Irene hesitates, I take the lead up the stairs.

I move slower than she has, one step at a time, starting and stopping to make sure nothing is creaking or groaning and giving me away. I catch myself wishing the stairs would be longer, that we would have further to go, because I'm still so scared of what we will find up there.

I didn't ask her what he's done to them, yet. What damage he has already wrought. Because I didn't want to hear it. Because I didn't think I could go through with it if she had told me what we were going to find.

I saw Caroline. I know what Adam is capable of.

The upstairs hallway looks like something half remembered, a memory from long ago. Muscle memory wants to take over, steer me to my room, to my bed, where everything is normal and sane and nothing bad is going to happen. But I look at Irene, and she indicates left with her head.

On the right are the bedrooms. On the left is a room that didn't seem to be in use. I hadn't asked what it was for. Quite frankly, I didn't even wonder.

The door is open. Just a sliver.

My ears prick up. I can definitely hear something. Muffled, yes, but it sounds like . . .

It sounds like crying.

Irene pushes me.

It's not hard, but it's enough to make me stumble in through the door, shock and fear rushing to my head, and I look around, trying to get my bearings.

It's a bedroom. An empty one. And they are all in there. All but Mikaela.

The walls are bare. There is no furniture in there but a chair. By the far wall, Lena, Anneliese, and Natalie are sitting, hands tied behind their backs, rags stuffed in their mouths. Natalie's eyes are closed, her head leaned back at an odd angle, her face so pale I'm not sure she's alive. I've never seen a living person that color.

Lena's eyes are wild with terror, but she's alive. She's been crying, but she doesn't look badly hurt.

Not like Anneliese.

Anneliese's got the beginnings of a black eye, a swollen, bloody nose, and she's struggling with the restraints behind her back, seemingly to no avail. She looks like she's been through hell.

But it's not the sight of her that makes me freeze in place.

Because Adam is standing there, in the middle of the floor, chewing on his thumbnail. He looks up in surprise at the sound of my entrance, his thumb still at his lips, and there is no aggression in his eyes.

There is shock, and what looks like fear.

I don't understand. I was expecting a monster. I don't understand why he would be scared to see me. He's the one who's done all this, after all.

Then I realize he's not looking at me, at all. He's looking over my shoulder.

"I told you I could get her up here without hurting her, Adam," a voice says behind me. "See, you didn't have to break the door down."

I turn.

Irene is standing in the doorway, holding a shotgun. And it's pointed at me.

CHAPTER 40

April 16, 2022

For a few seconds, my brain just flat-out refuses to process what it is I'm seeing. All I can comprehend are the abstract shapes. The cruel, sleek geometry of it all.

The straight perfection of the long, smooth barrels of the gun. The twin muzzles, black eyes staring at me. The long, competent fingers gripping the weapon, white lines folded over each other.

Irene clears her throat.

"Adam," she says, her voice that same soft command she used during sunrise yoga. She is not a woman who has to yell and scream to get her way.

I feel Adam grabbing my wrist, and I tear it away, staring at Irene.

"What do you think you're doing?" I say. It's odd, because I mean to shout, but it comes out strangled.

Adam's holding ordinary plastic zip ties, the white kind you can buy in any home improvement store.

For whatever reason, the thought that pops into my head is *You're not supposed to use those on people. They can cut off blood flow and damage the tissue. That's why you should get proper handcuffs if you're going to engage in bondage.*

My mind is fracturing.

"Tessa, I don't want to have to hurt you, but if you won't let him restrain you, I'm afraid I'm going to have to," Irene says.

When I look back at her, she appears infinitely tired.

My whole face feels numb. Shock, probably. I feel like I am about to start laughing, for some reason. Like this is all one big, funny joke.

Maybe it is. Maybe this is some stunt for Anneliese's bachelorette party. Maybe I'm just the only one who's not in on it. Maybe they forgot to tell me.

Yes, that makes sense. I'm going to tell them off later. I'm going to tell them they went way too far with this, and that it really wasn't very funny at all, and that I'm very angry with them.

That this isn't the sort of thing you do to your friend.

I feel Adam gathering my wrists behind my back. His touch is careful, even as I feel him threading the plastic over my wrists and pulling tight, until it cuts into my skin.

"Good," Irene says, and it feels absurdly reassuring.

I'm happy to have pleased her. I want her to be happy with me.

I don't want her to shoot me.

"Now sit down next to Natalie."

I don't move, so Adam takes me gently by the shoulders and guides me over to the wall. He turns me around, so I'm looking outward, and pushes me carefully down onto the floor. My legs fold like they were only waiting for permission.

He looks me in the eyes, and all I see is regret.

"Did you see Mikaela?" Irene asks Adam, and he turns and shakes his head.

Irene appears thoughtful for a second.

"I don't think she's coming back for anyone. She's a survivor, that one. She's probably trying to swim away right now." She sighs.

"I hope she doesn't. It's too cold. She seems like a strong swimmer, but the currents . . ." Irene closes her eyes for a moment, looking genuinely upset.

When I look to Irene, I open my mouth, and I don't recognize the voice that comes out.

"Are you going to kill us?"

Adam shoots Irene an alarmed glance. He's back on his feet now, standing by her side, and Irene catches it.

"I hope not," Irene says, as much to me as to him. "I just need you to stay calm. I don't want to hurt you."

She almost sounds wounded by the question.

"You hurt Anneliese," I say, and something else comes over her face. A flash of contempt.

"Well," Irene says, slowly. "Anneliese started screaming. Trying to hit Adam. She actually managed to scratch me, as you can see."

She turns her still-bloodied cheek toward me.

I can't help but feel a welling respect for Anneliese. Pride.

Good job.

Adam clears his throat.

"I could bring them downstairs," he suggests to Irene, the distress in his voice becoming more apparent by the minute. "It might be easier if they're not here. I could give them those sleeping pills you were talking about."

Irene shakes her head.

"No," she says. "I think it's better if we have everyone in one place. I want them to hear." Her voice shakes a little bit on the last word, and I see her gripping the rifle more tightly.

I see Adam turning toward the window, running his hand across his face. I hear him muttering something. All I can catch is:

". . . not the plan."

Irene takes a step toward him, raises one hand as if to touch his shoulder, and then lets it drop again.

"I know," she says, quietly, and when he turns back to her she presses her lips together, something I can't name radiating between them.

It's not romantic. Nor is it sexual. It's something else, something deeper and more painful.

He nods at her. Once.

Irene turns back to us, and when she sees me looking, she says:

"I'm sorry about this. All of this. I really am. It wasn't supposed to happen this way. If it hadn't been for . . . well, you were all supposed to be sound asleep in your beds by now. Most of you, at least."

She smiles, small and strange.

"You might not believe this, but I really wanted you to agree to let me call you a ferry," she says. "You were getting a little too close, and I was concerned you would figure it all out, but trust me when I say that I genuinely wanted you out of the line of fire. So to speak." She crouches down in front of me, rifle resting easily on top of her toned thighs.

"I like you, Tessa. You remind me of Matilda, in a lot of ways. Though you and I may have more in common. I think, when you hear what you're going to hear, that you're going to understand. I even think that if I'd had time to explain, you might have . . . though I guess we'll never know now."

I wish I could think Irene was crazy. But she doesn't look, or sound, crazy.

She looks sad, and very tired, and very, very determined.

"Irene," I say. "Please. I don't know what this is all about. But . . . whatever it is, whatever you want, we can work it out. We can fix it. Just don't do anything you can't take back."

She smiles again.

I can see that she knows I'm lying.

Because whatever line she was hoping not to cross, it's already far behind her.

It's all been leading up to this.

And no matter what she's telling us, no matter how many times she says she doesn't intend to hurt us, I can see in her face that it isn't true.

Irene stands up again, without responding, and turns to Adam. She nods in Anneliese's direction, and I see his face harden.

"Let's get started," she says, with a new, nasty edge to her voice.

CHAPTER 41

April 16, 2022

Irene crouches down in front of Anneliese.

Her face changes so completely it's as if she's been wearing a mask this whole time. The anger floods her face with an ugly red, and her lips twist into a harsh imitation of a smile.

"Now," she says. "For our guest of honor. Our *bride*." She spits the last word, and I see Anneliese recoiling. Tears are still running down her cheeks, but she's completely silent. The sobs have stilled. Her eyes are so wide I can see the whites around her irises.

"We're going to put you in that chair," Irene says, and nods toward the chair in the middle of the room.

"I'm going to cut your hands free and then tie them to the chair. If you start struggling, I'm going to shoot you in the foot. I'm not going to be careful. I might take most of your lower leg off. And I'm not going to stop the blood flow. I'm going to let you bleed out, and I'm going to watch you do it, and I really won't feel that bad about it. Do you understand what I'm telling you?"

Irene bites off the last word. I can see Adam behind her, pale but no longer hesitant, his eyes burning almost as bright as Irene's.

Anneliese is trembling. Irene raises her eyebrows.

Another few tears leak out the corners of Anneliese's eyes, but then she nods, once.

Irene takes ahold of her arm and stands up, yanking Anneliese with her.

I scream—"No!"—and try to throw myself forward, try to stop what is about to happen, trying to get to my feet. But my legs have gone numb, and I can't find my balance with my hands behind my back. I end up falling forward, hitting the floorboards with my chin, and my mouth fills with the taste of blood.

I try to roll over on my back, but a cool hand on the back of my neck stops me instantly.

I freeze, like a small animal. I can't see anything but wooden planks, smooth and lacquered, softly reflecting the cool light from the lamp in the ceiling.

But I can feel the shotgun behind me. Like some evil entity, the trigger just waiting to be squeezed.

A strong hand grabs me and lifts, pushing me back against the wall, gently but firmly. Adam isn't looking me in the eyes. His mouth is set in a slim line, and his gaze is still fastened on Anneliese.

Irene has dragged Anneliese over to the chair, and she now looks over to Adam, who gets to his feet.

"I need help with this one," Irene says, and Adam obediently shuffles over.

"Are you okay to hold this?" Irene asks, and Adam says, voice gravelly:

"Yes."

She hands him the shotgun. She lets her hand rest on his shoulder for a couple of seconds, until Anneliese makes a move to get up, and then the fury returns to Irene's face and she slams her back down in the chair.

Irene grabs Anneliese with both hands, pulling her up against the seat back. Anneliese looks hysterical with fear now, her face scrunched up tight, tears and snot leaking down onto the gag in her mouth, mingling with the dried blood under her nose.

Irene pulls a small knife from her pocket, reaches behind Anneliese's back, and cuts the zip tie holding her hands together. Then she presses Anneliese down on the chair and looks deep into her eyes.

"Remember what I said?" she asks in a low voice. "I want you to imagine Adam shooting you in the foot. I want you to imagine what that will feel like. Your foot and most of your leg will be gone. The force will shatter your tibia completely. It'll be nothing but meat, and blood, and bone fragments. Imagine what that would feel like before you decide to try to make a run for it."

Anneliese is white as milk. She looks like a ghost. Like she is already bleeding out, seconds away from death.

She nods again.

"Would you hand me the zip ties, Adam?" Irene straightens up again, all business, that low, menacing growl gone as though I'd imagined it, as if we were all having a collective hallucination.

Maybe we are. Please, God, let this all be my imagination.

But it just keeps going. It just keeps happening. Adam hands Irene the zip ties, and Irene yanks Anneliese's hand down to the seat of the chair, expertly zip-tying her wrist to the base of the armrest, and then does the same to her other wrist before moving on to her ankles.

It comes to me, then.

She has done this before. This isn't the first time.

When Irene has finished, she stands up once more, admiring her work. She walks a half lap around the chair, checking that Anneliese has been properly secured, all while Anneliese keeps crying quietly, the weeping of a child who has given up on ever being heard. Her face has fallen forward, and her body looks subtly contorted, her joints straining against the unnatural position she's been bound in.

I can't keep looking at her. It doesn't feel like something I was meant to see.

This is Anneliese. Bubbly, happy Anneliese, who took me under her wing in high school, who used her beauty and wealth and charm to bring people into the fold even as a teenager. Anneliese, who's about to get married in just a few weeks. Anneliese, who rode into the harbor in a limousine with a tiara on her head less than forty-eight hours ago.

Irene stops in front of Anneliese. She lingers there, for a second, as though taking it all in. Or savoring the moment.

Then she reaches out and yanks the fabric out of Anneliese's mouth.

"We're going to have a little conversation, you and I," she says to Anneliese, a little smile on her lips and a flat look of fury in her eyes.

CHAPTER 42

April 16, 2022

"Please," Anneliese says, speech garbled by her swollen lips and dry tongue. "I'll give you anything you want. Anything. Just let me go. Don't hurt me. Please. I'll get you money. I'll get you . . . I'll do whatever you want."

Irene keeps studying her face. Searching for something.

Then she shakes her head.

"It's not about money, Anneliese," she says. "But I can see how you would think that. I'm guessing you've never had to see consequences for anything, have you? You've always been able to buy your way out of any situation. First with Mommy and Daddy's money, then with . . . what was his name, again? Samuel?"

Anneliese hiccups at the sound of his name, a half sob somehow made worse by how quiet it is.

"I'm sorry," she whispers. "I'm not going to do that anymore. I promise."

It's the childish tinge to her voice that breaks me. None of the adult Anneliese remains. Nothing but fear and helplessness.

"Irene, whatever it is you think Anneliese has done, it can't be worth this," I say. "Just stop. Okay? You've made your point. She's terrified.

We're all terrified. Whatever this is about, you don't have to let it go any further than this. We'll never tell anyone. I promise."

When Irene turns to look at me, she does it slowly, in a near-mechanical way. It's like her whole body is straining against the movement, like she'd half forgotten I was even there. That any of us were there.

Anyone but Anneliese.

"Tessa, I'm going to need you to be quiet," she says, the implied threat blazing in her eyes. "Otherwise, I'm going to have to gag you. This has nothing to do with you. Stay out of it."

Irene pauses, and then she sits down on the floor in front of Anneliese, legs crossed and back straight. She watches Anneliese for a few more seconds, head cocked to the side, the only sound that of Anneliese's crying.

"You know, Anneliese," she says, "at first, I didn't think you even remembered. I was convinced you had forgotten about it. It must have been such a small thing, in your life. You were barely out of your teenage years, after all, and it seems like you weren't sober very often back then. I was a bit concerned, you see, if I'd be able to get you to remember enough." Irene chuckles.

"I had to needle you a little bit to get you to admit it," Irene says. "You see, I was sure it had happened. But I had to know. I had to know that you remembered it. And, you know, for a second there, I thought you'd caught me. I thought you had realized what I was getting at. I'm sure I wasn't concealing my feelings very well." She pauses.

"But then again, why would you notice anybody else's feelings but your own? You're the main character of your story, after all. Anyone else is just a bit player. No one else matters but you."

The rage breaks through, making her voice crack, contorting her face.

"I don't know what you are talking about," Anneliese whispers, her voice weak, her breathing labored.

Irene puts her hands on her knees, relaxes her shoulders. She looks like she's going to tell Anneliese to breathe deeper. Inhale through her nose, exhale through her mouth.

"I wanted to talk about that older man you mentioned," Irene says. "During that fun little game we were playing, earlier. Remember him? Tall guy. Good-looking, I guess, if you like that sort of thing. Short dark hair. Glasses?" She cocks her head again.

"Does that ring any bells?"

Anneliese doesn't answer.

Irene looks over her shoulder, up at Adam, whose face is set in a grim mask.

"Adam, do you want to help her out here? It seems like Anneliese can't quite place him."

Adam raises the rifle, ever so slightly. He's breathing in short, hard gasps.

"You were fucking him," he says, in a low voice. "You were getting high together."

Irene turns back to Anneliese.

"That's right," she says. "You were fucking him. Your friend had an apartment in the same building as him. You met one day, probably visiting her. Am I getting close?"

Anneliese doesn't respond.

"I don't really know how or when—in the stairwell, maybe? Coming in or out of the building?" Irene shakes her head.

"I guess it doesn't really matter how it happened. The point is that you started fucking him, as Adam so succinctly put it. And you were lying, during that little game we were all playing together, weren't you?"

Anneliese draws a deep, shaky breath, and looks up through her curtain of hair.

Irene's voice starts to climb.

"Because he had a girlfriend, didn't he? A fiancée, actually. And you knew that he did. You just didn't care that much. You were young, and it was just a fling, right? A cheap thrill? I bet you were feeling so bold. I bet it was all just *so exciting.*"

"I'm sorry," Anneliese whispers, and Irene raises her hand; Adam twitches, and for a second, I think Irene is going to hit Anneliese across the face, but then she lowers her hand again.

"You're sorry," Irene repeats Anneliese's words. "That's good. But the thing is, I'm not sure I believe you."

She gets to her feet and backs up a couple of steps, folds her arms in front of her.

Looks over at Adam.

"Do you believe her?"

Adam looks hesitant. His eyes are flying between Irene and Anneliese.

Then he shakes his head.

When Irene starts to speak again, her voice has once more grown softer.

"See, Anneliese, he doesn't believe you, either," she says. "Come on. You have to work with me here. We're not going to get anywhere if you don't help me."

"I don't know what you want from me," Anneliese says, her voice hoarse from crying. "I'm sorry. I shouldn't have done it. I didn't mean for anything bad to happen."

Irene leans in over Anneliese.

"Can you imagine how you would feel if someone did something terrible to Samuel?" Irene asks. "That wouldn't feel very good, would it? That would make you very angry, wouldn't it?"

"Yes." Barely a whisper.

"Wouldn't it make you even angrier if someone kept that person from being punished?" Irene asks, leaning in further. Her face is so close to Anneliese's now that they might be about to kiss.

Anneliese nods.

"Because that man, who you lied for . . ." Irene pauses, and then chokes out the words. "He killed my baby sister. And I loved her very much."

Now Anneliese looks up.

"And the thing is, Matilda had this group of friends," Irene continues. "She'd known them her whole life. Just like your friends, actually."

When she turns to look at us, I catch something like hesitation in her face. But it's gone in an instant, and when she turns back to Anneliese, there is no trace of it left.

"Matilda and her friends would go to a little island in the archipel-ago every year," she says. "To party, and relax, and just get away from it all. And then one night, ten years ago, they didn't come back."

Irene looks back at Adam, whose hands are shaking.

"My sister didn't come back," she says, on the verge of tears. "And neither did Adam's girlfriend, Linnea."

Adam closes his eyes momentarily.

"Four women," Irene says, once more facing Anneliese. "Matilda Sperling. Linnea Andersson. Evelina Banér. Anna Wittenberg. All gone, like they'd never existed."

"They went missing," Anneliese whispers. "Their boat turned over."

"NO!" Irene shouts, making Anneliese scream, and Adam jump. "No, they didn't, Anneliese. They didn't go missing. They were killed. And the police might have caught the person who did it."

She grabs Anneliese by the hair, and Anneliese whimpers as Irene pulls her head up to look her in the eye.

"They might have caught him," she says, her voice strained, "if you hadn't lied to the police. If you hadn't told the cops you were with him that night."

May 12, 2012

Carl turned the engine off once he saw Isle Blind in the distance and picked up the oars. They were heavy and solid, chafing the insides of his palms as he rowed as quietly and as quickly as he could.

His father was proud of those oars. Carl's grandfather had, according to family lore, carved them himself. He had been an old-fashioned man, a proud man, as good with his hands as he'd been with running the family business. Or at least that's how the story went.

Carl's father liked to bring up Carl's grandfather as the perfect example of what a man should be whenever Carl failed to live up to that standard. When Carl had been a skinny, acne-ridden teenager, his father had told him about how Carl's grandfather had worked down at the docks every summer. To build character and, it was implied, muscle.

Not like Carl, who'd spent his summers indoors, playing video games. Not like Carl, who wasn't good with his hands, who'd never carved an oar or even used one, before today.

He was proving his father wrong, though. Had been for years. There was more than one way to be a man.

You could get into the best university in northern Europe, get a degree in finance, and start building your own fortune as opposed to coasting on what your father had built.

You could make enough money to buy a beautiful, expensive apartment, start wearing perfectly tailored suits that made you look distinguished and made up for your smooth cheeks and weak chin. You could learn to show that money in ways subtle yet obvious enough for the beautiful girls who'd scorned you in high school to suddenly realize you were a good prospect.

You could find the perfect fiancée, have the perfect child, live the perfect life.

He was almost at the shore now.

In the distance, he thought he could hear voices. Music.

This was a crazy plan, but he didn't know what else to do. It had been a mistake. It was all going to stop, now that he and Matilda were getting married, now that they were having a baby. He had just been sowing his wild oats, getting it out of his system.

It was better than what his father had done, all his life. Cheating on his mother in broad daylight. Carl would never do anything like that. A girlfriend was one thing, but once they were married, he planned on being the perfect husband.

Henny, Anneliese, Evelina . . . they didn't matter. They weren't part of his real life. Matilda was. Matilda was someone he could build a future with, the kind of future he deserved. The kind of future they both deserved.

Evelina wasn't even his type. He wasn't even sure why he had kept seeing her, after that first time. They had run into each other at a bar, a few months back, both of them drunk, and Evelina had basically taken advantage of him. She had been throwing herself at him, for God's sake, wearing basically nothing.

It had just been a moment of weakness.

The second time, and the third, well . . . he wasn't perfect. He had never claimed to be. He worked hard to take care of Matilda, to see to her every need, and it got exhausting, sometimes. He loved her, but she could be a lot of work.

And Evelina had just been there. So easy, so available, asking for nothing. Only for him.

Frankly, he didn't even find her that attractive. It had all been a mistake. What Evelina had done was worse than anything he was guilty of; she'd been friends with Matilda since they were basically in kindergarten. She should have known better.

He couldn't let some misguided attempt at absolution from Evelina's side ruin what he had with Matilda.

They were perfect together. Everyone said so.

Evelina was just panicking. Carl didn't even think this was about a guilty conscience. If she'd been feeling guilty, she wouldn't have slept with him in the first place. She was probably just jealous. He'd never liked how Evelina treated Matilda. She didn't want to come clean because she was such a good, morally pure person, she just wanted to blow up Matilda's life because she couldn't take seeing Matilda happy, engaged, pregnant and glowing while Evelina herself was still single.

It was pathetic, really.

He just had to explain to Evelina how it would look. She hadn't thought it through. He'd always been good at explaining things to people. He explained things to Matilda all the time. When she'd told him she was pregnant, she'd said some ridiculous things about not being ready, but he had explained to her how good it was all going to be. How happy they'd be. What a beautiful home they could make together for the baby.

Sometimes, people just needed to have things laid out for them to understand.

When all this was over, when he and Matilda were married, he'd have to explain to her that she couldn't keep spending so much time with her friends. She would need to focus on their family, and they weren't the best influence.

Just look at how Evelina had betrayed her.

The beach was no more than a few yards away. He jumped out of the boat, steadying it with a hand as he started dragging it toward shore. The water was freezing cold, and he was going to be soaked on the way back, but it was all okay.

He was doing this for love, after all.

Just as he'd managed to pull the boat up a bit onto the shore, so it wouldn't float away, he heard steps approaching. He straightened up where he stood, frantically calculating an explanation for why he was there. He'd say he'd come to surprise Matilda.

No, that wouldn't work. They'd wonder how he had known where they were.

Maybe he could say Matilda's sister had told him. He was sure she knew. They were always whispering, those two, keeping their little secrets. It would have been cute, if her sister hadn't always seemed so stuck-up.

But, no, Matilda's sister would tell her they hadn't talked. She might even tell Matilda he was being "controlling," or some other such ridiculous thing. She had never liked him. She had always been opposed to their relationship.

He ran quickly across the beach, squeezing himself halfway into a deep crack in the bedrock. He saw the dark silhouette of a woman walking down the rocky slope to the beach, stopping at the water. Turning her head as she discovered the boat.

He saw a flash of red in her hair.

Evelina.

She had come down to the beach on her own.

Everything was going to work out. She was going to see reason, and everything was going to work out exactly as it should.

He walked out from where he was standing.

Evelina spun around.

"What—" she started, but then her eyes grew wider, and he recognized the expression on her face as fear. In a second, she was going to start screaming, and the whole thing would turn into a complete mess.

Carl managed to close the distance between them in what seemed like no time at all. He didn't think he had ever moved that quickly in his life. He clamped his hand over her mouth, and he saw her eyes tearing up.

"It's just me," he said. "Don't be scared. I just want to talk. I'm not going to hurt you."

She was squirming in his grip, but he kept talking, and he made sure he used his office voice, the one that sounded low and methodical. He'd calmed a lot of people down with that at work. People could work themselves up into hysterics, sometimes. All they needed was for someone to be the adult in the room.

"You can't tell Matilda about us, Evelina," he said as she kept squirming. "You're just going to hurt her. And what do you think people are going to say about you? You seduced me. I didn't want to cheat on Matilda. It was an honest mistake, and I feel genuinely sorry for what I did. But you're supposed to be her friend. You have known Matilda since you were kids. Think about how that is going to look. Really think about that before you do something you are going to regret."

She didn't seem to be listening. He needed her to stop struggling, so she would start listening. He felt anger swelling in his chest, tried to clamp his hand down harder over her mouth.

He didn't want to have to hit her, but he was willing to, if that's what it would take. She just had to listen. This would all have been so much easier if she had just listened.

This was all her fault, after all.

Carl tried to adjust his grip on her shoulder, but just as he moved his hand, she wrenched away, harder than before, and slipped out of his grasp.

She didn't scream. She just started running. But she wasn't very fast. It was all going to be okay. He just needed to catch her.

He caught up with Evelina in two steps. He reached out and grabbed her hand.

She lost her footing.

He saw it happening step by step. Time slowed down until all he could see were snapshots.

Her hand, slipping out of his.

Her head, hitting the outcrop on the rock.

Her body, falling, until it hit the ground.

She jerked. Twice. She opened her mouth. Nothing came out.

The blood looked black in the light of the moon.

He should do something. He should help her, somehow. His father would have known what to do. His grandfather as well. They would have known how to fix this. They would have known how to fix her.

It had taken only a second. Surely it could be undone. Nothing that took only a second to go wrong could be impossible to fix.

Your life wasn't supposed to change that quickly.

Carl didn't know how long he stood there, looking at her in the moonlight. Waiting for her to move. Waiting for the world to right itself again.

It was only when he heard the crunching of footsteps and a high, searching, joyful voice calling that he managed to come back to himself.

"Evelina?"

Linnea.

She would see them in no more than thirty seconds. There wasn't enough time for him to get away. Not enough to get the boat far enough away from the shore.

She was going to see Evelina, and see Carl, and draw all the wrong conclusions. There would be no coming back from this.

He was going to lose everything. Everything he had worked for. Worked, and sweated, and struggled for.

He could feel it all slipping away, and the injustice of it felt searing, blinding. It hadn't been his fault. They were all going to judge him on a single moment of his life, a single mistake, as if it had been his doing, as if Evelina hadn't pushed and pushed until he had no choice but to take action, as if that stupid bitch hadn't decided to try to run away and slipped on a fucking rock and ended her own useless life.

He could imagine how his mother would look, when she heard the news. Could imagine her silent crying.

And he could imagine the disappointment on his father's face, the twisted disgust as his son disappointed him, one last time.

It wasn't fair. It couldn't happen like this.

He didn't feel himself making the decision. He just watched himself, from a distance, going down to the boat, and reaching for the knife his dad kept there. The one his grandfather had supposedly kept in there to gut the fish he'd pull from the Baltic, early in the mornings, with naught but the cries of the seagulls to keep him company.

I'm just going to scare her, he told himself. I'm only going to use this to make her keep quiet while I come up with a plan. Right?

But he couldn't find an answer to the question.

All he knew, in that moment, was that the long, heavy blade of the knife made him feel calm and in control for the first time in weeks.

CHAPTER 43

April 16, 2022

Irene reaches down into a bag and fishes out a cell phone.

Of course, she's had it on her, this whole time. The taking of the phones was never about "mindfulness" or "living in the moment."

It was all, always, leading up to this.

Irene activates the screen on her phone and taps something before holding the phone out at Anneliese, casually, just as she would have shown her a picture of a new rug.

"Anneliese," she says. "Look up. Come on, pet. I know you can do it."

Anneliese raises her head, her eyes dull with pain and exhaustion.

"That's my sister," Irene says, and her voice breaks again, just the tiniest bit. "Matilda."

She turns the phone toward herself, and in the light from the screen, I see her eyes glossing over with tears.

"Beautiful, isn't she?" Irene continues, wiping her eyes with the back of her hand. "She was such a gorgeous girl. She didn't do great in pictures, never did. She hated having pictures taken of herself. Thought she had chubby cheeks. I always imagined she would have grown out of that. The hatred of photographs, that is, not the chubby cheeks. I thought her face was perfect."

Irene scrolls to the next picture and turns the screen back to Anneliese.

"And this is Linnea," she says. "Adam's girlfriend." She turns to look at him.

"Do you want to tell Anneliese a little bit about Linnea, Adam?" she asks, gently.

Adam opens his mouth.

"She was . . ." He stops, lowers his chin, shakes his head.

Irene nods toward Anneliese.

"You can do it," Irene says, with true tenderness in her voice. Like a mother encouraging her child.

Adam looks at Anneliese.

"She was . . . funny." He struggles to continue. "Beautiful. And very kind. She cared about people. She went to dentistry school because she'd been scared of the dentist, as a kid." His voice cuts out, and he lets go of the rifle with one hand, wiping his eyes roughly, before adding:

"I used to tease her about it. Say that no one wanted to be a dentist. But she was really set on it. She was very . . . passionate. About things. About people."

Anneliese has closed her eyes. As though she might be able to tune it out, make it go away, if she's just not looking.

"The thing is, Anneliese," Irene says, putting her phone away once more, "you weren't the only girl Carl was fucking on the side. No, Carl got around. I never understood the appeal, personally. I found him quite forgettable. I always thought Matilda could do better. But she loved him, and I thought they would break up sooner or later. I always had my suspicions about Carl, but he never did anything too overt, and Matilda wouldn't hear of it. She insisted he'd never cheat on her. And I had no proof, so what was I supposed to do?"

Irene presses her lips together.

She draws a deep breath.

"Carl had been fucking one of Matilda's friends on the side, too," Irene says. "Evelina. And Evelina had, apparently, started to feel quite bad about it. Unlike you, she had a conscience. So she told Carl that he had a choice: he could either tell Matilda what they had been up to, or she would tell Matilda herself. On their annual trip, that they had been going on since they were teenagers." She shakes her head.

"I guess she was hoping he'd have the spine to rip the Band-Aid off for both of them. But she overestimated him. He was still thinking he could get away with the whole thing."

"How do you know all that?" I try to ask, but Irene will not be interrupted.

"So, when Evelina texted him from Isle Blind, telling him she was going to tell Matilda everything, he panicked. He decided that he was going to come out here and stop her. Save his perfect little life from blowing up in his face.

"Evelina probably thought they were safe, since no one knew where they were. If she'd ever wondered about the safety of it, at all. Carl didn't seem like a very threatening guy, on the surface. Not the kind of guy who would lose control. He was methodical. And precise. Even when rattled. So when he decided he had to go out there, had to talk to them, he logged on to their computer and checked Matilda's find my phone app."

She stops, and draws a small, rattling breath.

"Such a simple thing, in the end. If she hadn't gotten that fucking iPhone, none of it might have happened."

Irene turns to Anneliese, and smiles, and it is a smile of terrible rage.

"Carl told me that he lost control and blacked out," Irene says. The thin veneer of thoughtfulness hides something black and ragged in her voice. "He said he couldn't remember what he had done, after. He said he cried. But, Anneliese, I'm not so sure about that. Matilda always talked about how rational Carl was. She was always going on and on about how *composed* and *logical* Carl was."

She wets her chapped lips.

"If you ask me, I don't think he panicked at all," Irene continues. "I believe him that Evelina fell. But after that, I think he just did the math. I think he decided that killing all four women, sinking their bodies in the ocean by the island, towing their boat out, and dumping it far away from Isle Blind was his best bet. It was a smart play, I have to give him that. He did everything perfectly. He admitted the cheating to the police immediately. Said the guilt was eating him alive. Cried about how they had to find his fiancée. He even begged them to keep the search going. He brought their phones with him and dropped them in the water at different locations. To make sure they wouldn't look in the wrong place, if you understand what I mean."

Irene smiles, thin-lipped and hollow-cheeked.

"I guess I have to admit Matilda was right about Carl being very organized," she says.

September 10, 2020

His mind was hazy, and his head felt too heavy. He couldn't figure out why his head felt so heavy, or why his wrists hurt. The world was rocking, ever so gently.

When he tried to open his eyes, he thought, for a moment, that Matilda was looking at him.

At first, he smiled. Matilda. Of course.

But then, through the fog, the relief of seeing her was replaced, first by confusion, and then by horror.

"You're dead," he tried to say, but the words came out garbled. His lips would not cooperate, and his tongue felt like a dead piece of meat, lying in his mouth.

"No," Matilda said, softly. She didn't sound like herself. "No, I'm not the one you killed, Carl."

He blinked, once, twice, and her face came into view.

It wasn't Matilda. Not the soft, rounded features that had kept coming to him, in his dreams, these last eight years.

Sometimes she said that she forgave him. Sometimes she said she understood. Sometimes she said it had all been a big misunderstanding, that it had never happened.

Sometimes, she was angry.

Those were the dreams he drank to forget.

No, the woman looking down on him was made up of hard eyes and sharp angles. He'd never liked those eyes, he remembered, groggily. He'd never liked how much they seemed to see.

"You're . . ." He couldn't find her name.

"Irene," she told him, and then she stood up from her crouch, and turned him over so he was lying on his back.

He recognized that wide, blue sky above.

He still saw it, sometimes, when the booze wasn't enough.

"No," he managed to say.

It was only when he started struggling to get up that he realized his hands were bound behind his back. He couldn't feel his fingers, only a low, searing pain below his wrists. His head was pounding, and he was very cold.

"I think I might have given you too high of a dose." He heard that horrible voice, as Matilda's sister walked around him in the boat. "For a while there, I was worried you wouldn't wake up."

"Please," he said. His mouth was so very dry.

His memories were coming back into focus. Fleeting, shimmering things.

Irene had called him. Told him she had found something, something that might help find out what had happened to Matilda. Had said that she was sorry for having accused him, and that she needed his help. That they had to work together, the two who had loved Matilda the most, to ensure she saw justice.

She had told him to get a boat and meet her.

And he had thought . . . what?

That he had to see what she had found.

That he had to make sure she didn't actually know.

Carl heard the sound of water splashing, and then her face came into view again.

He felt his eyes filling with tears, helpless as they slid down his cheeks.

"Don't do this," he said, and it almost sounded intelligible.

She must have understood. Because she smiled, again. So sweetly that he thought, for a second, that he must have misunderstood.

That it was all going to be okay.

"You're going to tell me where it happened," she whispered, putting her hand to his cheek. Her hand was burning cold against his skin. Her voice was almost tender.

"I'm going to take you there, and you're going to explain to me exactly how you did it, and where you buried her."

"You don't have to do this," he begged, tears still running and turning cold.

Her face changed in an instant. She leaned in closer.

"You know, they all told me that, Carl. They all told me to just let it go. To grieve, and move on. My father. My boyfriend. They thought I had gone crazy from grief. They told me that I was crazy. That I needed to stop. But I knew, all along. I knew you were bad news the first time I met you. And I know you took my sister from me. It's only right that you finally pay for it."

He tried to shake his head, body straining, through the sluggishness, with freshly minted fear.

"I didn't do anything," he started to say.

She put her hand over his mouth and nose, and squeezed, hard enough for him to hear the cartilage start to crack, for him to moan in pain.

She leaned in close over him. In the light of the sunset, her pupils were no more than pinpricks, and her smile was tinted red.

"No more lies, Carl."

CHAPTER 44

April 16, 2022

I can't stay silent anymore. Irene has been creeping closer and closer to Anneliese, circling her like a cat stalking in the night. Now she's standing so close to the chair her leg is brushing against Anneliese's knee.

"Irene," I say, and she twitches, turning to me. "Please, don't . . . I'm so sorry. I'm so sorry that happened."

The tears running down my cheeks aren't a tactic. I just don't know who I'm crying for. If I'm crying for myself, or for Anneliese, for Caroline or for poor Matilda or even for Irene herself, who looks and talks like an open wound, because I recognize something in her voice in myself.

Finally, I see the pain I've glimpsed in her all weekend laid open, and it's a wound so raw and infected as to inspire madness.

I wish I couldn't understand it. I can condemn her actions, but not her pain.

What would I have done if someone had killed Lena?

I would have wanted them dead. I would have wanted them to hurt the way I was hurting. It wouldn't have been done for justice, or for fairness, or for any of those lofty ideals we all like to pretend we live our lives by.

I would have wanted to hurt them to stop myself from slowly bleeding out.

"What Anneliese did was bad," I say. "She messed up. She made a mistake. But it's not worth all this. I understand you're angry, but all of this was Carl. Not Anneliese. Not Caroline."

Out of the corner of my eye, I see Adam start in surprise.

"None of us deserve this," I say. "You can't fix this by punishing us. You can't fix this by ruining your own life."

Irene laughs. It's short, and harsh, and ugly.

"You can't understand, Tessa," she says. "Don't try that shit with me. There is no possible way for you to understand."

She turns back to Anneliese.

"You lied for him," she says. "Carl came to you and asked you to lie to the cops. And don't give me that shit about not knowing why he needed an alibi. I know he told you. So why, Anneliese?" When her voice cracks this time, it's in rage, not sadness.

"Why did you lie for him, knowing he'd murdered his fiancée? My sister?"

"I didn't know," Anneliese says, her cheeks covered in tears and blood. "Okay? He told me he was in trouble, he told me he needed help. He said I was the only one who could help him. I thought I loved him. I thought he trusted me." Her voice is thick and slurred, but there is something more than fear and sorrow there. There is defiance, too.

"He hurt her," I tell Irene, trying to get through to her. "He hurt Anneliese, and he hurt your sister, and he hurt her friends."

I'm straining against my restraints, fear and frustration sisters within me, the need to reach Irene, to find the sanity within her so great it's making me ache.

"This isn't justice," I tell her. "This is just revenge. And it isn't even against the guilty party. Carl is the one who should be punished. Not Anneliese. Not Caroline."

"What is she talking about?" Adam interrupts, and Irene looks surprised, as though she's almost forgotten he's there.

"Who's Caroline?"

I stare at him for a few seconds, speechless. When I look to Irene, she's gone pale.

"It was you?" I ask her, still not wanting to believe it.

Wanting, even now, to believe that the woman I've gotten to know wouldn't have killed my friend. Wanting, still, for it to be the man I've feared. For Irene to have been so blinded by her quest for vengeance that she would have gone along with it.

"What do you mean?" Adam asks me, taking a step toward me.

"You killed her," I say, still staring at Irene. "Why? What did Caroline ever do? Caroline had nothing to do with your sister. Or with Carl. She never did anything wrong."

"It was an accident," Irene says, her voice wavering.

When Adam looks at her, it's as though he's seeing her for the first time.

"You said she left," he's saying.

"I . . . ," Irene says, and I can see her hands gripping the rifle tighter.

"It wasn't a fucking accident!" I shriek, anger ripping through me like a tidal wave, breaking down the barriers of self-preservation. "You slit her throat! You stabbed her in the *fucking eye*!"

Adam is backing away from Irene now.

"You said no one would get hurt," he says. "You said you wanted to get a confession. You said we were going to get her to sign a paper, so that we could take it to the police and get the investigation reopened. You said it would finally put him away."

Irene's face contorts.

"It wasn't supposed to happen like this," Irene says, swinging wildly between me and Adam. "If she hadn't overheard us talking . . ."

"But you said you took care of it," Adam says. His voice is flat, and all color has left his lips; he sounds like a child, looking to be reassured, begging his mother to explain away the monster under the bed. "You said you told her some story and put her on a boat."

"I did," Irene says, and there is a dark amusement in her words, deep down there, under the surface.

"I did tell Caroline a story, and when she didn't believe it, I made sure she would stay quiet whether she wanted to or not. And then I did put her on a boat. I cut the cord, and I sent it out to sea." Hearing the words out loud seems to shock even Irene, for a moment, but then she recovers.

"I told you what you needed to hear. I told you we could finally get justice for Linnea and for Matilda if we could just get Anneliese out here, if we could get her to confess that she'd lied. And we still can. If it hadn't been for her, and for Matilda's so-called friend sleeping with Carl, none of this would have ever happened. It's just as much their fault as it was his."

"That's insane," I say, and Irene snaps.

"No, Tessa, that's the truth!" There is nothing left of the woman I thought I'd gotten to know, thought I'd gotten to like. There is only wild, self-righteous pain.

Adam is shaking his head, a silent plea for the kindness of a lie.

"Please," I say. "Don't do this. You can still have your life back. I can help you explain it to the cops. You're traumatized. You're grieving. I know you didn't mean to kill Caroline. You panicked. We can tell them that." The sliding panic in my voice is taking over, making it high-pitched and frantic.

"It's too late for that," Irene says, seemingly more to herself than to me. "It's too late for all of it." She raises her gaze and lands it on me, and continues, lower now:

"It's been too late for a really long time."

"We'll—" I say, but she interrupts me, harshly:

"It wouldn't be enough. Someone has to pay. Four people. Four women who were loved. Who were *cherished*. Who had their whole lives taken away, in an instant. For nothing."

"Irene," Adam cuts in, and he takes a step toward her, puts his hand on her shoulder, hesitantly but firmly.

She turns to look him in the eyes.

"This has gone too far," he says, drawing from some inner strength I didn't expect him to have. "We have to call the police. We have to stop this. This isn't . . . this isn't what I signed up for. I don't think it's what you want, either. Come on. It's over. We're done."

Irene looks at him for a long, drawn-out moment, and then says, almost casually:

"I'm so fucking sick of men telling me what I want."

And then she grabs the rifle and swings it, swiftly, so the stock hits him over the temple.

I scream, and I hear Lena screaming, too; her gag must have fallen out. Adam falls to the ground, trying to grab ahold of Irene, bring her down with him.

He manages to roll over onto his stomach, reaches for Anneliese with one hand, but Irene runs at him.

"No!"

I don't know if I'm screaming. Someone is.

"Irene, no!"

Irene manages to get on top of him, right before he reaches the chair. She gets one knee on top of his right elbow, and he's trying to reach back, scratching for her, but she raises the rifle and brings it down. Twice.

The first one hits his half-upturned face, bone crunching and blood spattering.

The second hits the back of his neck, and his left foot twitches, just once.

CHAPTER 45

April 16, 2022

Irene is sitting there, rifle pointing upward, breathing in huge gasps. Someone is whimpering. Someone is crying. One of them might be me.

Black spots are dancing in my field of vision.

The silence is too horrible to comprehend.

Finally, Irene turns to look back at us, and I try to shrink back against the wall.

Her eyes are empty. Her mouth is slack. There are beads of blood on her cheeks.

"You asked me how I knew what happened to my sister," she says, to me, with a harrowing sort of intimacy in her voice. Like we're having a conversation, just her and me, and she's confessing to some small, negligible sin, committed long ago.

"It happened a little bit like this, honestly."

She looks down at Adam, and she wipes her nose, and I don't know if she's crying, and I don't know if I am, either.

"I wanted to do it right, this time," she says. "I thought Adam deserved to know what happened, too. I wanted to do something good. For someone else."

She smiles, the muscles of her face looking discordant, like her smile is hanging by strings.

"I guess I should have learned from what happened with Carl that it's easier to just bear the burden yourself."

She slowly gets to her feet, and I can't breathe, can't speak, can't think.

Irene shakes her head.

"I really wish it hadn't come to this," she says to herself. "I don't know how it all went so wrong."

Then she turns to me and says, eyes still so very empty:

"I hope you can find it in yourself to forgive me, Tessa. I think we could have been friends, if it hadn't been for all of this."

In one quick, smooth motion, she turns to Anneliese, raises the shotgun, and fires it right into her chest.

CHAPTER 46

April 16, 2022

My ears are ringing.

My ears are ringing, and everything is happening in slow motion. I'm faintly aware that I'm coughing, that the smoke is making the air taste charred.

I've never heard a gun fired before. I didn't know it would be so loud, didn't know the sound would swallow everything else.

I'm lying on my side, on the floor, one of my arms crushed under the weight of my body, and I don't know if I've fallen or if I've thrown myself to the side to try to escape whatever it is that might be coming.

When I blink, the colors of the scene start to come together, and I wish I hadn't. I wish I could close my eyes again.

You hear "gunshot," and you think about a small, neat hole. An entry wound and an exit wound.

I know how guns work. I've read enough about them to understand the small explosion creating enough energy to propel a projectile forward, quickly enough to let it penetrate whatever is in front of it. I've seen crime scene photos of gunshot victims. Gruesome pictures of bodies stiffened in death, blood having soaked into their clothes, matted their hair. I've seen pictures of murder victims with bullet holes in their heads, in their chests, in their faces, tissue ripped from bone by the force of the bullet.

But I've never seen anything like this.

Anneliese has imploded. The shot has shattered the window behind her. I can see the edges of her shredded skin, the red and black of her chest cavity, the white of her fragmented ribs poking through. It looks like a giant has stuck his hand into her rib cage and ripped her heart out.

The rest of her body is still impossibly and perfectly intact. A framework for the horror. Slim, immaculate arms and legs, sculpted through hours of running and yoga. So much lost time. So much work, and all for nothing.

A few weeks ago, she texted me about the bachelorette party, to confirm I was still coming. She mentioned she was almost at her target weight. She sent me a picture from the dress fitting.

She's never going to wear that dress. She's never going to walk down the aisle. All those hours she spent poring over magazines, picking the perfect flowers for the bouquet, choosing between ringlets and beachy waves, picking kale and grilled chicken over pasta, it's all for nothing.

It seems impossible that those arms and legs are going to go to waste. It seems impossible that she's never going to throw her head back, curls gleaming in the sunlight, and laugh that full, throaty, unexpected laugh.

Something moves in the gaping hole that used to be her chest. Lungs twitching, still attempting to draw breath. The body doesn't yet know it's dying. The body doesn't know the difference between wounded and obliterated. It's only a mechanism, after all. It tries to keep going even after it's too late.

Someone is screaming.

It's not me.

"Run!"

Sound comes rushing back into my ears, and reality snaps back into focus.

Suddenly I feel everything, again, the taste of vomit in my mouth, the shrieking ache in my shoulder where I've fallen, the painful pounding in my wrists. And I see.

I see Irene is on the floor, Lena on top of her. Her hands are still behind her back, but Irene's nose is bleeding, the rifle on the floor.

Irene grabs Lena's long hair and pulls, and it snaps Lena's head back for a second as she shrieks. Her furious, terrified, stark white face is blazing as she locks eyes with me and yells again:

"Run, Tessa!"

Irene's free hand finds the shotgun, and Lena desperately throws herself at Irene's arm, trying to stop it, and she tumbles off Irene.

I try to get to my feet. I have to run away from here. Anywhere. Throw myself into the ocean and try to swim. I would rather drown than die like Anneliese. I would rather sink to the bottom of the sea, the last bubbles of my breath rising to the surface, and rest intact on the ocean floor than feel my body ripped apart in an instant.

I fall again, but I get up. The floor feels like it's moving, like I'm in a boat caught in a storm, but somehow, I get up, bound arms throwing me off as I run out the still-open door, the grunting from the struggle behind me following me like it's clinging to me, and it's so dark out in the hallway, I don't know where I'm going. It's like I've switched over into a dark, alternate reality where nothing is quite the same and the island itself is a sentient being trying to eat me up and consume me whole.

The lights by the floor seem to be pulsating.

I trip down the first step of the stairs and throw my shoulder out to try to keep myself from falling down them, and I scream at the impact, at the pain, but I don't fall. I run downstairs, feet slipping and skidding, knowing that any moment she might be behind me, that I have to get out, have to get as far away as possible.

And then I'm on the ground floor, and I see the patio doors, the quiet outside. I keep running. Tears are streaming down my face, trying to blind me. I can still taste the smell of blood in the air. For the rest of my life, I will keep smelling that blood, keep smelling the moment when Anneliese died. No matter if the rest of my life is a few minutes or a few hours or years and decades, I will never escape it.

The sound of my steps changes as I hit the patio, turning from soft and pattering to reverberating thuds as the weight of me thrums through the wooden boards.

I stop, for a second, to try to orient myself, lungs aching from the effort, and I think of Anneliese's lungs, gleaming in the light, meat trying to remember its programming, trying to fulfill its function, and my stomach cramps violently. I feel the planks starting to roll under my feet, see my field of vision starting to shrink. I'm swaying. I need to stop that. I need to keep going. But I don't know how to make it stop. I don't know how to make the world right itself again.

Someone grabs my arm, and I instinctively try to tug away, but the one, small part of my brain that is still consciously thinking whispers: *It was always going to end like this. There is no way out.*

When I turn, she looks like a small, frightened woodland creature, back hunched, hair wild. She's holding a shard of thick, green glass.

Mikaela.

"Hold still," she says. "I'm going to cut you loose."

"I thought you left," I hear someone saying, and her voice sounds like mine, but it can't be mine, because I can't remember how to speak. "I thought you swam away."

Mikaela has turned me around with forceful hands, and I feel her pulling on my arms, and my breath leaves my lungs with a long, squeaking note, too tired to yell. The pain is part of me now. Like the smell. Like the image of Anneliese.

"I was always going to come back."

"She's coming," that strange, disembodied voice says, using my lips, reverberating through my vocal cords. "Irene. She shot Anneliese. Irene shot Anneliese, and Anneliese is dead."

Something snaps, and suddenly I can move my hands, and when the blood starts flowing back into my hands it feels like they are catching fire. I feel my eyes starting to roll back in my head, but Mikaela jerks me around again and grips me hard and shakes me a bit, and I blink at the sight of her furious face.

"Where are the others?" she asks.

Fragments of thoughts start knitting themselves together. I look into the dining room, raise my eyes to the second floor, the light shining out the shattered window, and then I take a step backward.

"We have to run," I tell Mikaela. "We have to run, right now."

"I'm not leaving them," I hear Mikaela's voice, still hushed, as though that matters, as though any of that still matters.

But I've already grabbed her wrist with my useless, screaming hand and I'm pulling her toward the patio stairs, stronger now than I ever have been before. She's trying to wrench out of my grip, but she can't. She doesn't have my clarity. She didn't see what I saw.

I pull her with me down the stairs.

All I know now is escape. To get away. To run until Irene catches up.

Don't wonder whether your sister is still alive. Don't wonder if Natalie is going to be next.

Don't try to calculate how long you have before Irene has reloaded, before she can make her way down the stairs.

Don't think about Anneliese's body. Don't think about Caroline's crushed eye. Don't imagine what it would feel like.

Just get away.

I've never known clarity before. I guess Irene really did manage to teach me mindfulness, after all.

All that exists is this second, and then the next.

All that matters is that I'm still alive, and in a moment's time, I may not be.

We're halfway across the beach. When I reach the far end of the island, I will just dive into the water and keep going until I can no longer feel the ground under my feet, let the water carry me home.

"There is nowhere to go," Mikaela says behind me. Her hand slips out of my grasp. I don't turn around. I can still hear her steps behind me. "There is nowhere to run, T—"

I don't hear her screaming. I just hear the gun going off. I feel the sound, more than I hear it, the shock of it, the closeness of it.

I turn. I see Mikaela's fingertips reaching out for me as she falls. See her eyes, wide open and unblinking, and then she's gone, face down, her hair caught like seaweed in the waves lapping at the beach.

And I see Irene, rifle raised, pointed right at me.

I do the only thing I can, and I run toward the trees. Hoping they will shield me for just a few minutes longer. Trying to steal as many more breaths as I can.

I do what my sister told me.

I guess Lena didn't manage to wrestle the rifle away from her, in the end.

CHAPTER 47

April 16, 2022

"Tessa!" Irene's voice rings out from between the thin, twisted trunks. I see her moving in the distance, a sharp, black shadow.

If she had taken a little longer, maybe I could have gotten in the water. But the clarity of the panic has started ebbing away, the singular purpose of escape getting muddled.

I can't run from her.

Mikaela was right. There is nowhere to go.

The tree I'm hiding behind is shorter and stouter than the others, shielded from the wind by its sisters. It's grown in the embrace of the grove, in the middle of Isle Blind.

It's just me and Irene now.

I failed them. Lena tried to buy me time to get away, but those precious few minutes weren't enough. Mikaela tried coming back for us, for me, yet again, and for her trouble she got shot in the back.

"I don't want to hurt you, Tessa," Irene calls out, and it's funny, because a part of me still wants to respond to her. That voice has grown familiar to me over the past couple of days.

She doesn't sound like she wants to hurt me at all. She just sounds tired.

"I'm out of shots," Irene calls to me. "I only had two. Listen. Can you hear this?"

I hear a loud clicking noise through the trees.

"That's the trigger. I wouldn't be able to shoot you even if I tried."

I stay perfectly still. I've lost track of her in the dark. She's blended in with the trees, and she's moving too quietly for me to get a handle on where she is. But the clicking came from my left. She must be moving in a half circle, stepping slowly through these twisted woods, trying to find me.

"Just talk to me, Tessa," Irene says, and her voice hitches on something. She sounds like she's on the verge of tears. "Just hear me out."

I draw a deep breath. Tense my body in anticipation.

"How are you going to fix this, Irene?"

I shout it, and then I get moving, as quickly and as quietly as I can. I was shouting to the left of me, and I move to the right, weaving through the trees, zigzagging between them. I stop after only a few seconds and press myself against another tree, heart pounding, legs trembling.

When she speaks again, her voice sounds farther away.

"I didn't mean for this to happen," Irene says. "I never meant for it to go this far. I panicked, with Caroline. And I never intended to shoot Anneliese. I was just going to scare her. When Adam turned on me, I . . . I made a mistake." A quick interlude of silence, something quietly rustling.

"I know you've made mistakes, too, Tessa. I know you know what it's like to hurt people without meaning to."

She's closer now.

The words hover on my lips, the shock and outrage surprising me.

That wasn't the same. I did an ill-conceived interview. You killed people, multiple people.

I fucked up. You're a murderer.

But I'm not going to get pulled into this. She just wants to get me talking. She wants to get me talking so that I will come out into the open.

The fact that she's out of shells doesn't mean she can't kill me. I saw that, with Adam.

I hear something. She's moved again. When I risk looking out beyond the tree, I see the shadow slinking by, only a few steps away.

I'm going to have to be faster this time.

I focus on a tree closer to the beach. The visibility looks better there, more light coming through, which is riskier. But she won't be expecting me to go in that direction.

I sit down on my haunches, moving painfully slowly, acutely aware that with every passing second, she might be getting closer. But I need to cloud the soundscape.

My fingers close around a rock.

I straighten to a half crouch. An amateur starting position. Ready to run.

To run, and to swim, and get as far away from Irene as possible before I sink.

One final act of rebellion.

"So what are you thinking, Irene?" I yell, and as I yell, I throw the rock as far as I can and take off in the opposite direction.

A twig snaps under my foot. I don't know if she can hear. I don't know if my steps were too loud. I don't know if she saw me. I don't know if throwing the rock worked.

As I stop, the silence pounds through my veins.

It stretches out for much too long.

"We can get our story straight," Irene says back. Her voice seems to be bouncing now, somehow, and I can't tell where she is, if she's closer than before or farther away. My palms are sweating, and the salt is stinging both the old wounds and the new.

"I know you're in shock right now. But I know you understand. You could understand, if you would only let yourself," she says. "I didn't want to hurt your sister. We can still save her, if you will just help me."

She's lying. I know she's lying. I can't let my ridiculous hope get the better of me.

I hear a crunch as she steps on something. The sound is too loud. I need to make my escape, but I don't know where she is, and if I try to reach another tree I might run into her.

The beach is my only option. But out there, I will be completely exposed.

"Do you really want to die for their sake?" Irene asks. "Just think about it. You're a storyteller. You can come up with a narrative that will work. You're good at that, I've heard."

I can't stay here and wait for her to stumble over me. I can't find another place to hide. I can't start running again.

There are no options left.

Except.

Except that I don't want to die. Except that I want to go back home, and I want to try to restart my life.

I don't want to be yet another woman who disappeared on Isle Blind, gone without a trace. I don't want my friends to be that, either.

I want their families to know what happened to their daughters.

They were my friends. I loved them.

They deserve to be remembered, even if I couldn't save them.

Irene can't shoot me. She's stronger, yes, and she's killed before, but I'm backed into a corner. There is no other way out, for me.

And Irene is underestimating me. If she thinks she can sweet-talk and seduce me into coming out, that means she thinks I'm either stupid or in so much shock I can't think.

And she's wrong about that.

There's a lot to be said for desperation. For the will to fight.

I may not be the predator, but even prey can fight, when driven into a corner. With tooth, and claw, and rage.

And I'm so sick of giving up.

"Think about it, Tessa," I hear Irene say, and now she sounds a bit farther away again. I don't have much time. But it might be enough.

"This doesn't have to be the end for you," Irene says. "It can be like none of this ever happened. You can move on with your life. I can, too. I think we both deserve that. Don't you?"

Keeping my eyes up, still listening for her, I reach down again, feel for a rock. As large as I can find.

I only need to hit her once, if I find the right spot. I don't even need to knock her out. All I need to do is hurt her enough for her to lose focus. I don't need to beat her, I just need to gain the upper hand for a second.

My fingers close around a rock. Not as big as I would have liked. But big enough.

I hear something shifting right behind me, and I turn instinctively.

Irene almost looks disappointed, as she stands, shotgun held in both hands with the butt of it pointed at my head.

"Sequins," she says, and she smiles sadly. "Catches the light. Bad choice."

And she brings the butt of the gun down on me.

CHAPTER 48

April 16, 2022

I throw myself to the side and roll away, feeling the vibration in the ground when she hits it. I kick in Irene's direction, but she swats me away, and I throw the rock still clasped in my hand at her head.

Not a perfect hit. But good enough to graze her, to make her head snap back. Good enough to buy me a second.

I get to my feet and run, down and out on the beach. The color of the night has started shifting, turning from blue and black to gray. Dawn is coming. The nothing between night and day, that quivering moment where everything looks both ghostly and achingly sharp for just a few minutes. When I reach the beach, I hear her behind me, and I turn, almost against my will.

Irene is bleeding. The sorrow has been wiped from her face, and there is nothing but rage left as she approaches me. I keep backing away, feeling the ground sloping under my feet, down to the water.

"What are you going to do, Irene?" I ask, out of breath and my voice high-pitched, but it doesn't matter. It's all out in the open now anyway. No more lies. No more hiding places.

"Seven dead bodies and only you left alive, right? There isn't a fucking story on this planet that could explain that. The police aren't perfect, but a five-year-old could figure this shit out."

Irene bares her teeth, not even attempting to make it look like a smile.

"It doesn't matter what I'll do," she says. "Not to you."

"Oh, because I'll be dead, right?" I say. The rocks beneath the soles of my feet have grown wet and slippery. In a few seconds, the water is going to be licking at my heels, and there will be no more retreating.

"I mean, you can kill me," I say to her. Irene's face is lit in soft shadows by the quickly approaching daylight. Shades of blue and lavender, silver and white.

She's got burns on her fingers from wrestling over the recently fired shotgun with Lena. She's holding it like a club. If you run out of shells, you can still use the rifle as a blunt instrument. Can't fault her pragmatism.

"But I want you to remember that you're just like him," I say. "You're just like Carl. Killing all of us to get rid of the problem. You're no better than the man who killed your sister."

I stop. The water is up to my ankles now. Irene is standing no more than two steps away from me.

"You really are a vindictive little cunt, aren't you?" Irene says, her face a twisted mask.

I feel hysterical, furious laughter tugging at my face.

"I guess it takes one to know one," I say.

Irene throws herself at me, and I try to put my arms up to defend myself, but I only make it halfway.

The shotgun hits me in the side of the head, and it feels like my skull shatters and explodes. When I hit the water, it doesn't feel cold. It feels inevitable.

I see my blood coloring the water red in wild, gorgeous ribbons. I feel hands closing around my neck and holding me under. I feel myself thrashing and bucking, feel my lungs begging for air, feel the skin on Irene's arms breaking under my fingernails, as I drag and scrape.

I don't know if she's screaming at me. All I hear is the water, the rapid beating of my heart. I wonder if I will hear it stop before I lose consciousness.

My body twitches, and it brings my face above the surface for a fraction of a second. The brackish water makes everything blurry, and Irene's face above mine is all I see, that cold, determined rage, the blood still running from her temple, the tiny pinpricks of her pupils surrounded by bright, vibrant blue. She's kneeling on top of me in the water. I wonder if anyone, anywhere has ever looked so alive.

And then the hands disappear from my neck. She falls to the side, her legs still entangled in mine in a more intimate embrace than that of a lover, and I burst out of the water, coughing and gasping, and when I see Irene trying to crawl onto the beach, that same foot kicks her again, a perfect hit in the face. Irene's nose folds against her skull, the blood appearing like a magic trick as she falls forward.

I draw myself onto the rocks, and Irene is still moving behind me, but I barely notice. I'm reaching for a rock, for something to hit her with, hit her over and over until she stops moving, my body pure animal.

I grab a stone, and I look up, just as I hear a cry and a thud.

Mikaela is standing over Irene's half-submerged body. Her arm and shoulder are a frayed, bloody mess, bone or tendon glinting through the torn skin. She's swaying where she stands. When she opens her mouth to speak, I can see that one of her teeth appears to have been broken.

"I told you," she says, the words thick in her mouth.

"I do Krav Maga. For fitness."

Then she bends at the waist, and she pukes next to Irene's unmoving body.

CHAPTER 49

April 16, 2022

There is a moment when it all threatens to overwhelm me.

That moment isn't when I open the door to the upstairs room and smell the remains of violence, still permeating the air.

It's not even when I see the ruins of Anneliese, still at last, still tied to that one single chair in the middle of the room.

No, it's when I see that Lena's chest is still rising and falling slowly, and hear the gurgling noise emanating from her mouth.

I sit down on the floor next to her and turn her over, and she doesn't open her eyes. She's clutching something in her hand.

But she's breathing. Still breathing, even though her scalp is split open from a blow, even though she is bleeding from a wound somewhere on her torso, even though her clothes are so encrusted with blood it flakes off on my fingers when I touch her.

My mind goes white.

And then I hear her forming words.

"... er oom," she says. Every syllable sounds like she's having to give birth to it, force it out of her body.

"Lena?" I say.

"'arger," she says. "'rensh room."

Had it been anyone else, I wouldn't have understood. But it's Lena. It's my sister. I know her way of speaking better than anyone's.

Charger. Irene's room.

She opens her hand, and I see my cell phone, the one I handed to her. To call for help, if they needed it.

I leave her there, because I have to, because there is nothing else to do but this. Mikaela has passed out. From blood loss or from shock, I don't know. I managed to get her as far as the beach below the patio before she collapsed.

All I can do for anyone here is to call for help.

I run downstairs, my surroundings passing in a blur. Everything looks just as it did yesterday morning, when we got up for sunrise yoga. When we all put our leggings and our sports bras and our over-size hoodies on for a morning of meditation and clarity and new light, not knowing yet that the wheels were already in motion, that one of us was already dead.

I run past the kitchen and the office and all the way down to the door at the end of the hallway.

It's not locked.

The bed is perfectly made with hospital corners. There is no clutter on the floor. Only a half-empty water glass on the bedside table, and that familiar abstract painting on the wall.

I don't see any chargers. I take a half turn around the room, open-ing the small drawers in the desk, finding them all empty.

Finally, I fall to my knees next to the bed, and reach under it.

My hand brushes against something.

It's a box. It's beautiful and simple, a sturdy, rectangular box carved from rosewood with a clasp lock.

On the box, *Matilda* is carved in elegant, black letters.

I already know what I'm going to find. I open it anyway.

The pieces all look like the one I picked up on the beach yesterday. Small, rounded, and yellowish white or light brown. I think I recognize the one I found at the very top, but I can't be sure.

She must have been walking the beach every day, searching for pieces of her sister. Collecting them in this box under her bed. The only way she could think of to one day get to bury Matilda.

Little pieces of bone that might once have been part of her, polished by the sea, washed up and collected and hidden away.

I close the box again. I wipe my eyes with the back of my hand.

When I turn my head to the left, I see a small, white iPhone charger plugged into the outlet under the bed.

The phone starts up after less than a minute.

I dial the familiar three numbers and put the phone to my ear.

I connect immediately.

"Hello," the smooth, collected voice of a middle-aged woman says in my ear. "You have reached 112 emergency response. How can I help you?"

CHAPTER 50

October 24, 2022

Hi, Tessa!

First of all, how are you doing? I hope that isn't an insensitive question—I genuinely want to know. If you want to get a drink sometime and catch up, or just meet up and talk, that would be absolutely lovely.

I don't know if you've seen my other emails. I'm sure you have more important things to do than check your email! But I wanted to reach out again to ask if you would be interested in collaborating with us on a podcast on your experience out on Isle Blind. I've heard that another network is planning a limited series about what they are calling "The Bachelorette Party Massacre" (which seems incredibly tacky and awful, if you ask me), and I figured you might want the chance to get ahead of all that and tell the real story. If some of your friends would like to participate as well, that would of course be fantastic, but we'd be happy doing it with just you.

I think this could be a really great thing for you. Knowing you as well as I do (and I think you would agree that I know you fairly well!), I think the chance to take control of the narrative would be very therapeutic for you. With your experience, we could really do this horrible story justice and shine a light on the tragedy. We might even win some awards! It would be the comeback of the century.

Please get back to me as soon as you feel able, and feel free to call me or text me if that works better for you. I hope your recovery is going well.

All my love,
Minna Jacobssen

I read the email twice before deleting it. The last seven she sent were easier to ignore, but something about the syrupy-sweet tone of this one gets my blood flowing. I allow myself thirty seconds to fantasize about writing her back, about calling her out for her shitty, narcissistic, predatory attempts at capitalizing on having known and worked with me once, but then I just sigh and put my phone away.

I'm stalling. I know I'm stalling. It's because I'm nervous. The scars around my wrists always itch when I'm nervous these days. My therapist says it's psychosomatic, which is ludicrously unhelpful. I know it's psychosomatic. That doesn't do anything to make the itching go away.

Other than her occasional overtly unhelpful observations, she's pretty good. I like her better than my last therapist. She's very non-judgmental. She lets me ramble, which I appreciate, because most of the time, rambling and crying is what I need to do. Rambling about the guilt, about what happened and all the little things I should have done differently. Rambling about Irene, and how I should have seen that there was something wrong with her, something more than just grief, and all the ways I let everyone down.

It all comes down to guilt, of course. It always does.

My therapist says it's not going to go away. Not in the way I think it will. She's tried to get me to put the blame on the people who deserve it, onto Irene and, to some extent, Adam, but I've found it hard to blame a dead man for a crime he didn't know he was complicit in.

My therapist compared it to grief. Guilt and grief, she says, are intertwined. You don't cure it. You learn to live with it, and little by little, it gets absorbed into your life and starts fading with time. Never completely. But enough to let you move on.

I laughed when she said that. A bitter, contemptuous laugh. It's new. I didn't have that laugh before Isle Blind. Now it seems to pop up daily. My therapist doesn't seem to mind, though. She just smiles serenely whenever I do.

Sometimes, when she smiles in that placid way, she reminds me of Irene.

Is that the trauma, too?

I should probably ask her about that, next time.

My shoulder is hurting, and I stand up from my chair to do my stretches. The physical therapist I saw after the hospital was very stern about needing to follow the schedule he'd created for me to the letter. I didn't, of course. For most of those first two months, I was busy trying to remember how to breathe, trying to figure out how to function, trying to sleep through the night without waking up screaming.

So my shoulder hasn't bounced back quite as much as I would have hoped. Neither has my head, but at least that isn't my fault; there are no exercises for a cracked skull. The splitting migraines might go away and they might not. Yet another thing I'm supposed to learn to live with.

A glimpse through the window informs me of the reason for my stiff shoulder. The sky outside is dark and overcast, heavy, gray clouds bearing down over Stockholm. I pull my hand down behind my neck and grunt when I feel the shooting pain, but I hold it there while counting to thirty, and it does start to release, just a bit.

I've turned into an old woman. Staying in my apartment all day, every day, with a witch cackle for a laugh and a shoulder that predicts the weather. All I need to complete the picture is a cane and a musty old shawl.

I feel my phone vibrating in my pocket, and I pull it out.

Shoulder ok to go out? Still on at 2?

I feel a small smile forming, despite myself.

Good to go at 2, I text back, and then I check the time and start getting ready, holding my cell all the while.

It's another one of my new quirks. I can never let my phone out of my sight anymore. If it gets below fifty percent battery, I start to panic. Franz has bought me a portable battery, so that it won't happen.

We've been spending a lot of time together in the last few months, me and Franz, as we've taken turns visiting Lena in the hospital. He's taken on the full financial burden of my recovery. He's even paying the rent for my new little apartment, "until I get back on my feet."

I've found a new appreciation for Franz, who never asks me questions I'm not willing to answer, and who's been there by Lena's side for the whole, drawn-out recovery process, one that will probably never end. The way he looks at her is newly informed with a painful tenderness, and sometimes I wonder if it really is new, or if I've just never been willing to see it before.

I apologized to him, once. For leaving Lena behind. For running, when she told me to run, instead of trying to help her.

He just patted me on the shoulder, in a manner so kindly it made me cry.

Some part of me was hoping he would blame me, since Lena refuses to. Her speech still isn't fully recovered, and the painkillers she's on make her tired. But the one time I tried to tell her I was sorry, she got angry with me. I could see it in her body more than in her eyes.

She leaned in, and told me, as clearly as she could:

I'm the one who got us all there. It was more my fault than yours.

I hope we can talk about it properly, one day. I hope she can tell me what happened when Irene befriended her, if only so that I can tell her that none of it was her fault.

I was taken in by Irene too, after all.

I guess we all carry the burden, in our own way.

Actually, the only one of us who doesn't seem to be feeling guilty about anything is Mikaela. Last I saw her, a couple of weeks ago, she was waxing rhapsodically about some new collaboration she had lined up with a beauty brand specializing in covering up burns and scars.

If nothing else, she's a survivor.

I close the zipper on my backpack and look around the apartment. Franz rented it fully furnished, but I've taken care to fill it with color and soft things, every surface covered in fuzzy blankets and thick pillows. Nothing too clean or sterile. Nothing that could potentially remind me of Baltic Vinyasa.

My shoulder really is aching. But I'm not going to miss this.

The air outside is colder than I expected, and the humidity makes it worse. I've been hoping for an early snow this year, but so far we've had no luck. Late October is the worst part of the year in Stockholm, so dark and colorless and wet it feels like being smothered by a damp wool blanket. But I soldier on, pull my beanie down lower to avoid recognition, and start walking down the street to the water.

If only the media hadn't run our pictures, it might not have been so bad. But since I had once been a so-called public figure, I guess they figured it was fair play. We were all catapulted to fame, or infamy, depending on your point of view, which hasn't exactly helped with my feeling of being followed. It's harder to tell yourself you are safe and no one is coming after you when people keep staring at you and approaching you wherever you go. At least October helps with that. The summer months were hell. I don't think I left the apartment for all of July.

Well, not until she came and physically pulled me out, that is.

I see her hair first, that short, bright blond pixie catching what little light there is. It still seems to glow, even without a speck of sunshine. I haven't figured out how she does it.

"How's the shoulder?" Natalie asks when I get closer. She's more smartly dressed than I am, has got a thick, matching set of navy-blue activity gear on.

"Fine," I shoot back. "How's the brain damage?"

She laughs.

"Do you have everything?" Natalie asks, and I nod. "You didn't forget your lens cleaner this time?"

"I didn't forget my lens cleaner this time," I say, somewhat crankily, just to make her smile.

Up close, you can tell that she drags a bit, occasionally. The right side of her face is ever so slightly less expressive than the left. Between the homemade chloroform Irene had given Adam to try to subdue us in the basement, and the hit to the head when that didn't turn out to be as easy to use as the movies had made it out to be, Natalie suffered two small strokes that night.

Unlike some of us, however, she has recovered beautifully. Some words don't come out quite as clear as they once might have, and her smile is the teensiest bit lopsided, but it's nothing you would notice unless you knew.

Unless you were there.

"I picked out a spot for us," Natalie says as she starts walking. "It's really gorgeous, even with this weather. I figured we're going to work on composition today."

She's been dragging me out with her to take pictures once a week for the last two months. She says it's therapeutic. I don't know if the photography is therapeutic, but being around Natalie is, so I go along with it.

Sometimes we cry. Sometimes we talk about the nightmares, those first few gasping moments in the dark, waking up in the middle of the night and thinking we're back there. On Isle Blind.

Sometimes we don't talk at all.

I always feel a little bit lighter, after, though.

She's the one who convinced me to reach out to the family of the man I hurt, finally. To apologize to them. Not in the media. Not to gather virtue points.

Just to say that I was sorry, that I deeply regretted having contributed in any way to him feeling he had no choice but to try to end his life.

My lawyer has said she thinks they may withdraw the lawsuit, after everything that happened. My therapist told me I should be grateful, if they do; my gut tells me I would feel ashamed to earn absolution through the deaths of my friends. Natalie told me not to overthink it.

There aren't a lot of people out today. It's just me and Natalie on the street by the water. All the boats have been taken out for the season, and the water is iron gray, the bare hint of wind not enough to cause waves.

"Just a little bit further," Natalie says to me, and smiles.

Her fingertips brush against mine.

I hesitate before reaching out and grabbing her hand.

She doesn't say anything. She just smiles, and doesn't let go.

It's not all going to be okay. I've come to accept that. Sometimes there is no such thing as okay. Sometimes all there is, is good enough.

Sometimes you have to accept that you can't go to your oldest friend's funeral, because your body is still too broken. Sometimes you have to let go of any idea you ever had of reclaiming the person you were before, because that person is gone. Sometimes you have to learn to live in the "after," because you can't go back to the "before."

But right now, holding Natalie's warm hand in mine, trying to work up the courage to ask if I'm the only one feeling something more than friendship, it feels good enough.

And good enough might just be enough.

ACKNOWLEDGMENTS

Writing the acknowledgments section of a book is by far the most difficult, and the most stressful, part of the process. At least if you are me. Writing about fictional people and their bloody, gruesome trials and tribulations is fun, but having to be up-front and heartfelt about the depth of gratitude I owe the people around me for all their help and support? Absolutely terrifying. But I will do my best. (And if you should be on this list, and I forgot you, please know that I still feel very, very grateful, and you have my permission to hold your omission over my head for the rest of my life.)

First of all, I have to thank my agent, Anna Frankl, who agreed to hear me out in 2021 when I called her and said that I wanted to do something a little bit crazy. Anna has been with me since I was just a little baby writer, and the value of her trust and support in the process of creating this book is impossible to overstate. This wouldn't have happened without you, Anna.

Next, I have to thank my remarkable editor, Alex. Working with Alex has been a revelation; I don't think I've ever had as much fun editing as I have working on *The Bachelorette Party*. Thank you for seeing the potential in that initial, clumsy pitch, and thank you for all the notes, big and small, that turned this book from a first draft into something I hope we can both be truly proud of. Thank you to the entire team at Minotaur, for all the work you've put in—the cover design, and the typesetting, and the marketing, and, maybe especially, the patience and the kindness. If the world was fair, all of our names would be on the cover. A book, much like a child, takes a village. Thank you to all of you for being the village. Thank you to my incredible friend and fellow writer Katie for agreeing to read the script and give me feedback, even when I was so nervous I couldn't stop reminding her that "English is not my native language." Thank you for reading, thank you for the smart and incisive feedback, thank you for being my friend, and, most of all, thank you for not making fun of me for not having figured out where the apostrophes go. (I've almost got it, now. And in my defense, the English language uses too many apostrophes.)

Thank you to Saga, my "other spouse," for listening to me whine about my objectively quite wonderful job when it's hard, and for celebrating with me when it's fun, and for generally being the best friend a person could have. Thank you to my mom, for being so proud of me, and for giving me the initial seed of an idea for this book by getting really into yoga. Thank you to my dad, for always, always giving me his real opinion on my books, which makes the times he likes them that much sweeter. Thank you to my two furry little editing assistants, Rufus and Rizzmatizzle, both for making me laugh when I'm stressed and for deleting only three or four pages by stepping on my laptop. I know you could have done worse, and I appreciate your leniency.

Thanks to you, the reader, for picking up this book. I hope you liked it. I sincerely apologize if you like yoga and feel that I made fun of it too much. I hope I'll see you for the next book, too.

Finally, thank you to my husband, Mark. This book is for you. You made it happen. You are the one who told me you liked my English writing. You are the one who told me you thought I could, and should, write a whole book directly in English, even though I told you it wasn't "the done thing." You are the one who encouraged me to take a leap of faith and go for it. You were the one who suggested that a yoga retreat would be a really fun setting for a thriller. You were the one who helped me figure out the ending. You were the first one to read the book, and the first one to love it, and seeing you sitting on the couch engrossed in a book I'd written is an experience I will treasure until my dying day. I am so lucky to have you.

ABOUT THE AUTHOR

Elvira Glänte

Camilla Sten has been writing stories since she was a young girl. In 2019, Camilla published the now internationally acclaimed, hair-raising novel *The Lost Village*. Rights for *The Lost Village* have been sold to nineteen territories around the world, including film and television. Her third novel for adults, *The Resting Place*, was one of Goodreads Most Popular Horror of 2022, and in the same year Camilla was longlisted for the prestigious Viktor Crime Award in Germany. An ever-prolific author, Camilla has released the third part in her YA series and continues to write new thrillers.

Find her on Instagram: @AuthorCamillaSten.